Touchdown

BLUE SAFFIRE

Perceptive Illusions Publishing
Bayshore, New York

Blue Saffire/Perceptive Illusions Publishing Inc.
PO BOX 5253
Bayshore, NY 11706
www.BlueSaffire.com

Publisher's Note: This is a work of fiction. Names, characters, places, and incidents are a product of the author's imagination. Locales and public names are sometimes used for atmospheric purposes. Any resemblance to actual people, living or dead, or to businesses, companies, events, institutions, or locales is completely coincidental.

Ordering Information:
Quantity sales. Special discounts are available on quantity purchases by corporations, associations, and others. For details, contact the "Special Sales Department" at the address above.

Touchdown/ Blue Saffire. -- 1st ed.
ISBN 978-1-941924-38-9

Life will hit you hard. Love can hit you harder as it heals.

—BLUE SAFFIRE

CHAPTER ONE

The Return

Bentley

I walk out of the tunnel onto the field and inhale the scent of the freshly cut grass. So many memories wash over me. Though the stadium is currently empty, I can hear the roar of the crowd like it's my first game all over again.

I've had a great career. It's the one thing in my life I've done almost perfectly. My personal life, not so much. I'm still making mistakes there. However, when I'm out on this field, I have it all together. I know where I fit and what I'm supposed to do.

My heart belongs in the end zone. That moment when I get my team in the red zone gets my blood pumping every time. Getting close to scoring is as heady as making the touchdown.

I wish I could apply the rules on the field to my life. Heck, I wish I at least knew the rules to play by. Maybe then I'd know how to get this right once and for all.

My biggest dream was to get to the pros. I did that despite all the obstacles that got in the way.

The one thing I didn't see coming was her. I should have. She has always been there.

Zahirah Nickels was the girl next door. Being an only child, my family drew her into our crew. I'm the oldest of six.

As much time as Zah spent at our house, I should say I'm the oldest of seven. Zahirah and my sister Erica became friends almost from the moment they met. As a result, Zahirah became a fixture in our home.

"Hey, mister." I turn to look down at the little boy peering up at me.

"You're Bentley Coswell, right?"

I squat to get eye level with the little guy. His green eyes light up in his little face. Reaching out, I ruffle his blond hair.

"That's me, kid," I say.

His eyes grow wider. He's a cute kid. I can only hope to have my own someday who is just as cute as he is.

"Can you sign my football. You're my favorite. I want to be a quarterback too when I make it to the pros."

"Sure, of course," I say and take the ball he has tucked under his arm. "Love the confidence, kid. Never let go of that. What's your name, little guy?"

"Sean."

"Nice to meet you, Sean."

"You're coming home, right? I mean, you're here to win us a championship. My dad says we can do it with you here. I think he's right. Besides, I hate rooting for you when you play against us."

I burst into laughter. Signing the ball, I hand it back to him and ruffle his hair again. I give him a wink.

"Can you keep a secret?"

He nods his head and mimics zipping his lips and throwing away the key. I stifle more laughter. This is the lightest I've felt since stepping off the plane.

"That's the plan. While I'm here to visit with family, we're looking to see if this is a fit for me. I might just get you that win."

"You will. I can see it. You're going to deliver the game-winning touchdown too," he says excitedly.

"Thanks for the support, bubby."

He gives a sage nod. I look up to see Christian Darity, an offensive lineman the team has been trying to re-sign in order to entice me. He places a hand on the boy's head and looks down at him.

The boy looks up at him with a smile. "Hey, Dad. Look, it's Bentley Coswell."

"I hope he's not giving you any trouble," Christian says.

"Not at all, man. He may have sealed the deal for the organization," I chuckle and stick my hand out for him to shake.

We shake hands and he grins. This team has done a lot to get me to sign. Christian was on my list of players it would take to get me to come here.

"That's good to hear. The ink is just drying, but I'm hoping to play with you this coming season. You were a big deciding factor for me."

"Yeah, I was amped to hear they were in talks with you for a new contract. They're putting together a strong squad. It's kind of hard not to consider taking the leap."

"Do you mind if I ask what's stopping you?"

I pull a hand down my face, then fold my arms across my chest. Placing my weight on my right leg, I try to figure out the best way to say this. I want to come home.

It's long overdue. My family has been through so much and it's time I get my shit together to be there for them. My mom's words exactly.

"I've made a lot of mistakes. I don't want this to be another one. Coming home might not be the right thing to do," I say.

Yeah, I'm here to claim what's mine, but that might not work out. I can't see myself living here and watching my biggest regret breathing in my face. It's why I came here first.

I need to clear my head before I jump into the fire waiting for me. This day has the potential to turn into shit real fast. My gut twists when I think of why I'm truly here in Arizona.

"Well, I hope things work out," Christian says as he lifts his son into his arms.

"Same here, buddy. Same here."

"You ready for that ice cream?" he says to his son.

"*Yes*," Sean cheers.

"You enjoy your ice cream. I hope I see you around sometime," I say to my new little friend.

"You want to come with us?"

"Not this time, bubby. I have somewhere to be."

"Aw, okay. It was nice meeting you, Mr. Coswell. Thanks for signing my ball."

"We'll have to get a pic next time."

His eyes light up and he nods excitedly. If only everything else in my life could be this simple. If it were, I wouldn't be here, ready to tear my hair out.

My dad used to tell me what makes a man is not the things he does wrong, it's how he takes the lesson and does better from it. You never fail; you learn. I've done a lot of learning.

"Bentley."

I turn to my youngest brother, Eddy. He has a somber look on his face. "Mom's been blowing up my phone. If we're going to make the rehearsal dinner, we need to head out now."

"Well then, let's go crash a wedding."

Zahirah

I look in the mirror at the sexy black dress I have on. I chose it because it says classy but confident in who I am. I need the reminder to get me through this.

"What am I doing? What am I doing? What am I doing?" I keep repeating the words as I shake my hands out in front of me.

"I've been asking you that for the last four months," Erica, my childhood best friend, grumbles at me.

She's not happy about this. I think I get why. It has nothing to do with my fiancé, Gilbert. Well, not really.

Things were never supposed to get this far. Gilbert is a nice guy; he should be engaged to someone he loves, not me. I'm still trying to figure out how we got here.

"Erica, I don't want to fight about this again," I mutter.

"Then don't. Just call it off and fix your shit. I don't thin—"

"No, not this again. I don't have time for this right now."

I'm getting ready to leave for the wedding rehearsal before our rehearsal dinner. The rehearsal dinner for the wedding that was never supposed to happen. Yet here I stand.

The wedding is tomorrow, and it doesn't look like we're going to pull the plug on this charade before I walk down the aisle and say I do to a man I don't love.

"Zahirah, have you asked yourself why you're doing this?" Erica says from her perch on the arm of the accent chair in my living room.

I turn from the mirror to look at her. We lock eyes and her brother comes to mind right away. He has the same hazel eyes she does.

Eyes I know so well. I stop myself from going down that road. This isn't about Bentley.

That was another life, another time. I had to let that dream go. No matter how much it hurt.

It was better to let go than to keep hurting each other. I shake my head clear. I can't blame this mess I'm in on Bentley, not this time.

"He's my friend. His grandmother is so sweet. It would break her heart if we told her the truth."

Erica gives me a pointed glare. She's the only one I've told the truth about all of this. What started out as a simple favor has blown up in my face.

I chew on my lip and begin to shake my hands out again. The ring on my finger feels so heavy and as if it doesn't belong. I thought it was too much for a fake engagement from the time Gilbert gave it to me.

However, it did make sense that he needed to give me such an expensive and over-the-top ring. It would have looked strange otherwise. My fiancé is a wealthy man.

Another reason for me to freak out. This could all go so wrong. What the hell have I gotten myself into?

"So you're about to marry a man you don't love because you don't want to hurt his grandmother's feelings?" Erica scoffs, folding her arms over her chest. "God, I wish I never talked you into that first date. This is all my fault."

"It's not your fault. It's no one's fault. We should head out. Gilbert and I will figure something out before tomorrow evening. I just need to make it through tonight."

"Really? You're going to go through with this? What about your mom? What about Aaron?"

"Erica, the last thing I want to do is make this more complicated than it already is. Mom will understand. I'll figure everything else out."

She sighs and stands. "I think I should tell you something before we leave."

A nervous look comes to her face. I know my friend too well to think anything about to come from her mouth right now is going to make any of this better.

"If it's not going to better my mood, I don't want to know. Save it for after tomorrow."

Her cheeks turn pink, and I almost tell her to spill it. However, a glance at the clock tells me we need to go. My childhood friend will just have to hold whatever it is in. I'm grateful to Erica for all her support.

Over the years, she's had my back even in times she probably shouldn't have. I love her like my own sister. I have love for the entire Coswell family.

I try not to feel guilty as that thought crosses my mind. There's so much I've been trying to keep from them. The lies have been adding up. Gilbert has been doing me as big a favor as I have been doing for him.

Erica pulls me into a tight hug. When she releases me, she cups my face in her palms. Tears are brimming in her eyes.

"Whatever happens tonight, promise me you will follow your heart and do what's best for you, not everyone else," she says.

"I promise."

"Good, I'm holding you to that. I love you, best."

"I love you too. Stop it before you make me cry," I choke out.

My phone begins to ring. I groan and go to pull it from my purse. Looking at the screen, I see it's Gilbert. I chew on my lip. I was sure he would have called this all off before now. He's spent so much money on this wedding.

From the lavish engagement party to this rehearsal dinner and the wedding itself. It's been a never-ending fountain of money being poured into a wedding that shouldn't be happening. I sigh and answer the call before it turns over to voicemail.

"Hello."

"Hey, gorgeous. Grandma is concerned about you. Where are you? Are you on your way?"

"Yes, I'm on my way right now. No need to be concerned. But Gilbert, we should talk before the night is over."

"I told you. Everything will be fine. I'll see you when you get here."

"See you," I murmur and hang up.

CHAPTER TWO

Not the Same

Bentley

"Are you sure you want to do this, man? This is Zah. All I want is to see her happy, bro. I don't know what all happened between you two, but she's family.

"Haven't we all been through enough? Gilbert can give her a nice life and stability. Why come back and get in the way of that now?" Eddy says as he pulls up to the reception hall and parks.

"I love you, Eddy, but shut the fuck up and mind your business. You're right about one thing. You don't know what happened and you don't know what the fuck you're talking about," I grumble.

"Bro, what I do know is this is crazy. It's her wedding rehearsal dinner."

"What's your point, Eddy?"

"It's always about you, Bentley. All my life, it's been about you. I'm asking you to stop and think about her.

"Think about how this affects everyone else around you. I don't want to lose her too. Zah is important to me. I don't want to see her hurt."

As the youngest, he thinks everything has always been about me. My family did a lot to support my dream. Heck, our entire community has.

I feel for him, but he's wrong. It's never been all about me. This dream was my father's first. He ingrained it in me, and I did all I could to see it through. Then life called an audible.

"I'm not here to hurt her. I've done enough of that," I bellow. "I'm fucking tired, bro. I'm tired of fucking up. I'm tired of saying the wrong thing. I'm tired of being without her.

"Yes, I'm going to do this because nothing makes sense without Zahirah in my life. Nothing."

I shake my head with my last words. I didn't come all this way to turn back now. Call me selfish, but I need to do this.

I have to hear from her lips that she doesn't want me. If she looks me in my eyes today and tells me I'm too late, then I'll walk away. Then and then only.

"Well, there she is. If you're really going to do this. Here's your chance. Don't fuck this up, bro. Don't cost us all her light."

I tighten my jaw and close my eyes. I'm not here to take her away from my family. I know how much she means to everyone.

When I open my eyes, I glance out the window and the sight before me takes my breath away. Zariah looks like a fucking knockout. Her hair is flowing down her back in loose brown waves.

The black dress that's hugging her body is sexy but classy. Her dark-brown legs look amazing. That body still screams track star.

I clear my throat and reach for the door handle to open the door and step out. Three things happen at the same time. I step from the vehicle and run a hand through the front of my hair. Gilbert Manning walks up to Zahirah and places a hand on her back.

Zahirah looks in my direction and freezes with her mouth open. I can't help but smile at her. A smile brightens her face for a brief second before it falters and she frowns.

I inhale deeply and force my feet forward. This is it, it's now or never. Strolling across the lot, I close the gap between us.

"Bentley?" she breathes as I stop before her.

"Hey, Zah."

I can't take my eyes off her face. Zah has the clearest skin I've ever seen. Her dark-brown complexion has this glow about it. It looks like the purest dark chocolate kissed by hues of bronze and gold.

"What are you doing here?" she asks, looking up into my eyes, searching.

"You're getting married. My family was invited."

"Coswell, I wasn't expecting you. This event is by invitation and RSVP only. I don't know that there's a place for you tonight," Gilbert says with a smug grin on his face.

"Oh, that's not a problem. My mother RSVP'd. I'm her plus-one," I reply, returning his smile with a shit-eating one of my own.

"Oh. My. God. I should have known our mothers were up to something. Gilbert, I'm so sorry about this."

"What is there to be sorry about? We grew up together. Gilbert and I were once friends. I don't see the problem."

Zahirah sighs and rubs her temples. "Bentley, can you and I do this some other time?"

"No, not if it means you'll be married to someone else."

She looks at me with wide eyes. "Are you serious?"

I give her a pointed look. Gilbert moves her behind him and steps forward to get into my face. I roll my shoulders back.

The nerve of this asshole. I've always known he's wanted Zahirah. He's not who she thinks he is.

"Maybe you should go. She doesn't want you here and after tomorrow, I don't want you around my wife."

"Gilbert," Zah gasps. "Can I talk to you?"

I release a grin. Gilbert growls in my face but takes a step back and Zah tugs at his arm.

Pussy.

"I'll be waiting right here for my turn," I say as they begin to walk away.

Gilbert stops and turns toward me with his fists balled. I don't even flinch. I will lay his ass out if he jumps at me. Gilbert ought to know better.

While we were once friends, I've kicked his ass more than once. I'd be happy to do it again.

I can't believe he went after my girl behind my back. I'm not surprised. He has always been a pretentious asshole.

I can't begin to fathom why Zah has gotten involved with him. He's not her type. The jerk has to be putting on airs to get her to fall for his shit.

Gilbert opens his mouth to spew some crap when a loud cry fills the air. We all turn to see what's going on. I sprint into action as soon as I see what's taking place.

My heart is in my throat. This can't be happening. I stop breathing until I make my way over to my mother, sisters, brothers, and ...

"Mom?" Zah cries as she drops to her knees.

Zahirah

"Mom? Mom," I cry as my mother lies on the ground.

My ears are ringing, and my heart is racing. What is going on? I can't lose my mom.

"She said she wasn't feeling well in the car and passed out as we were making our way inside," Mrs. Coswell says as she wrings her hands.

My mom and Mrs. Fran have become as close as Erica and I are. They have seen each other through a lot. The two are inseparable.

"Someone call for an ambulance, please," I sob.

"I already did. They're on the way," Bentley says from beside me.

He has taken his jacket off to place beneath my mother's head. I shouldn't be so grateful to have him here. However, I am.

He wraps an arm around my shoulders and tugs me into him. It feels like coming home. He smells so good, and his arm banding around me feels so strong and warm.

Memories try to flood my mind, but I push them back. I don't have time for that right now. I need to focus on my mom.

"It's going to be fine. I'm here," he whispers in my ear.

A shiver runs through me. I shouldn't want to cling to his words so easily. However, I'm on the verge of falling apart.

This is the last straw. All the pressure feels like it's going to cave my lungs. In this moment, Bentley is like a lifeline I didn't know I needed so much.

"Zah, baby, Dr. Richards hasn't arrived yet, but he should be pulling in soon. He'll be able to look after your mom," Gilbert says.

Dr. Richards is a friend of Gilbert's. I'm sure he does his job well, but I'm not waiting around for him or taking any chances. I'm taking my mom to the hospital to be checked out.

"I'm taking her to the hospital," I say firmly.

"What about our guests?"

"Fu—"

"I will go inside and let everyone know what's going on," Erica says, cutting me off before I lose my shit.

"You can let them know tomorrow isn't happening while you're at it."

"What? Zahirah, I'm sure your mom will be fine by tomorrow night. Let's not be so hasty."

I shove out of Bentley's arms and stand. Grabbing Gilbert by the arm, I tug him out of earshot. He looks back at me nervously.

"That is my mom lying there. Take this as the sign it is. We need to call this off. Tell everyone my mom has fallen ill. She's supposed to walk me down the aisle.

"I think everyone will understand if we postpone for now. In a few weeks, we'll part amicably. Too much stress and needing to slow down or something. We'll figure all that out," I bite out.

"Is this because of him?"

"What? What are you talking about? What aren't you getting? My mother just collapsed."

I drop my voice. "This isn't real. We should have called it off weeks ago. It has nothing to do with him."

"Are you sure?"

"I'm sure I'm about to lose it on you. What's the matter with you?"

I turn to go back to my mom as the ambulance pulls up. Gilbert grabs my arm to halt me. I turn to look at him with my brows knit.

"He's only going to hurt you again. Don't do this," he pleads.

I shake my head to clear it. I've been missing something here, but I don't have the time to process what. I need to get to my mom.

"Whatever, Gilbert. I'll talk to you later. I have to go," I say and pull my arm from his hold.

He bites out a curse but allows me to walk away. My mind is moving in a million directions. I'm not able to process any of it as I follow my mom into the ambulance.

I sit with my head in my hands, sobbing as we ride to the hospital. Once we arrive, Mom is rushed to a room and examined while I pace and wait.

It doesn't take long before I'm led back to her room. Denzel, Bentley's sister Lauren's fiancé, is the attending doctor. I'm so glad to see him. He gives my shoulder a squeeze as I enter the room.

"She's going to be fine," he says before he walks out.

I take a seat by her bed and drop my head into my hands like on the ride here. I'm so confused and lost right now. My mother is a healthy woman, this is so out of the blue.

A hand on my shoulder causes me to lift my head. My mother is smiling at me with her soft-brown eyes.

"Now that I have your attention and that boy isn't around to cut my questions off, I'd like you to explain to me what's going on. Why are you hell-bent on marrying someone you don't love?"

I scoff. "Aw, hell nah. Mom, did you just fake all this?"

"I'm a mother, I did what I needed to do to protect my baby. Now start talking, Zah. I know you've been hiding things since you came back home.

"I think Gilbert has been playing on your secrets and has been trying to trap you into a marriage he doesn't intend to end."

"Wait, you know?"

"That this entire wedding is bullpoopy? Girl, you think I'm one big fool, don't you? You're lucky I haven't bopped you upside your head. You're dragging a lot of good people into this mess, and most of all, you have Aaron smack in the middle."

She shakes her head and purses her lips. Guilt begins to rise in my chest. I'm not even sure how I got here anymore.

"I can see you're lost, baby. It's written all over your face. Maybe if you talk it out with me, you will hear your answers for yourself," my mother coaxes.

I look back at her as she searches my face. I try to think of where to start. I've wanted to tell her so much over the years, but the secrets started a long time ago.

"Start from the beginning, child. I'm here to listen."

I take a deep breath and blow it back out. I open my mouth and the words begin to spill. It's like a burden has been lifted from my shoulders.

I go all the way back to the beginning. I was so young and naive back then. If I could do it all over, I would. There's so much I would take back and change.

"It all started with my first day of college."

CHAPTER THREE

Cold Greetings

Zahirah

I did it. I got the full-ride scholarship to the same university Bentley Coswell has been attending for the last two years. I can't wait to surprise him. Bentley is my best friend's older brother.

I've had a crush on him for years. When Erica told me she was thinking about going to the same school as her big brother, I worked my ass off to be able to get in too. I didn't change my mind even after Erica did.

My parents aren't too happy about it, but they're not paying for it, so it's my choice. I earned that scholarship and here I am. I can't stop smiling and my face is starting to hurt.

So far, so good. I like my roommate and my dorm room is cute. I've spent the morning setting up my space and getting to know Arlene.

"What do you say, girlie? Want to head to the student center and have a peek around? I'm starving," she says as I place away the last of my clothes.

My stomach gurgles in answer for me. "Need I say more?" I laugh.

She's sitting on my bed, looking through my high school yearbook. My senior year was a blast, but I'll admit, I spent most of it thinking about Bentley and his reaction once I got here. I've missed him the last two summers.

If I wanted to get here on a track scholarship, I had to train my butt off. Unfortunately, that meant missing out on time with Bentley during his summer visits, as he would be off heading back to school for summer football camp by the time I returned from my camp.

"Come on. This room will be here when we get back. I need a nice, juicy burger and fries. If I can get a milkshake with that, I'll be a happy roomie."

"Sounds good to me. Is the food really that good here?"

"A-mazing. Come on, you can find out for yourself. Hopefully we'll run into some of the football team or the swimmers. We're golden either way," she says with a bright smile.

"Do the teams hang out there a lot?"

"I've only been here two days, but they've been there every time I've been so far. The teams sort of clique up, but some of the guys have come by to flirt." She wiggles her brows at me.

Arlene is going to be fun to live with. Her outgoing personality and infectious smile are only icing on the cake. I had been so nervous about meeting my roommate and if we would get along.

"I thought I was going to barf waiting for you to arrive. I'm so happy you're so cool. I think we're going to make great friends," she says as we walk out of the dorm and head for the student center.

"Oh my God, I was just thinking the same thing."

"See, it was meant to be," she sings.

We fall into excited chatter as we walk the path to the center. I'm so engrossed in our conversation, I don't see the guys or the football they're tossing around until it hits me in the side of the head. I fall over and grasp the side of my face.

"Oh shit, are you all right?"

I look up to find three big guys staring down at me. The one who spoke squats down to check on me and help me up. My face is throbbing, but once my eyes focus and lock with those hazel eyes, I break into a smile.

"Bentley," I squeal and throw my arms around his neck.

"Hey, he's the one who tossed the ball, gorgeous. I can take you to get an ice pack and carry you to your dorm," one of the other guys says.

I look up and find a pair of blue eyes fixed on me. He's handsome, but I have the only boy I've ever wanted in my arms. However, Bentley pulls my arms from around his neck and places them into my lap.

"I'm sorry about that. Are you all right?" he says.

I look at him, confused. He searches my face and then a light bulb goes off. I see the moment shock sets in.

"Zah? Wh … what are you doing here?"

"I go here. I got a track scholarship," I say excitedly.

"Oh, um … that's cool," he says and rubs the back of his neck.

"Bro, what's wrong with you? Hey, sweetheart, are you okay? Let me help you up," the third guy says.

Bentley stands and takes a step back. This wasn't the reception I was expecting. I'm a little thrown off by it.

"Thanks," I say to the guy who helps me up as I look down at my feet.

"No problem. I'm Corey. Can I take you to get an ice pack or something?"

"She's a big girl. She can find one on her own," Bentley bites out.

Corey throws his hands in the air. I look at Bentley, stunned. He's never been like this with me.

"Hey, babe. I've been looking all over for you," a girl in a miniskirt and crop top sings as she rushes over and tosses her arms around Bentley's neck.

She plants a big, sloppy kiss on his lips, then turns to look me over. I take a step back and wrap my arms around my middle. With each second, I start to feel like a big dummy.

What in the world did I think was going to happen when I showed up here? Bentley almost kissed me once—the summer before he left for college—it happened so fast, I have to wonder if I made it all up in my head. That would explain why he's looking at me like I'm crazy.

"Seriously, you should get some ice on that. I'd even say go see the med staff. You look new. I can show you where it is," Blue Eyes says.

"I'm sure she can find it on her own, Jason," Bentley snaps. He then looks at me and his eyes widen as I shake my head and take a few more steps back. "If anything, it was my fault; I'll show her where to go."

"But, babe, we're supposed to head out for that movie. I don't want to miss any of it."

"I'm fine. You don't have to worry about me," I say and turn to leave.

I grab Arlene by the hand and take off back toward the dorm as fast as my legs will take me. This was all a big mistake. I should've never come here.

Bentley

What the fuck just happened? There's no way Zahirah Nickels is a student here, and when did she turn into a fucking knockout? She's always been so pretty, but now ... how am I supposed to control my feelings?

It took everything in me not to kiss her that summer. I had been so close to pressing my lips to hers, but my phone buzzed in my pocket, stopping me. That was for the best. She's two years younger than me and my little sister's best friend.

No matter how much I've always been drawn to her, that shit can never happen. Zah is like family. I should see her like one of my sisters.

I've been telling myself that for years and still it hasn't stuck. For two years, we've missed each other during summers and holidays. I rub at my chest as I realize how much I've missed her.

I snap out of my shock and groan. I was just a total dick to her. Not that I meant to be.

No matter my feelings, Zahirah is still a friend. At least she was before that shit I just pulled. I shake my head clear and tug my arm from Carly's grasp.

"Zahirah, wait," I call out.

"Bro, you're too late. She's gone," Corey says.

I clench my jaw as I see Zah and her friend turn the corner as they rush away. My stomach sours. Could this all have gone any worse?

"Which is a shame because she's super cute. Dude, do you think she's going to be all right? I hope she doesn't have a concussion or something," Jason says.

"She's fine. I mean, are you sure it really hit her? She could be faking. You guys are all on the football team, you have to be careful, you know," Carly says.

"Zahirah isn't like that. She doesn't care about any of that shit. She'll be at the Olympics before I ever make it to the pros," I grumble.

"You know her?" Carly asks bitterly.

"Yeah, she's my next-door neighbor. My little sister's best friend. That's Zah," I say, but stop myself before I can blurt out more.

No one here needs to know that's the girl I've had a thing for since I was thirteen. Back then, she was all bony limbs with the biggest smile and brightest eyes I've ever seen. God, she's morphed into a supermodel.

I palm my forehead and allow it all to sink in. Zahirah Nickels is on campus. She's a freshman here at my college.

"What the fuck does this mean?" I say under my breath.

I'm stuck in a daze as I process the fact that she's here and will be attending the same college. The track program here is phenomenal. With her talent, she's sure to go far.

I smile as pride fills me. I don't know why I'm surprised. If Zah puts her mind to something, it's hers. I just didn't know she wanted to come here. Erica had tossed about the idea, but for whatever reason, she changed her mind.

"Jason and Corey, why don't you guys go check on her if you can find her. Bentley, we can go. We still need to get our tickets and make it to the concession stand before the movie starts," Carly says.

I roll my eyes. Things haven't been great between us. I don't know how an us even started.

One drunken almost hookup turned into her clinging to me at every party, every event, and nearly every moment of my life for the last three months. I've only kept it going because she scares off the other girls. I'm trying to keep my head focused on the game. I'm not into chasing after girls.

Doesn't mean they're not into chasing me. I close my eyes, feeling like an asshole. I had thought Zah was one of these chicks around campus trying to throw themselves at me when she first hugged me. Carly's thoughts were my own at first.

I had wondered if she had intentionally fallen to get my attention. She had it from the moment she went down, but I shook it off. I mean, she felt and smelled nice, but I didn't want to fall into a trap set by some pretty groupie on campus.

"Way to go, Bent," I mutter to myself.

I just fucked that up so royally. For years, since I've started to see Zah as more than my little sister's best friend, I can't seem to do or say the right things around her. I'm two years older, but I would swear I'm the younger one with how tongue-tied and twisted up I get.

Damn. Nothing I said today came out right. I was stunned to see her and then I was jealous as Corey and Jason tried to come to her aid. The girls here on campus are pretty, but Zah ... she brings the light with her.

"You live next door to her, bro? Please tell me you've—"

"Finish those words and I'll put my fist through your face. It isn't like that. That's like one of my sisters," I grind out.

"Sure didn't seem like it. I would hope you'd treat your sisters better than that," Corey murmurs. "I'm concerned.

"I know that chick with her. Maybe they're in the same dorm. I'm going to go check on her. I've had enough concessions. I'd feel more comfortable making sure she's okay."

"I'd come with you, but I booked a workout. I need to be there in ten minutes," Jason says.

"I'll come with you," I say.

"What? Come on, babe. She'll be fine. Corey can call you if anything happens," Carly whines.

I look at her and roll my eyes. Opening my mouth, I go to tell her I'm not going to the movies, and I think we should break things off. However, my phone rings, cutting me off.

Seeing it's my sister, Erica, I pick up and walk off without another word.

"What have you done, Bentley?" Erica growls before I can get a word out.

CHAPTER FOUR

Here for Myself

Zahirah

My head was throbbing by the time we made it back to the dorm room. I didn't know if it was from being hit with the football or from the tears I tried to hold back. I almost didn't answer Erica's call because of it.

However, she's the only one I can talk to about this. Arlene was kind enough to go get us something to eat while I took the call. I was grateful for that.

I don't want my roommate to know how stupid I've been. Now, after crying into my phone—telling my best friend what happened between me and her brother—I get how huge this mistake is. I don't know what made me think this was going to be some great love story.

"Hey, I'm here for you if you need to talk," Arlene says as she devours her fries.

"Thanks," I murmur and run a hand under my nose.

I'm still curled up on my bed, sniffling and feeling too pitiful to eat. I just don't understand. The Bentley I know would have treated me with kindness and made sure I was okay.

This Bentley felt so cold and distant. Why was he so rude? He was even curt with his friends.

Okay, he has a girlfriend. I can't really be upset about that. Bentley Coswell is gorgeous. All that thick chocolate-brown wavy hair, those hazel eyes, and that sexy grin.

At six-four, he has always towered over me. Every time I would have a growth spurt, I used to pray to be taller like him. Only for him to shoot up several inches. When I capped at five-six, I gave up hope of at least getting to six feet.

I'm not too hopeful for that last four inches. That girl had to be at least five-nine with her long legs. If she's Bentley's type, I really am delusional and should have gone to the school my parents wanted me to go to.

I had hoped I had a shot. Bentley dated Vanessa Stanley his senior year. They broke up right after prom.

She was pretty and brown like me. Almost my height and everything. People at school often mistook us for sisters.

"Your food is getting cold. You should at least try to eat something," Arlene says with a plea in her voice.

"I don't have an appetite."

Her shoulders sag and she turns back to her burger. I sit and continue to remain lost in my thoughts. I mean, how did it come to this?

I should've known he would be attached to someone. I guess I was so deep in my delusion I never took any of that into account. I would be fine with that. I would have still had my friend at least.

I get that once he graduates from college, his life is going to change and I probably won't be a part of any of that, but I thought we'd have these two years to make a few more memories.

I've seen all the Coswell kids as friends all my life. Bentley is no different. He used to carry me around on his back, the same as he did with Erica, Lauren, and Tara.

He's bandaged a knee or two for me and has handled a few
bullies to protect me. Not wanting to lose any of that as a child
who grew up without siblings, I thought this was a fantastic idea.

"I'm so stupid," I sob to myself.

"I highly doubt that. You got into this place. You can run like
a Tasmanian devil and this place wouldn't have accepted you if
your grades were crap," Arlene says.

"Like my mom says, book smarts and common sense don't
always hang out together."

"I like that one. I'm stealing it," she says and comes over to sit
on the edge of my bed. She reaches to tuck a lock of hair that has
slipped from my ponytail behind my ear.

"Let's see how good I am at reading between the lines. From
his reaction and yours I gather you know Bentley Coswell.
However, that reunion didn't go as you had expected.

"Now you're questioning yourself and your decision to come
here. Am I right?"

"Yeah, something like that. Bentley is my next-door neighbor
and my best friend's older brother. We were both going to come
here together. She changed her mind, but I thought I'd still come
since Bent and I have always been friends.

"I have no idea who that was. He treated me like a stranger.
I've never been so embarrassed in my life. And I've torn a swimsuit
during a swim meet before.

"I still think that was sabotage, but I didn't feel this humiliated
then. I don't understand why he was so cold to me," I choke out.

"Boys are stupid. I stopped trying to understand them a long
time ago."

"Yeah, well, maybe I should do the same."

"Honey, you're gorgeous. There are plenty of mistakes to be
made on this campus and I can't make them all by myself. That
means you have to make the other half.

"I say you forget all about him and find someone else to
welcome you to campus properly. There's a party tonight. I was
invited while getting our food.

"How's your head? Do you think you're up for a frat party with your new bestie?"

Erica's words come back to me. *This is your first year of college. Fuck my brother, he can be such an idiot. Forget about him and make the best of your college years. You've made this too much about him; now make it about you.*

She had a point. Both she and Arlene are right. Bentley can do whatever he wants. I'm here for my education and a chance to run competitively.

Heck, they have a great swim team here as well. I turn eighteen in two weeks and I'm not going to do that while sulking over a stupid crush. My tears dry up and I sit up.

"Sure, why not?"

Bentley

I haven't been able to get my sister's words out of my mind. I never thought of how much my life would change when it comes to those close to me once I get drafted. Yeah, I know the fame and money will come. But I didn't think about how much I'm not like Erica and Lauren. They plan to return home after college to work in our hometown and start a family there.

I've always taken for granted that they will all be there when I return. Like frozen figures in a snow globe, waiting for my attention to return to them. To hear that Zah doesn't think she'll fit in that picture doesn't make sense to me. However, now that it's been said, I can't get it out of my mind.

"Fuck, she came here for one last chance to be a part of my life," I say as I stare down into my lap.

Like a little sister missing her big brother, and here I've fucked it all up. I don't know where life will take any of us, but I understand what Erica tried to get through to me. We're all growing up and life is changing.

Our paths might not meet up the same and with my future set to be in the league, I might not have the same circle when I do return home. This has been a huge dose of reality for me. I'm also flattered Zah would choose to come here to have this time with me.

"You're an absolute moron," I breathe.

I should be getting ready for the party we're throwing tonight, but I've been sitting here with my towel still around my waist, lost in my thoughts. I feel like such an asshole. There has to be a way to make this up to Zah.

Erica has never chewed me out so badly before. Knowing I hurt Zah's feelings makes me sick to my stomach. If only she didn't reduce my brain to mush.

"Bro, they're looking for some muscle to help with the kegs downstairs. You almost ready?" Corey pops his head into my room.

"Yeah, I'll be there in a bit. Hey, man, did you catch up with Zah and her friend?"

"I ran into her friend Arlene in the cafeteria, she's her roommate. I gave her my number and told her what to look out for. She said your girl was fine, just a little shaken up. I think when Jason tipped the ball, it took some of the speed off as it slipped through his hands."

"Bro, it wasn't a dart. It was a floater. Jason was complaining they were stinging his hands. I took some of the heat off," I say, hoping like hell I only hurt her feelings.

"I hope so. Maybe she'll feel up to coming out tonight and you can apologize in person. Jason is going to have to tighten up on those butterfingers, though, if we're going to make a bowl this year."

"You're telling me. It's no wonder they've been recruiting new receivers so hard," I snort.

Corey raps his knuckles on the doorjamb as he laughs. "See you downstairs, bro. Tonight is gonna be epic," he croons and turns to walk away.

I stand and walk over to the mirror in my room. I run my hand through my wet locks as they curl and wave wildly around my face. For all the confidence I give off, I'm nervous as fuck when it comes to the thought of Zah showing up for this party.

I flex my pecs. I'm a lot bigger than I was the last time she saw me back home. Does she like shit like this? Should I cut my hair? *Fuck.*

Why does she fuck with my head so much? It should be easy between us since I've known her all my life. Zahirah is the only girl who can make me blush and turn my stomach into knots. Yet I seem to put my foot in my mouth every time she's near me.

"Pull it together, bro," I say to my reflection.

I shrug my thoughts off and head to get dressed. There's no way she's coming tonight after getting hit in the head. Besides, tonight I need to break things off with Carly.

The tantrum she threw when my sister called was a turnoff. My family will always come first. That includes Zah.

It's time I bring an end to our annoying situation. It's been a long time coming. What's the point in dragging it out?

Tossing on a pair of jeans shorts and a polo shirt, I then shove my feet into a pair of high-top sneakers. I spray on some cologne and brush my hair to try to tame it. One last glance in the mirror and I'm off to help out downstairs.

I try my best to clear my mind of what happened earlier and the call from my little sister. Tomorrow I'll figure out how to make things right with Zah. Her birthday is coming soon.

Maybe I'll get her something nice or take her out somewhere. She doesn't know the area yet. She might like that. A new memory.

"Yo, Bent, where you been? I could use your help, man," Dustin calls as I come down the stairs.

"I'm here now. What do you need?"

"I have two more kegs that need to go out back. The DJ needs a table and there's something wrong with the bathroom down here again."

"I'll get him the table. We should lock that bathroom for the night, send everyone upstairs. Let's get to those kegs after I bring in the table. Cool?"

The guys call me the organizer. They all act as if they can't put *A* and *B* together without a coach. As team captain, I'm used to it.

"Yeah, that works. I'll lock the bathroom. That's a good idea. It will only be busted halfway through the night anyway," he says and heads to lock the bathroom.

I get to work on my tasks and have the DJ set up in no time. It's as I'm helping with the last two kegs that I feel eyes on me. I turn to find Carly staring at me.

Yup, this ends tonight. Perfect timing.

CHAPTER FIVE

Jealousy

Bentley

"So wait, you brought me up here to dump me?" Carly seethes, tossing her long hair over her shoulder as she sits on my bed.

The tight red dress she has on barely contains her breasts and is short enough to expose her ass if she bends over. Heck, I think it might be visible without her bending. I'm getting quite the view from where I'm standing. Honestly, it's not how I would want my girl to dress.

Other guys might find it hot, but not me. It's one of the reasons I've never slept with her. I sobered up before I made that mistake.

"Would you have preferred I had done it in front of everyone?"

"I would have preferred you not try to dump me at all. Is this because of that new bitch? She's a fucking freshman."

"Don't call her a bitch. This has nothing to do with her. I haven't been feeling it for a while," I bite out.

"Whatever," she huffs and stands. "If that's what you want. Just remember this is your loss."

"I'm sure," I mumble.

"Excuse me?"

"Nothing. I hope you have a good time tonight. I don't want this to ruin your vibe," I say and force a smile.

She stomps her way to the door where I'm standing and shoves her way by me. I don't even care when she slams the door behind her. Leaning my back against the door, I close my eyes and exhale.

I already feel like I can breathe. I don't know how I get myself into shit like this. Now that it's over, maybe I'll enjoy this party tonight.

I blow out a breath and push off the door. First things first, I need a beer. I'm not trying to get shit-faced, but a good buzz is welcome for sure.

I jog down the stairs. The party is now in full swing. Carly is in her usual spot with her friends, twirling her hair around her finger as she glares at me. I ignore her and her friends and head for the keg in the kitchen.

I fill my cup and turn to people-watch. A couple of my buddies surround me and start to chat. We're in the middle of a conversation when the air in the room shifts.

"Dude, where has she been hiding? I've always wanted to hook up with a Black chick. She has to be the one," Terry says, causing me to look toward the door.

Zah and Arlene have just walked in. Zahirah looks amazing. Her hair is down from the ponytail she was wearing earlier.

Her thick locks are now in deep waves, framing her pretty face as they fall down around her shoulders. She has on a pair of short shorts that show off her shapely, sexy brown legs, which I know come from years of running track and swimming.

On her feet are a pair of wedge heels that tie up her ankles, drawing attention to her toned and defined calves. The blue short-sleeved button-down she's wearing clings to her breasts in a way that's appealing but not a turnoff. Zah is effortlessly sexy.

Terry takes off in her direction, but I grab him by the back of his collar and lift him off his feet. He turns to look at me in shock. I don't take my eyes off Zah as I speak my next words.

"Don't even think about it. She's off-limits," I growl.

"What the hell, bro?"

I drop him as Jason walks over to her and tosses his arm over her shoulder. I bare my teeth and finish my beer. It's when Corey walks over—pushing her hair back from her face, before pinching her chin between his fingertips to lift her head—that I'm in motion.

Jealousy courses through me, making me feel like I'm going to explode. I should probably take a moment to breathe and think, but I can't get my feet to stop.

I walk over and tug Zah from Jason's hold. Corey drops his hand away from her face and looks at me like I've lost my mind. I turn to look down at Zah, she's looking up at me with knitted brows.

"What are you doing here?" I say without thinking.

"Arlene was invited. I'm with her," she says.

"You shouldn't be here."

"Why not? I don't plan to drink. I'm not a liability."

"Why would you want to be here? You should—"

"Bentley, I don't know what I did to you, but you can back off. I'm not here to tag along or be up under you. I'm not going to kill your vibe and I would hope you'd do the same for me. Enjoy your night," she says, tugging from my hold and storming off with her friend in tow once again.

I stand staring after her for the second time today. I close my eyes and groan as I think over what all I just said to her. None of it came out right.

What I meant to ask was why she was here after getting hit this afternoon. She should be home resting. I keep putting my foot in my mouth.

I start to go after her to clear things up, but my frat brothers come and surround me, dragging me into a drinking game. Not wanting to make this worse and ruin her first college party, I go with them and try to ignore the fact that she's here.

"There's more going on there than you're saying, am I right?" Jason says in my ear as I down a shot.

"I don't know what's going on. I'm not trying to be an asshole. It's just when she's around, my brain-to-mouth function never works right."

He laughs and pats me on the back. I look at him and scowl. I'm not sure what the hell is so funny.

I shrug his hand off and turn to look around for Zah. My blood boils as I notice a group of my teammates has surrounded her and her friend. However, my head explodes as I watch Carly toss a drink on Zah's shirt then try to act as if it's an accident.

"Well, damn," Jason breathes in shock as we watch what happens next.

Zahirah

I can't believe Bentley. I mean, who does he think he is? Corey and Jason don't even know me, and they've been so nice to me and shown me so much concern.

If not for wanting to show him I can go to any party and enjoy myself with or without his permission, I would have left. However, I'm not going to allow him to ruin my first college party. My head is fine and I'm having a good time.

Arlene did a great job curling my hair and helping me pick out an outfit. I was surprised by her knowledge of how to work with my hair until she told me she's from a blended family and has a stepsister who's African American. I totally lucked out when it comes to my roommate.

She's making this party fun and has taken my mind off the big idiot across the room. I've been doing my best not to look in Bentley's direction even as his friends make a ruckus while tossing back drinks and horsing around.

"So you're going to be on the track team?" a guy whose name I can't remember asks.

"That's the plan. I'm excited to meet the team and throw myself into the new routine," I reply.

"You guys have a great program. I look forward to seeing you compete," he says as his gaze rolls over me.

I turn to the guy on my right to keep from sending mixed signals. He seems like he might be a nice guy, but I'm not interested. He's been undressing me with his eyes since he came over here.

To be honest, most of the guys here seem to be more interested in hooking up than anything else. I'm not taking this that far. I'm offered another beer and decline.

"Come dance with me," Arlene says as she leans into my ear.

I nod and go to turn with her to head to one of the open areas where everyone is dancing. There are a lot more people than I was expecting. Which is why I'm not that surprised when someone's drink ends up on me and my shirt. I jump back and shake my hands out.

When I look up, Bentley's girlfriend stands looking back at me with a nasty grin on her face. She gives a fake gasp and covers her mouth with her hand.

"I'm so sorry. I didn't see you there," she says dramatically.

I see right through her. Her friends snickering around her only confirms what I already know. I ball my fists at my sides. The last thing I'm about to do is allow this chick to bully me.

"I'm sure it was an accident," I say dryly.

"Those seem to be happening a lot around here. How's your head?" she says in the snarkiest tone I've ever heard.

"My head is fine."

"So you admit you're a lying, boyfriend-stealing slut," she hisses at me.

"Excuse me?"

She pulls a face and steps closer into my space. I refuse to step back. She's not about to intimidate me.

"I said you're a liar, a boyfriend stealer, and a nasty-ass slut. Look at you all up in our star players' faces. You skank-ass bitch," she says and goes to push me.

The next thing I know, my hand is stinging from slapping the shit out of her before she can put her hands on me. Corey is at my side right away. He gets between us before this disrespectful heifer can try something else.

I look down at my clothes and groan. My white shorts are ruined, and my thin top is now see-through and stained red. I peel the top away from my front.

A yelp leaves my lips as I'm suddenly picked up bridal style. I look up into the angry face of Bentley. He starts for the stairs that lead to the second level of the house.

I'm in shock at first. Then annoyance runs through me. Is he angry because I slapped his girlfriend after she attacked me?

"Where are you taking me?" I hiss.

"Your top is see-through. You need something to cover you up."

"Bent, put me down. I can walk on my own."

"Your bra is as thin as this shirt. I can see your nipples. I'm not putting you down for anyone else to see," he says tightly.

I look down at how he has me pressed tightly to his chest. My cheeks heat. I am wearing a thin-panel bra with no padding. Instead of protesting, I wrap my arms around his neck.

He walks into one of the bedrooms and kicks the door closed behind him. Then he places me on my feet. His chest is heaving as he looks down into my eyes. My shoes are giving me a bit of height, but I still have to tilt my head back to make eye contact.

He opens his mouth as if he's about to say something, but clamps it shut and shakes his head. Turning, he then heads for the closet. He peels the shirt he's wearing off.

His back comes into view. The way it flexes and ripples with the motion causes me to pull my lip between my teeth. He's so much bigger than the last time I saw him—more muscular and bulky.

He reaches into the closet and takes out a dress shirt. When he turns to face me, my mouth drops open. His body never used to be this sculpted.

He comes over to hand me the shirt. I take it as I eat him up with my gaze. He flexes his pecs, breaking me out of my trance.

"Put that on and I'll take your things down the hall to clean them."

"Thanks. Why did you take your shirt off?" I say just above a whisper.

"The front is covered in red shit from where you were pressed against me. I need to change it. Why? You see something you like?" he says with a cocky grin on his sexy lips.

Bentley has a nice white smile and a wide mouth. His lower lip is fuller than his upper one, but his upper lip makes the perfect bow. He would make a great male model.

"No, I ... I ... I um, can you turn around so I can change?"

He looks me over lazily. I bring the dress shirt up in front of me, clenched tightly in my hand. He lets out a small laugh and turns to head back to the closet.

Nervously, I place the dress shirt down on the bed and start to undress. I strip down to my panties and slip the dress shirt on. It swallows me, so I pull the belt from my shorts and wrap it around my waist.

"Zah, we should talk," he says as I turn to find him staring back at me.

"Were you watching me, asshole?"

CHAPTER SIX

Crazy Actions

Bentley

"What? No."

"You were staring at me when I turned around. I didn't tell you I was done. You were watching me, you perv," she tosses at me.

I wasn't watching her. Not really. I glanced in the mirror a few times. On the last glance, I saw she was done and turned at the same time she did.

I close my eyes and throw my head back. "I'm not an asshole or a perv. I turned the same time you did. Why has everything been so hard with you today?" I growl in frustration.

"Oh. Well, I can help you with that," she says and goes to storm out.

I snap into action to stop her. "Zah, wait," I say as I reach her and hold my hand against the door.

I dip my head and inhale her sweet scent. I can't help placing a hand on her waist. The pull I feel to her is so strong, she has to feel it too.

"Wait for what?" she says without turning.

I slide my hand down the door until I reach her shoulder level and then place my palm on it. I turn her to face me and look down at her face. Her lips are so full and plump looking. They sit under the cutest nose I've ever seen. Her whiskey-brown eyes are so pretty with their oval shape and long lashes.

I lift my index finger and ghost the backside down the bridge of her nose. God, she's gorgeous. I bite my lower lip and drop my gaze to her mouth.

"I'm not an asshole, Zah. I was taken by surprise earlier. I didn't know it was you. I had no idea you were coming here.

"I was worried about you when you arrived here tonight. I wish you would have stayed home to rest." I brush my thumb against her hairline, wiping away the beads of sweat that are starting to gather. I keep my eyes on the movement and swallow hard. "I'm sorry I hit you with that ball. I've been fucking this up all day."

"Fucking what up?" she says and frowns.

"This," I murmur and lean in to take her lips.

She gasps as I brush her lips with mine, allowing me to slip my tongue into her mouth. I slip my arm around her and tug her flush with my body. A deep groan leaves me as I deepen the kiss.

I reach for her neck and hold her in place as I explore her mouth with my tongue. Kissing her is better than I could have imagined. The deeper I kiss her, the more I want.

I feel like I'm high from her sweet mouth. When she slips her fingers into my hair, my restraint breaks. All thoughts of why this is wrong and why I can't have her fly out the window.

I bend my legs to wrap my arms around her thighs and lift her up onto my waist. Neither one of us breaks the kiss as I pin her to the door while devouring her mouth. She whimpers as I palm her ass beneath the shirt I gave her.

"Bent, wait," she breathes as she turns her face away from me.

"What's wrong, baby?" I say against the side of her face.

"I don't do cheaters. You have a girlfriend."

I go to tell her Carly isn't my girlfriend and I'm not seeing anyone else, but banging and shouting start on the other side of my door. I knit my brows and place Zah on her feet. When I tear the door open, a frazzled-looking Jason stands on the other side, shouting my name.

"What's going on?"

"Bro, Carly is down there beating the shit out of your car with a baseball bat. She's busted all the windows out," he says quickly.

"Are you fucking kidding me?" I snarl and take off out of the room.

My father just gave me that car as a birthday gift. That car costs more than Carly's tuition. My dad works hard for our family.

That was a lot of money for him to put out on me with a second child just going to college and four more still at home. I'm fuming as I run out of the house to see what she's done to my car. Campus security already has her in cuffs, but the damage is done.

"My fucking car," I growl as I tug at my hair.

The hood is dented in, and all the windows are smashed out, including the sunroof. The door looks like she got to it too. Tears burn the backs of my eyes; it's not the material item that hurts my heart. My dad was so proud when he handed the keys over.

Business wasn't as great as he let on last year. Mom told me how hard he worked and how much he sacrificed to do this for me. I'm super close with my dad. This is going to break his heart.

"Are you fucking insane?" I roar.

"Fuck you. You better go after your new bitch," she snarls back at me.

I turn to see what the fuck she's talking about. Zah and Arlene are rushing into a vehicle up the block from the house. I clench my jaw and ball my fists at my sides.

"Zah," I bellow. "Zah, stop. Wait."

I start to run after her, but Arlene peels out and takes off. I want to run after them, but I need to handle pressing charges for the vandalism of my car.

I stop and close my eyes, tugging at my hair once again. This day fucking sucks. Suddenly, my father's voice plays in my ear.

See the positive, Bent. Never allow the negatives to take over the good moments.

I reach to touch my lips and smile. I kissed Zariah and it was amazing. Once I clear things up, she's going to be mine.

"This isn't over, Zah," I mutter to myself as I stand in the middle of the street.

CHAPTER SEVEN

We Need to Talk

Zahirah

The student center is alive and buzzing with chatter as Arlene and I walk in. I look around nervously. I haven't been around this large a group of the student body since the frat party.

My classes have been small, but more students are filling them up each day. The campus has been lively, but nothing like this with such a concentrated group in one area.

This is my first time having dinner in the student cafeteria. I've been eating takeout in our room to avoid running into Bentley. I didn't tell Arlene what happened up in his room. In all honesty, I'm still processing that entire day for myself.

"Let's get our food and find some place to sit," Arlene says.

"Sounds good," I murmur.

"I wonder if they have that pasta dish I was telling you about. That was so good. I wouldn't mind having that again today."

"I hope they have some fresh fruit. I need to get back on my diet. I felt a little sluggish out there yesterday," I reply.

"Girl, if that was sluggish, I need to think about my life and my diet. I've broken wind slower than that."

I burst into laughter and shake my head. "You're a mess."

We grab our food and go to find a table to sit at. There aren't many options. A group gets up from one of the larger tables and we rush to take it.

"Hey, look. There's Terry. You remember him from the party, right?" Arlene says as she waves him over.

"Not really." I shrug.

It's been two weeks since I arrived on campus and went to my first frat party. Totally overrated in my opinion. I'm in no rush to go to another.

Though Arlene hasn't stopped trying to talk me into going to several parties over the last two weeks. I haven't had time for that. Between orientation and learning my way around the campus, as well as training with my new team, I haven't had much time for anything else. Which is how I've avoided Bentley since the party.

There are several rumors flying around about what Carly did to his car. Some say she did it out of jealousy because he was at the party flirting with others. Others say they broke up and she wanted revenge because he hooked up with someone else.

I don't know what to believe and at this point, I honestly don't care. Bentley is allowed to do whatever he wants to do. I'm done with my stupid crush; he's not at all the person I thought he was.

"Nickels," Corey croons as he comes over with Terry to sit with us at our table.

"How do you know my last name?"

"One of my best bros is interested in you. I made it my business to find out everything I could," Corey says.

"Your best bro? Who's your best bro?"

"Coswell, of course."

I groan and roll my eyes. "Bentley is not interested in me. We grew up together, that's all."

"If that's what you think, we'll go with that," he says noncommittally. "How's campus treating you so far? Are you finding your way around?"

"It's been okay. My schedule is keeping me busy."

"I hear you're like a bullet out there. I can't wait to see you in action. You're keeping off the injured list, I hope."

"Haven't taken a football to the face, if that's what you mean."

"I guess that's easy to do when you're avoiding the quarterback."

I sigh and rub my hands on my jeans. I don't want to talk about Bentley, but it seems his friend is hell-bent on getting me to. That kiss has been plaguing my thoughts and dreams.

I left that party confused and so conflicted. I decided that night that it would be best to steer clear of him to keep from embarrassing myself anymore. Although he kissed me, I can't help feeling like everything that went wrong that night was my fault.

Erica told me their dad bought him that car. I know how much it means to Bentley. If it weren't for me, his jealous girlfriend wouldn't have ruined it.

Then there's the fact that he was about to cheat on her with me. I never would have forgiven myself if I had allowed it to go any further. I still feel a little guilty.

"Now this looks like the place to be," Jason calls out as he comes to take a seat.

Our table is beginning to fill up with members of the football team. I had hoped to be able to come here and eat in peace. However, it seems I'm a little more popular than I thought I was.

Everyone begins to joke around as conversations spark around the table. Corey and Jason sit talking to me animatedly. They are hilarious. I get a big brother vibe from Corey, and Jason is like a big, goofy teddy bear.

I'm doubled over in laughter when the energy around the table shifts. I swipe at the tears leaking from the corners of my eyes and turn to see what has changed the atmosphere. Bentley is standing over me, glaring down at me and Corey, who's sitting next to me.

I stare back at him, wondering what all the tension is about. The way he's looking back at me, you would think I was the cheater. I'm so confused when it comes to him.

I don't know what happened to my friend and I'm not sure why I ever had a crush on him. I should be happy that he was my first kiss ever. However, that moment will forever be tainted by the fact that he had a girlfriend. A girlfriend who trashed his car after he made out with me.

"Can we talk?" he asks with that scowl on his face.

"No, we can't," I reply and turn back toward my food to pick at it.

I've completely lost my appetite. The laughter around the table has died down as well. I can feel everyone's eyes on us.

Bentley doesn't seem to care as he places his hands on either side of me on the table, caging me in, then leans into my ear. My heartbeat picks up and my hands start to sweat. I scoot forward a bit in my seat, trying to put some space between us.

"Don't make me do this in front of everyone."

"Do what?"

"Have a conversation that should be just between me and you. You have everything wrong, Zah, and I'm not giving up until you see that."

Bentley

She smells so nice, like cocoa butter and peaches. It's taking everything in me not to tilt her head back and take her lips. For two weeks, I've been thinking about that kiss. Longing to duplicate it.

Zah has been the only thing on my mind. I haven't been focused at practice or class. I'm useless. That's why we need to have this conversation so I can keep my head clear.

It frustrates me that she has this so wrong. Technically, Carly was never my girlfriend. So it's hard for me to even think of her as my ex. This shouldn't even be a problem.

"You can come take a walk with me, or we can have this conversation here in the cafeteria in front of everyone," I say into her ear as I keep her caged in with my arms.

She cranes her neck to look back at me and narrows her eyes. "I'll take a walk with you, but I don't know what for. I'm not going to change my mind."

"Coswell, give the girl some space. It's bad enough you've warned half the team off," Henry G calls out from the far end of the table.

I stand up straight and glare at the asshole. I overheard him the other day talking about Zah to some of the other guys. Damn right I told them all to stay away from her.

Like I don't know they play for points when it comes to girls. Zahirah isn't a toy for anyone to play with. I'll put my fist down their throats if they try me.

"Mind your business, Henry," I bark back.

"You've been warning guys off?" Zah snaps, grabbing my attention.

"Yeah, I have and will continue to."

"You're an asshole. You have no right, Bentley," she says and stands to push me out of the way.

I stumble back as she marches off, dumping her trash as she stews in her anger. I place my hands on my hips and shake my head as I watch her go. She's still as stubborn as ever.

"Bro, you're still striking out. Why not step aside and let someone show you how it's done?" Henry taunts.

I point a finger at him. "You and I have a problem. I suggest you steer clear of me."

With that, I turn and head out to the weight room to blow off some steam. It's been a long day. I got the news that Carly will not be expelled. She's only going to get a slap on the wrist.

They're blaming it on the alcohol and giving her a pass because her father is a big donor and an alumnus. Total bullshit if you ask me. If I had trashed her car like that, I would have been out on my ass and in a jail cell.

However, her father did write a check to cover the damage to my car and then some. After getting the news about Carly, I received a call from my dad. He wants to come for a visit.

I haven't decided whether or not I will tell him about the car, so this isn't the greatest time for that. Now I have Zah pissed off at me for another reason. And all I want is to pull her into my arms and tell her how much she has always meant to me. I know I said no girls, and this is why. However, this is Zah.

***

"Coswell, calm the fuck down," Coach barks at me as I beat the shit out of Henry G.

I told him to stay out of my way. Coach already warned the team not to touch me in practice. However, Henry decided to sack me like the grade-A asshole he is. I tore my helmet off and stripped off my pads, then ripped his helmet off his head and started to beat his ass.

I lick my lips in satisfaction as I watch blood pour from his nose. The asshole deserved it. He's been taunting me since practice started.

"You two, in my office after practice. You're done for the day," Coach bellows.

"I think he needs a medic first," I snort.

"Bentley, I'm warning you."

I throw my hands up in the air as I walk backward. "I'm only stating the facts, Coach. My teammate needs some medical attention. He looks pretty banged up," I say with a smug grin.

"Fuck you," Henry snarls.

I lift my arm and flex my muscles then kiss my bicep before I turn back to Henry and wink. He growls and tries to lunge at me.

Coach grabs him by the shoulders and shoves him back. "You didn't get enough? Want him to close the other eye? I told you not to touch him in the first place. You're lucky I didn't let him beat your ass some more. You've lost your starting spot. Make me sit you down for the season," he says to Henry.

I laugh and blow Henry a kiss from behind Coach's back. Jason and Corey come to grab me by an arm each, tugging me off the field. I shrug them off and start for the locker room.

"Bro, he's an asshole. We all know that, but are you sure it's wise to mess with the chemistry in the locker room?" Corey says, always the voice of reason.

"It's my locker room. If anyone wants to get behind him, they can all find another team to play for. He broke the rules. I showed him the consequences. Fuck him," I say and shrug.

"I kind of agree with you both on this one," Jason says. "Coach clearly stated not to touch Bentley or the receivers in this practice. If he can't show self-control now, I can point out who will cause all our penalties during the season."

"Exactly."

I freeze in my tracks as the word falls from my lips. Standing across the field watching me is Zah. Fuck, I can't catch a break.

CHAPTER EIGHT

Flowers

Zahirah

"When did your brother turn into a complete bully?" I say into the phone as I talk to Erica.

"I don't know. That doesn't sound like him. That guy had to have had it coming for something," she replies.

I can't tell her the guy ratted her brother out for blocking guys from talking to me. I don't want to raise any questions. I can't lie to Erica. She'll know something more is up.

Instead, I try to change the subject. "How is school going for you so far?"

"You mean this lame campus where I know no one and have no friends? Yeah, go on and call me an idiot. I should be there with you and Bentley. This was such a dumb idea."

"I still don't know what made you change your mind."

She heaves a heavy sigh. "If I tell you something, will you keep it between us?"

"You know I will. Of course."

"I overheard Mom and Dad talking. They were thinking about selling the house. Dad lost a few million dollars in some bad investments. He needed to turn things around, or we were headed toward losing everything.

"I couldn't follow you and Bentley. You're both on scholarship. I would have been counting on Mom and Dad to pay my tuition. I couldn't put that on them, so I chose the affordable option once I couldn't pull off a scholarship like you guys," she explains.

"Oh, Erica. I didn't know. Is everything all right now?"

"Now, yeah. Dad was able to turn it all around. I might transfer next semester or something. I really hate it here," she groans.

"I would love that. I miss you so much."

"I miss you too, best. It will be like old times. The three of us taking over the world."

"I don't know about that. Bentley is … I don't know. He's different."

"Still think there's something going on you're missing. You should talk to him and see what's up," she says.

"*I don't know*," I drag out. I glance at the clock and see I'm running late. "Erica, I have to go. We're doing evening training this week and I should be on my way to practice. I'll talk to you later."

"Love you. Call me later."

"Love you too. I will. Promise."

I hang up and grab my gym bag to rush out. I'm going to have to run for it so I'm not late. I take off as soon as I step out of the dorm building. As I run, a shirtless Bentley catches my eye in the grass outside the training facility. He's surrounded by a bunch of girls while he laughs and smiles at them.

I roll my eyes and keep running. I don't miss that he pauses and watches me as I pass by. I still can't get over how he beat that guy up earlier. If Arlene didn't have to drop off those notes to one of Bentley's teammates, I wouldn't have known my childhood friend had turned so violent.

Sure, I've seen him lose it on the field before, or go at it with guys at school, but that was different today. It seemed so personal. Bentley meant to hurt that guy.

I shake the thought off as I pull the door open to the gym. We're using the indoor track today. I sigh as I glance at my watch. I'm not late, but I'm right on time, which is late to me.

I chide myself for not paying more attention to the clock. My dad would give me an earful right about now if he were here. You waste no one's time and respect every minute you're given. If you're a Nickels, you don't give people a chance to say you're ever late.

"Hey, this is the first time we've all beat you anywhere. I had thought you weren't coming," Tori, one of my teammates, says.

"No, I got caught up and lost track of time."

"Could you have gotten caught up with a certain quarterback? Rumors are flying around that you two are together," she says excitedly and wiggles her brows.

I look at her and my mouth falls open as we stretch for practice. I release my arm and shake both out. Maybe I heard her wrong.

"What did you say?"

"I heard you two are hooking up. That's why he's telling all the guys on campus you're off-limits. Anyone who touches you ends up like Henry G," she says with stars in her eyes. "I wish I had a guy that possessive over me."

"We are not hooking up. People around here gossip too much. It's sad."

"Well, I overheard it from him. Someone asked him and he said you were his and everyone needed to back off," she says and bites her lip.

"What?" I growl and stumble as I release my leg and lose my footing.

"I swear. I was in the quad when I heard him say that," she says and holds her hands up.

"I'm going to kill him."

"Girl, I would love it if he were spreading those kinds of rumors about me. He's so freaking hot."

I press my fingers to my temples and groan. I look like a boyfriend stealer, just like Crazy Carly said. What the hell is Bentley thinking?

Wait until I see him again. I'm going to give him a piece of my mind. I try to shake off this new information and focus on practice.

However, my anger simmers even as I make my first warm-up lap around the track. I distance myself from everyone as I stew in my thoughts, not wanting to hear anything else about Bentley or this fake relationship he's spreading around.

"Big idiot. Just wait until I get my hands on him. Why would he tell people we're together?"

"Nickels, did you hear me?" Coach calls out to me as I finish the first lap.

"I ... I ... um."

I can't spit my words out because Bentley is standing in the training gym shirtless with a bouquet of roses in his hands and a smile on his face as Corey and Jason hold up a sign that says.

Happy Birthday, Zah.

Bentley

The look on Zahirah's face was not what I was expecting. I know her birthday isn't until tomorrow, but I wanted to do something nice for her after earlier today and her seeing me beat the shit out of Henry. I need her to see me as the guy she's always known.

However, that doesn't seem to be working. Is she really that mad at me for kicking Henry's ass? If she knew the things he said about her and all the other girls on campus, she wouldn't spare him a single thought.

The dude is trash. No one on the team cares for him much. He has a few friends here and there, but they've been pulling away as well.

Determined to get through to Zah this time, I wait out her practice. Jason and Corey, God love them, stand cheering her name as they hold up their sign the entire time. I've put on my shirt that was in my back pocket and I'm still holding the two dozen roses when she stalks over to us.

"Thank you, Corey," she says and lifts on her toes to kiss his cheek.

"You're welcome, gorgeous."

Then she moves to Jason and kisses his cheek as well. "Thanks."

"Anytime," he replies.

I stand waiting for her to take the roses and thank me, but she glares at me and bites out an order for me to follow her. I'll take that over her ignoring me. We need to talk anyway.

We step outside the gym, and she whirls on me as soon as the door shuts behind me. I stop and look at her with my brows knit. She looks beautiful even with sweat drying on her face.

"Why are you telling people we're together? What the heck are you thinking? Especially with your psycho girlfriend lurking around campus."

"She's not my girlfriend. That's what I want to talk to you about," I say and close the distance between us.

"Could have fooled me. You didn't press charges, that's the only reason she's still here. Only a jealous girlfriend would do something like that to your car."

"I broke up with her before the party started. I didn't know she was going to lose it and trash my car. As for the rest, I don't know where you're getting your information from. I did press charges and got a restraining order against her once they didn't expel her.

"She's only still here because of her father. He's a big donor and alum here. As long as she stays away from me, they're allowing her to finish the year. They've blamed the whole thing on her having too much to drink," I say in frustration.

She looks at me in surprise. "Are you shitting me? She's a danger to others. She should have been thrown out that night."

"Well, when Daddy's throwing money around, you kind of get away with anything. Listen, Zah, about that night—"

"No, Bentley. We've been friends for a really long time. I think we should keep it that way. I'm here for my education. The last two weeks have already shown me I don't have much time for anything else. Let's forget what happened so we don't confuse our relationship."

My nostrils flare and I swallow hard. I can't allow this to end with her pissed off at me again. I frown as I think fast. "Will you at least take the flowers?"

"Fine, give me those." She takes them and holds them up to her nose.

A small smile comes to her lips. I know that smile. It's the smile she gives me right before she forgives me.

"What are you doing for your birthday tomorrow?"

"Nothing, because apparently, I have a boyfriend who's threatening every guy on campus to stay away from me."

I grab her by the front of her sweaty shirt and pull her to me. She looks up at me cautiously. I bite my lip and look down at hers.

I want to kiss her so bad my heart is hammering. I dip my head until we are face to face and my lips are all but a breath away from hers.

"In that case, you should let me take you out for your birthday. I'm not afraid of your boyfriend and his threats," I say against her lips.

"I guess you could, to make up for stealing my first kiss and making me look like a boyfriend stealer."

I lift a brow in question. Her first kiss? I was her first kiss.

I grab the back of her neck and kiss her hard. Fuck, I want to be her first everything. I devour her lips as she whimpers into my mouth.

I kiss her deeper and drag her body as close to me as I can get it with the bouquet between us. Why the hell does she taste so fucking good?

"I'm sorry for everything. I'm so happy you're here. Can we start over?" I say as I break the kiss and look down into her eyes.

"I don't know. I remember you saying something about staying focused while you are in college. I don't want to be a distraction," she says and bites her lip as she looks up at me through her lashes.

"That was before my crush dropped on campus like an angel out of heaven," I say as I cup her face and run my thumb across her lips.

"Well, when you put it like that. I'd like to start over, Bentley. Let's be friends and play our game. If you win, we can be more. If I win, I'll think about what's next and if it fits into my schedule."

I laugh as I think of the game we used to play. Zah is as competitive as I am. This could be fun.

"You know I never lose. Baby, you're on. You're as good as mine."

"We shall see."

"That we shall," I growl into her neck as I hold her close.

CHAPTER NINE

Happy Birthday

Zahirah

It's early morning and I'm at the football field waiting for Bentley to arrive. The morning chill on campus is real and something I'm not used to. This is a different type of cold.

Bentley and I spent last night texting back and forth. It started with a birthday text at midnight. We continued to text until I couldn't see straight and nearly dropped my phone on my face.

I woke up this morning wondering if I dreamed it all. That's when I saw the text from Bent telling me to meet him on the field. So here I am.

I exhale deeply and watch my breath mist in front of me. Needing to stay warm against the morning chill, I begin to bounce from foot to foot. Bringing my hands up to my mouth, I blow on them.

"Good morning, birthday girl," is breathed into my ear, causing me to jump and turn.

Bentley is smiling back at me as he holds out a cup to me. I take the cup, and it warms my hands up right away. I take a sip, and the warm, sweet flavor bursts against my tongue.

"Thank you. It's my favorite. Carmel hot chocolate," I say and give him a little goofy grin.

I can't believe he remembers what kind of hot chocolate I like. It's perfect too. He places his hands on my hips and kisses my forehead.

"I remembered and thought you would want something to warm you up. We're not in Arizona anymore. This cold will get to you," he replies.

"So what are we doing out here? I thought our date was for tonight."

"It is, but can you blame me for wanting to spend the day with my girl on her birthday?"

"Not your girl yet. You haven't won, or did you forget already?"

"I haven't forgotten at all. That's why we're here." He nods to the stairs. "Challenge number one. First one to quit is the loser."

I smile wider. I should have known. This is our thing. Our game is to challenge each other mentally and physically.

"Oh, you're on."

I finish my hot chocolate and toss it into the bin a few paces away. I begin to roll my neck from side to side and then start to stretch. Bentley is already stretching as he watches me with a smile on his lips.

Once we're done, we move to the bottom of the stairs and stand side by side. I don't need my speed for this, I need my endurance. Bentley has always been full of energy. All I have to do is match that.

"I win this round, I get another date this weekend," he says.

"We haven't even gone on the first one. What if it's a bust?" I tease.

He bumps me with his hip. I laugh as I dodge him. He reaches for me and pulls me into him.

"I have the perfect date planned for tonight. I'm confident you'll want another."

"If you say so. What do I get when I win?"

"I never thought about that because you're not going to," he says.

"Is that right? Fine. I win, I get to pick the next two challenges, and you have to show me all the need-to-know spots on campus. I still haven't gotten around to exploring much."

"Deal, I would do that anyway. Let's go."

He turns and starts to run up. I'm right with him. It only takes a few seconds for me to get where I went wrong with this one. Bentley has been here for two years. He's used to the altitude here. I'm not.

My lungs are burning, and we've only been up and down once so far. I want to curse and fuss, but I suck it up and keep going. I'm no quitter.

"You okay, baby? You ready to quit?" Bentley taunts as we start up again.

I frown at him and keep going. How the heck is he talking while doing this? At this point, I'm no longer feeling the cold.

I push through and keep going. However, exhaustion from not sleeping much begins to catch up with me as we get to round four. Once I turn and get back down to the bottom, I'm ready to throw the towel in.

I stop and place my hands on my knees. I grind my teeth as Bentley hoots and fist pumps. I'm so mad I could spit, but my body is telling me I can't go any further.

"You cheated," I pant.

"Come on, baby. Don't be a sore loser."

"Don't baby me. It's my birthday. You should've let me win." I pout.

He laughs and tugs me into him. "I'll take you to breakfast at my favorite spot. You can get some strawberry French toast and corn beef hash."

I'm smiling so hard right now. That's my favorite thing for breakfast. Bentley is definitely showing how much he knows me.

"Sounds good to me."

A huge smile comes to his face. He leans in and takes my lips, kissing me breathless. When he pulls away, I can't stop smiling up at him.

He cups my face and runs his thumb across my lips. "Then we can hang out in my room at the frat house until we need to get ready for our date," he says.

"At the frat house, huh?" I say teasingly and lift a brow.

"Or we can hang in your dorm room." He shrugs.

"No, your room sounds good. As long as I can get some reading done."

"It's your birthday and you still want to do homework. Nothing has changed. You're still the same old Zah." He shakes his head at me.

I scoff. "As if you're not going to be watching film. I just gave you an out to do so."

He gives a little laugh and holds his hands up. I love how natural this feels. When he wraps his arm around me and begins to lead me away from the field, I can't help feeling like something has changed between us that will never be the same again, but I like it.

Bentley

We're sitting on my bed in my room at the frat house. I have my AirPods in as I watch film on my tablet. I glance up from the screen, and a smile comes to my face. Zah has a highlighter in hand and a textbook in her lap. However, I don't know how much she's retaining.

Her head is lolling to the side as she nods off. She jumps as she almost falls forward off the bed. I chuckle, causing her to turn and look at me with a frown.

Pulling one of my AirPods out, I then lift my arm out at my side. I do feel bad for waking her so early this morning after keeping her up all night texting. I just hate when I'm not with her.

"Come here," I say and wave her to me.

Zah sets her book aside and crawls her way to me. She turns and sits beside me, snuggling into my side. I palm her forehead and tug her head against me.

"Get some sleep, baby. You can finish studying later," I murmur.

She turns her face up and gives me a sleepy smile. I lean in to kiss her lips. When I go to pull away, she cups the back of my head and holds me to her, so I deepen the kiss.

My tablet forgotten, I grasp her waist and lower us onto the bed. She moans into my mouth as I drink from her lips. I'm growing so hard as I nestle between her legs.

Wanting to test the waters, I finger the hem of her shirt then brush the skin just above the waist of her leggings. When she doesn't protest, I reach beneath her shirt to cup her breast in my hand.

"Bent, wait," she calls as she breaks the kiss.

"Too much?" I ask and go to lift up.

She sits up and looks back at me worriedly. I return to my place against the wall and sit. Zah tucks back into my side.

"It's just ... well, I'm tired. I want to enjoy my first time, but I don't think I will like this."

"No problem, baby. We don't have to rush. Go ahead and rest."

I kiss the top of her head. I can't say I'm disappointed. I've waited this long for Zah; I'm willing to wait so much longer.

"Bent?"

"Yeah, Zah."

"Thank you."

I look down at her. Her eyes are already closed. She's such a beautiful girl. I can't believe she's mine.

"Anytime. I always want to make you happy," I say.

I release a laugh as her snores start to fill the room. Replacing my AirPod, I go back to watching film. A few moments go by, and I begin to realize I don't miss home. For two years, I have missed home every day.

I glance down at Zah and my heart swells. You can't miss home when you're there. I kiss her lips and allow mine to linger for a few moments.

***

"Thanks, buddy," I say to Corey as he hands over the keys to his pickup truck while we're standing in my room.

I wanted to make this date special. I spent hours online watching videos for inspiration as I thought of the things Zah loves. I think I have a nice balance of something romantic, something Zah will love, and something that will be special for us both.

I'm excited to make new memories with her. I'm still kicking myself for rushing things earlier. Zahirah deserves better. I want to give her better.

That's why this date is so important. It's our first and I get the feeling it might be her first as well. The thought of being all her firsts makes my chest swell with pride.

"No problem, we put everything you asked for in the truck bed. I even found a tent in case it rains. I hooked it up. The remote is in the glove compartment," Corey replies.

"I've been watching the forecast. We should be all right. Seriously, thanks. I couldn't have pulled this off without you and Jason."

A smile comes to his face, and he nods. Corey and Jason have become my closest friends here on campus. I get the feeling we'll be friends for life.

"It was my pleasure, bro. It's good to see you like this. Carly never seemed right for you. Zahirah is different. Your eyes light up around her."

I can't help but smile. It feels right to have Zah here. When she woke up and left to get ready, I felt an ache in my chest seeing her go. I know we'll be together again soon, but my heart left with her.

"Listen, I better get ready. I'll see you later," I say.

"Have fun. Don't do anything I wouldn't and if you do, be safe."

I laugh and shove him in the shoulder. I'm not doing this to get into Zah's pants. I genuinely want to see her happy. I can't wait for her to look up at me with that big old smile.

"Whatever," I murmur.

Corey pats me on the shoulder and nods before he walks out of my room. I turn to look at the stack of clothes on my bed from before Corey knocked on the door. I still don't know what to wear.

This feels like my first junior high school dance all over again. I blow out a breath and settle on the blue button-down and a pair of blue jeans. I race to hop in the shower and get dressed.

Once dressed, I look in the mirror and question myself. I'm questioning the outfit, the date, everything. I groan and palm my forehead.

When it comes to Zah, I always fuck things up. What if I'm screwing this up too? I cut my rambling thoughts off and take a deep breath the way I do before every game.

"You've got this, Bent," I mumble to myself.

CHAPTER TEN

First Date

Zahirah

Looking at the clock, I note I'm running out of time. I need to make a decision. I'm so nervous.

After my nap in Bentley's room, I left to get ready for our date. I can still feel his lips on mine after the kiss he planted on me before I left. I didn't want it to end.

Now I can't wait for this date, but I need to pick something to wear. I have changed my outfit a hundred times.

I finally settle on a pair of light-washed jeans and a black off-the-shoulder sweater. I finish the look off with a pair of black suede calf-high boots. I pull my hair up into a half ponytail and put the bottom half in large waves.

I can't help chewing on my lip. Frustrated, I blow out a breath and groan. Arlene flops on my bed and picks up a few of the items I've tossed aside.

"What's wrong? This one was cute on you," she says, holding up a dress I chucked.

"Did I go too casual? Should I change one more time? I want to be more than cute. It's my first date," I reply.

"Zahirah, you are gorgeous in anything you wear. I wish I could pull off everything like you. Like, you have the perfect amount of everything."

"Ugh, it doesn't feel like it today. Okay, okay. I'm going to try one more outfit. You can pick between the two and I'll wear whichever you pick," I say as she looks back at me pointedly.

I rush to pluck through the pile to find something else. Arlene grabs a dress from the mess and hands it over. I take it and hold it up.

"It's cute and flirty. The color looks great against your skin. Trust me, this is the one."

I purse my lips and nod, then quickly undress to slip the dress on. Once I'm in it, Arlene comes over to hand me a pair of toeless espadrilles. I look in the mirror and smile. This does look good.

"That's it, that's the one. Here, use your shimmer lotion and spray on this mist. You always smell nice when you wear it."

"Thanks," I say as I go to sit on the bed and lotion up again.

When I'm done, I spray on the mist. Looking over myself in the mirror, I can't help but smile. The dress is yellow and looks perfect against my skin.

"I don't know why I changed my mind about this one. It's perfect," I say.

"You've been overthinking everything. Don't think I didn't see you styling your hair a hundred times."

"Speaking of which, maybe I should change that too."

There is a knock on the door before she can reply, although she's sending me a glare. I curse under my breath and stomp my foot. I was going to try one more style. A glance at the clock tells me it's Bentley at the door and I'm out of time.

Arlene jumps up and answers the door as I smooth a hand over my hair and take one more look in the mirror. I release a sigh. This will have to do. When I turn to face the door, Bentley is standing there with a smile on his face and a bouquet of roses in his hand.

"We're running out of room to place all these flowers," Arlene teases.

"I'm sorry. I can't help wanting to spoil my girl. It's her birthday. She deserves these and more."

"I can't say I'm mad at all. Keep up the good work," she says.

I move to the door and take the flowers, then give them a sniff. A smile comes to my lips as I look up into Bentley's eyes. He gives me a crooked grin and leans in to kiss my lips.

I'm a little disappointed when he pulls away too soon. Arlene takes the flowers and hands me my bag. I give her a smile and step out the door.

Bentley places a hand on the small of my back, causing tingles to run up and down my spine. His hand is so big and warm.

My mind goes back to his room earlier. I was tired and things were moving a bit fast, but I really stopped because I didn't want to rush into making that type of decision. I was grateful for his understanding.

"Where are we going?" I ask as we get outside.

"They're still fixing up my ride, so I borrowed a friend's."

"You didn't answer my question. Where are you taking me?"

He shakes his head and smiles, then opens my door for me to get in. I roll my eyes and bite my lip. Bentley tugs me to him by my waist and pecks my lips.

"That will be a surprise. Just trust me."

When he pulls away and looks down into my eyes, I know I trust him. This is the Bentley I've always known.

I can trust him. He would never hurt me. This is who I expected to find when I first got here.

I relax and hop into the pickup truck. Bentley closes the door and rounds the truck, tapping the hood as he passes by. I give him a big smile as he climbs behind the steering wheel.

He leans in and cups my face, then connects our lips. My stomach flips and butterflies come to life as he deepens the kiss and consumes me.

"Ready?" he asks as he pulls away and pecks my nose.

"Never been more ready in my life. Let's see what you've got, Coswell."

"You've got it, gorgeous. One birthday date coming up," he croons.

I can't stop smiling as he pulls off. I'm so excited. How did I get here with my longtime crush and neighbor?

I hope this isn't a dream I'm going to wake up from. Bentley reaches over to place his hand on my thigh, causing my skin to tingle beneath his palm. This is the best birthday ever.

Bentley

"I need you to do me a favor and wait here," I say as I place the blindfold over Zah's eyes.

"A blindfold, really?" she says.

"Yeah, I need to set up, and I want you to get the full effect during the reveal," I say.

"Okay, fine."

I kiss her lips quickly, then turn to drive the short distance to our final destination. My heart is racing as I pull out of the trees and onto the overlook. Leaning forward, I look out of the windshield. The sky still looks clear, but I'll use that tent just in case.

It has a little viewing panel I can open up. I think Zah is going to love this. I glance at my watch and note I have enough time to set up before dinner arrives.

Looking to Zah before I hop out, I find her with a huge smile on her face, even as she sits with a blindfold on. I'm crazy about this girl. Her smile is infectious.

I turn on the radio, then hop out of the truck before I get sucked into her bubble. Quickly, I grab my stash from the back seat. Rounding the truck to the bed, I let down the gate and pull out the blow-up mattress and the pump.

As I wait for it to inflate, I work on the speaker system. When the mattress is done, I focus on getting a sheet on it.

"Great idea, Bent," I groan as I take a breath and wipe my hand across my forehead. I'm sweating from all this work.

I should have thought this part through a little better. Once I'm done with the sheet, I toss a blanket and a few pillows in place. As I peek in at Zah through the back window, I find her singing and bobbing her head.

I shake my head. She's a great swimmer and runner, but she needs some more singing lessons. I've always teased her about it. She loves to sing, but she sure as heck isn't great at it.

I get back to work, setting up the projector screen and stringing up lights for a romantic vibe. Like clockwork, Jason and Corey pull up with dinner. My face breaks into a smile as I look over my work.

"This looks great," Jason says. "I'm stealing this one next time I want to impress a chick."

"Yeah, whatever," I laugh. "Thanks, guys. Now get the heck out of here."

"You see this? This is how he treats us?"

Corey looks at him and rolls his eyes. He then grabs the back of Jason's shirt and drags him off. I laugh at them as I watch them climb back into Jason's car.

Now that the food and snacks are here, I set up the little trays I got for us. Turning on the projector that has a screensaver that says, *Happy Birthday*, I nod to myself and go to get Zah out of the truck.

"All right, come on. Careful now," I say as I help her out of the truck.

She releases the sweetest giggle as she tightens her hold on my hand. As I back up and guide her, I take her in. She looks gorgeous in the yellow dress. It's perfect against her rich, dark-brown skin. She wobbles a little, causing me to look down at her shoes.

Shit, I should've told her to wear flats. I would feel like shit if she hurt herself. I tug her to me and lift her in my arms.

I set her on the tailgate. Then I bend to take off her shoes, unfastening the straps around her ankles. Placing the shoes aside, I then reach to take her blindfold off.

I hold my breath as I watch her take her surroundings in. She turns to look behind her and then looks back at me. Her eyes fill with tears, causing me to start to freak out.

"Bentley, this is so beautiful," she chokes out.

"You like it?"

"Duh, is this a movie projector? How do we get inside? Something smells delicious."

I lift her up and walk to the side of the truck, where I help her to climb in. Once she's settled, I kick off my shoes and climb in behind her. I can't help staring at her as she looks at me with sparkling eyes as she nibbles on a fry from one of the trays.

"Are you comfortable?" I ask, fussing with the pillows.

"Yeah. Seriously, Bent. This is amazing."

I lean in and capture her lips, then pull away to place the tray across her lap. As she starts to tear into her favorite lemon pepper wings and fries, I get the movie started on the projector. For her, I'm willing to sit through *16 Candles* for the millionth time.

"*Awww*, this is so sweet. I love it," she coos as the movie starts to play.

"We have snacks when you're ready. Popcorn and fruit snacks. I also have a few of your other favorites."

"Thank you, Bentley. This is the best date I could have asked for."

My chest swells. I actually got it right. With the realization, I finally breathe easy. I'm able to tuck into my own food on my tray.

In no time, I've scoffed down my burger and fries. Zah is totally focused on the movie, and her food is gone as well. I dig into my backpack and pull out two bags of popcorn, handing her one.

"Thanks," she says softly.

The date continues to go smoothly as we watch the movie and enjoy each other's company. At some point, we end up holding hands. Zah has snuggled closer to me and is tucked into my side. We're on our second movie and the stars have come out.

"Shit," I mutter when I realize I didn't roll out the tent, and the sky is beginning to look like it might rain.

"What happened?" she asks.

"I think it's going to rain."

"Oh no. I don't want this to end."

"It doesn't have to. Corey added a tent. I just forgot to roll it out. It will cover us up and keep us safe. We can still stargaze through its viewing panel too."

"That sounds perfect. Is it too late to roll it out? I can help."

I kiss her lips. "I've got it. I'll collect our trash and set it up."

CHAPTER ELEVEN

Old and Gray

Zahirah

"Hurry, hurry," I squeal as the sky opens up just as Bentley gets the tent in place.

He's getting soaked out there. I feel so bad. We should have packed up and gone home. Bent climbs back into the truck bed quickly.

"That came out of nowhere," he laughs and pushes his wet hair from his face.

I love the way his hazel eyes are sparkling at me. I wish I could see him look at me like this forever. It's different from the way he looks at anyone else and makes me feel like I'm special to him.

We both look up as the sound of the rain beating down on the tent gets louder. When I lower my gaze, I find him releasing the buttons of his soaked shirt. His chiseled chest comes into view.

I bite my lip and my cheeks heat up. He looks at me, and an embarrassed look comes to his face. I look away and busy myself with pulling the blanket over my legs.

"I look nothing like I did last time you saw me poolside. I've bulked up a lot. I had to to compete on the college level," he says, almost like he's apologizing.

"It looks good on you," I say just above a whisper.

"Really? Are you sure?"

I look back at him and knit my brows. He seriously looks a bit nervous. I lift to my knees and crawl closer to him. I place my hands into his opened shirt and run them up his chest as I look him in his eyes.

"You're perfect. You're always perfect. When you're old with a beer belly, I know I'll feel the same," I say.

He cups the back of my head and crushes his lips to mine. I glide my hands up to push his shirt from his shoulders, allowing my hands to run over his chiseled muscles. He shrugs the shirt the rest of the way off and tosses it aside.

Lightning and thunder crack and roll outside, causing me to jump and fall back on my butt. Bentley snickers and shakes his head. He then pulls his phone from his pocket.

"I'll turn on some music."

I smile and nod. Soon, the sound of Elvis's "Can't Help Falling In Love" begins to float around us. My smile widens because our parents play this at the end of every function. It's their way of saying the party is over as his mom and dad and my mom and dad take the dance floor one last time.

We've sat and watched them all dance together more times than I can think to count. I think I've imagined dancing to this very song at our own wedding just as many times. He has just made this date untouchable in my mind.

"Dance with me," Bentley says as he looks me in my eyes.

"Here?"

"Yeah, come here. We'll make it work."

I get back to my knees and move to him. He wraps his arms around me and pulls me into his chest. He's so warm, I can't help sinking into his warmth.

"You know, I've dreamed of what it would be like to do this with you when we're old and gray. So I really hope I am perfect in your eyes, beer belly and all. I know you will be perfect to me, no matter what.

"You've always been a part of my life. I've never realized how big a part you have been until now," he says as he sways us on our knees.

"You've been there when I had no front teeth and then when I had to get braces. All my worst moments," I laugh.

"All the best in my mind. I lived for those toothless smiles and your cute pigtails. I want to be there the next time you don't have teeth too."

I lift my head from his shoulder and look into his eyes. He searches my face with his gaze. I'm speechless.

Bentley leans in slowly to take my lips, and I allow him to kiss me passionately. The next thing I know, I'm lying beneath him on my back. I don't panic.

I actually welcome his weight on top of me as I run my hands up and down his smooth skin. Frustration fills me when he doesn't move to touch me, only kissing me as he tries to hold his weight up off me. I moan into the kiss and wrap my legs around his waist, tugging him to me. He groans and reaches a hand into my hair.

"Zah," he groans against my lips.

"I'm ready," I whimper.

He lifts his head to look into my eyes. "Are you sure?"

I nod. "Yes, I want you to be my first. This feels like the right time."

I reach for the tie at the shoulder of my dress and release it. Then I pull the fabric down to reveal my bare breasts. Bentley looks down and his eyes dilate.

He palms my breast and runs his thumb across my nipple. I cry out when he dips his head and takes the hardened peak into his mouth. He sucks harder as he reaches to push my dress up.

My belly coils with nerves and lust as he slips his fingers beneath my panties and runs them through my already wet slit. I stare up through the viewing window as the rain pounds down against the panel. I run my fingers through his hair as he keeps sucking and begins to pump his digits in and out of me.

"Zahirah," he moans. "I want you so much, but I want you to be sure. If you want me to stop, it needs to be now. I can make you come and we can cuddle, but once I take you, we can't go back. It will change us ... who we are to each other forever."

"I know. I'm ready. It's you. It's always been you."

CHAPTER TWELVE

Our First

Bentley

"I know. I'm ready. It's you. It's always been you." Zahirah's words ring through my head, causing my heart to race.

I can't believe what I'm hearing. As a matter of fact, I can't believe what I'm seeing and feeling. Zah wants me to take her virginity.

This is really happening. There's no turning back once this is done. I've thought about this so many times—never thinking it would really happen.

She's allowing me to finger her, and it feels so good. She's gorgeous. Her tits are so perfect.

She's perfect. I'm excited as fuck but nervous as shit at the same time. This isn't my first time, but this is Zah. It means more to me.

"Okay, if this is what you really want," I breathe against her lips.

I capture the plush flesh with my lips and kiss her passionately as I continue to finger her. She moans as her tight pussy tightens around my fingers. When she throws her head back, breaking the kiss to cry out, I almost lose my mind.

I watch her come for me, taking her in beneath me. I'm almost too transfixed to make my next move. I'm painfully hard and know if I move things too fast, I'm going to come even faster.

Zah deserves more than that for her first time. With that in mind, I pull my hand from her panties and move to kiss my way down her neck, back to her breast I had in my mouth before. Flicking my tongue out against the tightened peak, I then blow on it.

"Bent, please," she whimpers.

I turn my gaze back to hers and see the pleading in her eyes. I need to get us both undressed. I want to see the rest of her sexy body.

I guess she's thinking the same thing as she pulls the other shoulder of her dress loose and begins to wiggle free of the dress. Reaching to help her, I peel the dress over her hips. My mouth waters when her little lacy black panties come into view.

She lies before me, looking like a dream. I release my belt and pull out my wallet to grab a condom before I forget in my excitement. I grow harder as I think of the day this won't be necessary because she will be my wife.

That's the dream, to one day go pro and live in a house with this girl right here. We'll have kids and we'll travel. Zah will have Olympic medals, and I'll be the happiest husband in the world.

Placing the foil packet between my lips, I toss my wallet aside and unzip my pants. Zah sits up with her arm covering her breasts. I pull the condom from my mouth and cup the back of her neck to kiss her again.

She wraps her arms around my neck as I devour her lips. I lean in so she falls back once again. We continue to kiss as she runs her hands down my back. I groan into her mouth and nip her bottom lip.

Taking my time, I kiss my way down her body. When I get to her belly button, I lick, kiss, and nip at the skin around it. Hooking my fingers into her panties, I drag them down her legs and toss them aside with her dress.

I suck in a breath as I look at her glistening lips. Even her pussy is pretty. I lower to my stomach and dive in for my first taste.

I need her nice and wet for me. It's important to me that she enjoys this. My dad has been drilling in my head since I was fifteen that a woman worth keeping is a woman worth pleasing. Zah needs to be thoroughly pleased after tonight.

"If I do something you don't like, talk to me. Tell me what you like, okay?" I say as I look up her body.

She nods as she bites her lip while looking back at me nervously. Opening her slick lips with my thumb, I dive in with my tongue. She tastes so fucking good.

I hum and groan as I get into it. Zah starts to move her hips against my face, bringing a smile to my lips. I give it my all as I see she's enjoying it.

When I add my fingers with my tongue, she bucks away and turns to twist and turn away from me. Reaching for her thigh, I lock her in place as I keep devouring her.

"Oh my God," she cries out.

"Good? You like that, baby?"

"Yes, I think I'm coming."

"Come for me, Zah. Let go."

She laces her fingers in my hair and rides my face as I bring her to climax. When she catches her breath, I climb her sexy body and grab the condom to bite it open and roll it on. I shove my jeans down and palm my shaft to get the rubber on.

When I look up, I find Zah's widened eyes on me as she chews on her lip. I grin, then lean in to take her lips. She's kissing me with such hunger.

This is it. I line up with her entrance and place my weight down on top of her. We lock eyes and she gives me a nod.

My mouth falls open as I begin to slide into her. My heart is pumping so fast. What if she hates this? What if she hates me after?

"Bentley, it's going to be okay. I want it to be you," she pants as if reading my mind.

I pull back, then push all the way in. I work my jaw as I push through her barrier. Zahirah clings to my back and buries her face in my neck.

I still and take a deep breath. I kiss the side of her face as I regain control. She feels so good around me.

"Are you okay?" I breathe.

"Yes, I think so. Can you move? You're really deep. It feels weird."

"It will get better," I say as I peck her lips and begin to roll my hips.

Zahirah

He's right, it is getting better. The more I relax, the better it gets. My juices are flowing and making it easier for him to move in and out of me.

His hands are everywhere, but he keeps bringing them back to my breasts. I get the feeling he likes them. I know I love the way his hands feel on me.

I can't believe we're doing this. We've known each other for so long, this kind of feels weird. Although it also feels so right.

"Ah," I moan as he thrusts into me.

"Baby, you feel so good. Zah, I want you so much."

"Bent, you're so hard. It feels so good. Oh God," I cry out.

He's so deep inside me. It still hurts a bit, but the pleasure is overriding the pain. He dips his head to pull my nipple into his mouth as he tilts my hips up and continues to stroke into me.

My stomach coils and my toes curl. Bentley looks into my eyes as he groans and squeezes my boob. I run my hands up his chest and look away from his intense gaze. He reaches beneath my chin, causing me to lift my eyes back to his.

"Don't be shy. I want to connect with you. We should connect with each other.

"You're mine, Zah. I want you to feel me deep inside you. In your body and in your heart," he pants.

I whimper as he pushes my legs back and gets deeper. I didn't think he could get any deeper. Bentley's dick isn't small. I feel so stretched and full.

He keeps working his strong body into mine, making me so wet. Suddenly, he stills to kiss me hard and deep as he pulses inside me. I whimper as he breaks the kiss and pulls out.

I'm left feeling his absence. As if he's still there, but my body knows he's not and craves to have him back. The rain is still falling outside the tent, creating a soundtrack for our lovemaking.

"Bentley," I cry as he goes down on me again.

I look up at the sky through the panel and stare at the stars as he devours me. This is not what I thought it would be like. It's so much better.

I'm barely coming down from my orgasm when he rolls me on my side to enter me again. He wraps one arm around me tightly and palms my breast with the other as he pumps his hips against me.

"Zah," he groans into my ear. "Ah, baby. *Mm*, you're gonna make me come."

"I want you to. I want you to feel as good as you're making me feel."

He squeezes my breast and starts to thrust faster and harder. My body starts to shake, and my walls squeeze around him. He groans deeply and bites down on my shoulder.

"Bentley," I scream as I feel like I've lost control of my body.

It's too much, but not enough at the same time. Bentley grabs my hand and laces his fingers with mine, holding them tightly. I cry out and throw my head back.

"Fuck, baby. Fuck," he growls as warmth fills me.

***

The rain has stopped, but we're still lying here as Bentley spoons me and nuzzles my neck. This has been the best birthday ever. Bentley drags his hand down my side, then runs his fingertips back over the same path.

The gesture draws goose bumps across my skin. I sigh happily and snuggle closer to him. He kisses the top of my head, causing me to look back at him.

"How are you feeling?"

"I don't know. Happy, sore, like I want to do it again," I say and bite my lip.

He chuckles and pecks my lips. "I have one more condom in my wallet. We can make that happen if you really want to."

"Was I okay?"

"Okay? Zah, you were amazing. That was amazing. Better than I ever dreamed."

"You dreamed about having sex with me?"

"More times than I want to admit," he says with a blush.

"It was better than I dreamed too."

"It will only get better. We already have a deep connection."

I sigh and close my eyes. A part of me was so afraid he wouldn't want this after. Hearing him talk like this isn't the last time is such a relief.

"What are you thinking?"

"This is so unreal. I never thought this would happen. I didn't think you felt this way for me. I guess I was nervous you would change your mind after."

He reaches beneath my chin with his finger and lifts my face. I stare into his eyes as he looks back at me. God, he's so beautiful.

"I'm crazy about you, Zah. This night was so special to me. I'll never forget it."

"Thank you."

"For what?"

I smile back at him. "This night was amazing. The date ... and everything else. Thank you for making this birthday special for me."

He crushes his lips to mine and kisses me deeply. I shiver as he glides his hands over my body. I never want this night to end.

I don't think I'll need more time or our game to figure out if I want to be his girlfriend. I'm hooked. I've been in love with Bentley for so long; this all feels like a dream.

However, I just might make him sweat a bit since he was such a jerk to me when I arrived. Time will tell. For tonight, I'm just going to bask in the moment and enjoy what he's doing to my body.

I lace my fingers in his hair as he goes down on me again. God, I don't think I'll ever get tired of this. My back bows off the blow-up mattress as he pushes his face in deeper.

"Bentley," I moan as my toes curl.

Nope. Not going to get tired of this at all.

CHAPTER THIRTEEN

Shattered Pieces

Bentley

"Bro, can you explain this to me again?" Corey says as he flops down in the seat across from me in the library.

I look up at him and frown as others at surrounding tables hiss at him to be quiet. I wouldn't expect him to get it. This is a me and Zah thing.

"There's nothing to explain. I'm getting my assignments done for class," I mumble.

"Yeah, I get that. You've always been on top of your classwork, but this ... you have a whole hot girlfriend. She looked great out there on the track the other day, by the way. Yet you guys don't hang out together, you don't study together. Instead, you two have some type of competition going on. If that were my girl, I'd be trying to get in those cute little running shorts ..."

He lifts his hands up in the air as I snap my head up and glare at him. Trust me, I would love nothing more than to be somewhere alone with Zah, wrapped in her arms and legs. However, we've both been busy.

She has track and I have football. When you add in classes and classwork, plus assignments, we hardly have time for ourselves. The last two weeks have been brutal. We only see each other in the mornings. The rest of the day, we text as much as we can, but our schedules conflict like crazy beyond that.

We tried studying together once and got nothing done. When we set our second challenge in our game, we decided to make it an academic challenge. The goal is to see who will be the first one to get straight As and keep them up for the semester.

We both agreed to see each other during mutually scheduled times. Our competitiveness outweighs our horny hormones. As much as I crave Zah, I'm not going to lie and say our challenges aren't making me better.

My coach isn't complaining. I have the best grades on the team. Zah and I are currently tied for best grades as student athletes. It might sound nerdy, but this is us.

This is the most fun I've had in my college career. I wake looking forward to my morning runs with Zah, where we plan out our day and text to check in throughout. I'm falling so hard for this girl. I've always had love for her, but now I know I'm in love with her.

"Why aren't you focused on your books? As captain, no one is failing on my watch. Did you turn in that paper?"

"I'm nowhere near failing. You know my dad would kill me. I turned in that paper a week early. That's my point, bro. What happened to taking care of business and then having some fun?"

"Just because I've been turning down parties doesn't mean I'm not having fun. My version of fun is just different from everyone else's. I've got two more years.

"This can't be it for me. I need to go pro. It's all I've dreamed about since I can remember. The work starts here," I say, looking him in the eyes.

"I get that. More than you know, but we live once. A few parties aren't going to keep you out of the league. Tell Zahirah to come along."

I shake my head. "She's focused. Besides, the track team is traveling this weekend for a meet. She'll be back Sunday. We have a date planned for then."

"Good, you have a few days to kick back with your boys."

I get this feeling in the pit of my stomach and know this is a bad idea. Things have been too good. I have so much peace. Yet I look him in the eyes and cave.

"Fine, I'll come out tonight, but tonight only."

***

I sip at my soda and shoot a text back to Zah. She won her meet and broke two records. I'm so proud of her. They have one more day of meets to go before they head back home.

I almost text her that I love her, but I want to tell her in person for the first time. I can't keep the smile from my face when she sends back a bunch of heart eye emojis. I return the same emojis and tell her I miss her.

"You're the only guy here texting. Not having fun?"

I look up to find Carly's friend, Pacey. My first reaction is to look around quickly for Carly so I can leave to get away from her before she sees me. Just my luck, her father pulled some strings to have my restraining order blocked after I didn't press charges.

Fucking asshole. I never should have agreed to his terms in the first place. For the most part, Carly has been staying away from me.

"Don't worry, she's not here. No one really wants her at these things after what she did to your car. I hate that for you, by the way. That was so messed up," Pacey says as she bats her lashes.

"Yeah, well, the last thing I want to do is talk about her or what happened," I say and go to walk away.

Pacey places a hand on my arm to stop me. I turn to tell her I'll see her around, but I'm bumped from behind and she wraps her arms around my neck. I'm shocked at first, but jerk my head back as she's too close and reach to pry her arms from my neck.

"Come on, Bentley. Dance with me," she purrs.

"I have a girlfriend."

"And?" she pouts.

"And I'm not going to disrespect her. Back off. I'm not interested."

"Are you kidding me? You're really going to pretend to have a girlfriend instead of hooking up with me?"

"Whatever," I say and walk off.

As I go to find Corey and Jason, I see Carly watching me with a grin. I get a sour taste in my mouth and decide to leave without finding my friends.

Zahirah

I sit in my hotel room with a smile on my face. I've been texting with Bentley because I miss him. I can't wait for our date on Sunday.

He's been so patient with our conflicting schedules. I can see in his face he wants to have sex again, but we never have the time. The most we've been able to do is kiss during and after our morning runs.

His frat house and my dorm are too far from our classes and we would never make it on time if we detoured for sex. Skipping our run wouldn't sit well with either of us. I appreciate how he's been handling all of this.

I decided to stay in and work on a paper I have due next week. There is no way I'm going to let my grades slip.

I'm going to kick Bentley's butt in this challenge. We're neck and neck for now. All I need is an A-plus or two to pull ahead.

"Hey, Nickels. Did you see this?" One of my teammates pops her head into my door to ask.

We've kept our doors open to each other, so I'm not startled when she pops in. I look up from my book and give her a questioning look. I haven't been on social media. I don't like the distraction.

I have only looked at my phone to text Bentley and Erica. India comes all the way into the room and hands me her phone. I sigh and take it.

My heart drops when I look at the screen. It's a picture of Bentley hugging some girl. I force a smile and hand the phone back.

"We're not official. It's no big deal," I say, trying not to burst into tears.

The worst part is, I still have two races tomorrow. It's not the time for this. I can't call Bentley to ask him what's going on.

"You sure you're all right?"

"I'm fine. I'm going to finish this paper and call it a night. Can you push in the doorstop on your way out?"

"No problem. My door will be open if you want to talk."

Sure, I bet it will be. If I don't perform well tomorrow, she's next in line to take my place. She didn't bring that pic in here to be a friend.

She leaves and I sit staring into space. I want Bentley to explain it away, but if I call him and he can't, I'm not going to be focused. I'm on scholarship. I can't let Bentley get in the way of my schoolwork or my performance on the track.

However, the more I sit here, the more I think about that picture. I pick up my phone and log in to my account. I find the account of the girl who posted the picture. The picture is still there.

How could he do this to me? I thought we had something special. When I read the caption, I think I'm going to be sick. The caption keeps playing in my head over and over.

Spending time with the QB. Tonight is just heating up. It's going to be a good one. My man, my man, my man.

I toss the phone down and cover my face with my hands. I guess this is why he's so okay with us not having time for sex. I feel like such a fool.

"Hello," Erica says on the other end of the phone.

I didn't even realize that I called her. My heart is aching so badly, I can't even speak as I hear her voice. I can only sob.

"Zah? What's happening?" Erica says.

I shake my head as if she can see me. I'm sobbing so hard my body is shaking. Why would he do this?

I open my mouth to tell Erica what's going on, but I haven't told her that I'm dating her brother. Well, I had been dating her brother, or so I thought.

"I ... My ... the guy I was seeing cheated on me," I sob.

"Oh, Zah. I'm so sorry. You want me to call Bentley and tell him to kick the guy's ass?"

I sob harder. If I wasn't so heartbroken, I would laugh. Imagine him trying to kick his own ass.

"No, this is none of his business. I just needed someone to talk to. I really liked him, and I thought he liked me. I ... I had sex with him and everything," I cry.

"Oh, honey. I'll come and kick his ass myself. He's not worth your tears. You're too good for him in the first place. If it were me, I'd hook up with one of his best friends and make him feel my hurt."

I sort of laugh. Not only because I know that's something she would do, but also because I know Bentley would lose it if I did hook up with Corey or Jason. However, I'm too hurt to think about doing something like that.

I can't even imagine being with someone else. I'm so devastated. This was something special to me. I can't believe he would throw it away like this.

"I'm sorry, Erica. I didn't mean to call you with this. I'll text you later. My head hurts," I sniffle.

"Call me whenever you need. I'm here. If you change your mind and want me to call Bentley to handle the guy, let me know."

"Thanks, Erica," I say and hang up.

I burst into more tears and get up to climb into the bed to sob myself to sleep. Hopefully in the morning, I will be able to shove this all down and focus on my races.

Right now, I hate Bentley so much and I never want to see him again. He has ruined everything. Our friendship, this relationship, and so much more. I don't think I will ever forgive him.

"I hate you so much, Bentley Coswell," I sob.

CHAPTER FOURTEEN

What's Going On?

Bentley

My phone has been annoying this morning. It's been buzzing and pinging nonstop. The one morning I want to sleep in and get my body to agree, the world won't leave me the heck alone.

Suddenly, it dawns on me it could be Zah. She might need me to wish her luck before her meet. Not wanting to disappoint her, I sleepily reach for the phone to answer.

"Hello," I say after I take in a sharp breath.

I'm still trying to clear the sleep fog from my head. I went for a run last night after I left that party, allowing me to blow off steam and make the decision to sleep in this morning. To be honest, I miss Zah so much and didn't want to run without her.

"Bentley," Erica says on the other end of the line.

The sound of her voice brings me wide awake. If someone hurt my sister, I'll be on the first thing smoking to her. I was disappointed when she didn't come here like she said she wanted to. I couldn't believe she didn't get in. I'm still questioning that.

"Do you know this asshat cheater Zah has been dating? I want you to kick his ass for me. No one makes my best friend cry like that.

"She said she didn't want me to call you, but after thinking about it. Fuck that. This is my bestie and you're my big brother. You're there and this is Zah. I want you to kick his ass," Erica rants.

My brain is so confused. Zah is my girl, but why would she think I cheated? I would never cheat on her. She was crying?

My heart begins to ache with the thought of her in tears over anyone. However, the thought of me causing her pain guts me. I haven't done anything, so I'm even more hurt and confused.

"Wait, what the fuck are you talking about?"

"Zahirah called me last night, crying. She said the guy she was seeing cheated. She was balling her heart out. I think she really liked him. Bentley, please, can you do something? I hate not being there for her."

My heart aches even more to hear how upset Erica is. My sister and Zah are tighter than tight. When we were younger, you couldn't find one without the other.

"Have you spoken to her today? What makes her think this guy cheated?" I ask, trying to gain some clarity.

"No, she's locked in for her meet. We only texted once this morning. She said she'd call me after. I don't know any more than the fact that she had sex with the douche, and he cheated. You're going to kick his ass, right?"

I groan and close my eyes. What the fuck is going on? I don't tell Erica that I'm the guy. Clearly, Zahirah chose not to. I'm going to respect that until I can talk to her to straighten this all out.

I rub at my chest. This can't be happening. I was looking so forward to our date tomorrow.

I have it all planned out. It was going to be epic. How is this happening?

"Yeah, I'll make it right. Let me know when you speak to her again. I'm going to find out what's going on."

"Thanks, Bent. Love you. You're the best."

I scoff as I hang up. She doesn't realize I'm the guy she's trying to get fucked up. I can't believe my baby was crying, thinking I cheated on her. I would never, could never cheat on Zah.

My brain begins to fully wake and clear. I groan as I remember Pacey trying to throw herself at me and Carly watching with that shit-eating grin on her face. I'd bet my career on those two being the source of this problem. This is some bullshit.

I knew I shouldn't have gone to that party last night. I throw my legs over the side of the bed and go to text Corey and Jason to see if they might know something. Before I can open my phone to send a text, I see all the text messages waiting for me.

Jason and Corey have been blowing up my phone trying to find out what's going on. I open Corey's text first and find a screenshot of a picture of me and Pacey. When I read the caption, my head nearly explodes.

"Son of a bitch," I growl.

I glance at the clock and note I have about nine more hours before Zah makes it back on campus. While I would love to spend that time tracking down Carly and Pacey, I focus my attention on how I'm going to prove the truth to Zah. I shoot a couple of texts off in reply to all the messages from Corey and Jason.

"*Fuck*," I roar once I'm done and it all sets in.

We haven't even made things official yet. I'm supposed to be proving myself. This is going to go a long way to kill that for sure.

I can't allow that to happen. I love Zah. That's it … that's how I fix this. I need to show her how serious I am about her, how much I love her.

With a clear plan in my head, I rush to take a shower and get dressed. I have a lot to get done in the next nine hours. After I'm showered and dressed, I make my way to my first stop. I can't help checking my phone every five seconds to see if Zah or Erica calls or texts.

I have to force myself to focus after I almost rear-end someone in town. I toss the phone into the glove compartment and keep my eyes on the road. My mind is a mess as I think of how fucked up this is.

"You're going to pay for this shit," I growl to myself as I think of Carly and her stupid friend.

Zahirah

I won both my races and broke another three records. After crying myself to sleep last night, I woke this morning and channeled all that heartache into my superpower. I ran like I was running from all the pain and hurt. I ran as if Bentley was chasing me to laugh at me.

Now, as we make our way back to school, I'm balling all over again. I have my hoodie on with the strings pulled tight as I sit in the back of the bus, curled up in my seat. My AirPods are in as I listen to sad songs, wondering how I got here.

A part of me is trying to wait to get back to campus to address this. Then there's a part of me that wants to call Bentley and yell at him. He's been texting, but I refuse to read any of them yet.

This is so embarrassing. Arlene has texted me to check on me because she saw the pic as well. I just want to get home and curl up in my bed.

The app on my phone says we're five minutes away from campus. I wipe my nose and start to gather my things to be one of the first off the bus so I can do just that. I wish I had a bathtub to soak in.

"What the heck is going on?"

I pop my head into the aisle to see everyone moving to the other side of the bus to look out of the window. Not caring what's happening outside of the bus as long as I can get off and head home, I turn back to gathering my trash and putting my books away.

"Zahirah, I think you should come see this," one of my teammates calls.

I knit my brows and stand, slinging my backpack onto my shoulder. I walk up the aisle a few rows before I find an empty row and look out the window. I scowl when I see what's going on.

The school band is the reason the bus is having trouble pulling into the lot. They are surrounding the bus as they march in place. The drum major points when I come into view and the band begins to play.

They are playing "Can't Help Falling In Love". I frown and purse my lips. The band changes formation and that's when Bentley comes into view. He's sitting on the roof of his car with a huge teddy bear in his arms.

I guess Corey and Jason are the official sign holders. This time, they are holding a sign that says *I love you, Zahirah Nickels*. I turn from the window and go to storm from the bus.

I mumble to myself the entire way. This makes him look guilty. I hate him for continuing to embarrass me.

Clearly, he's trying to get ahead of his bullshit. Why do all of this if he's not guilty? My blood is boiling as I go to get off the bus.

I step off the bus and head straight for my car. However, I stop in my tracks as my parking spot comes into view and it's empty. Confused, I look around, trying to figure out where my car went.

My dad had it shipped to me a week after I made it to school. I know I parked it in this lot in spot number eleven. I remember because that's Bentley's number and I smiled to myself when I took the spot.

"I called in a favor. I had a feeling you were going to try to run off. Besides, I would prefer if you ride with me for our getaway," Bentley says in my ear as he comes up behind me.

"Where's my car?" I bite out.

"It will be in the student lot when we return Monday morning. Congratulations, baby. I heard you killed it," he says, his hand splaying across my belly.

I close my eyes and curse my treacherous body. Shaking my head, I pull away and turn to face him. Tears are soaking my face again and I can't stop them from falling.

"Zah, come on, baby. Please stop crying. That picture was bullshit. Pacey is Carly's friend. They set that shit up. They're trying to break us up," he says as he palms the side of my face and swipes at my tears with his thumb.

I shake my head, not able to speak words just yet. He moves closer to crowd my space. I look up at him as he searches my face.

"I love you so much. Don't let them take you from me. She had her arms around my neck. I wasn't touching her. I left the party right after she pulled that stunt and tried to get me to hook up with her."

When I still don't say a thing, he tugs me to him and takes my lips. I don't kiss him back at first. My mind is all over the place. I think back to the photo and remember what I saw.

He wasn't touching her, but her arms were all on him. I want to believe him. If I didn't need to focus on my meet, I would have called him last night to ask him about it.

"Zah, listen to me. I didn't even know about the picture until this morning. I've been going crazy for over nine hours now.

"I can't lose you. You make me so happy. Why would I ever cheat on you? You're amazing," he says against my forehead.

"Why did you do all of this if you didn't do anything wrong?" I ask.

"Because it dawned on me I haven't told you how much I love you and I wanted you to know. Erica might have called me to kick your boyfriend's ass too, I knew I needed to fix this if you called her crying.

"I never want to hurt you, Zah. Say you believe me, so I can take you on the date I have planned. I want to celebrate with you. Please."

I search his eyes and see the sincerity within them. As if knowing I believe him, he wraps his arms around me and crushes my lips with his. I lift on my toes and wrap my arms around his neck. We both laugh when the teddy bear hits us in our faces.

Bentley breaks the kiss. "Are we good? Will you come with me?"

I bite my lip as I look up at him. Then I give him a small nod. "I love you too."

"God, baby. I was going crazy thinking they took you away from me," he croons before kissing me again.

CHAPTER FIFTEEN

Romantic Escape

Bentley

I don't know what I would have done if Zah hadn't heard me out. I did nothing wrong to lose her and I would have been devastated. Lifting her hand to my lips, I kiss the back of it as I drive us to the surprise I have set up for us.

I was able to book an extra night for the cabin I had rented for our date tomorrow, since she lives in the dorms and I live in a frat house. I thought she might like having the privacy of the cabin for us to spend the night.

I also thought it would be romantic. There's no doubt we need the alone time. The sexual tension in this car has my pants so tight I might burst through them.

I can't wait to get there so she can see what all I've been working on all day. I did as much as I could on short notice. Tomorrow night is the big night.

"Are you hungry?" I ask.

"A little. I couldn't really stand to eat on the plane," she says softly.

"Babe, I want you to talk to me if you ever doubt me again. I have nothing to hide and I'm not going to lie to you. I could have put your mind at ease last night."

"And if you couldn't, I wouldn't have been able to focus."

I think her words over. My head would have been fucked if I had a game tonight. I would have had to do all I could to block my personal life out to get my job done. As an athlete, I get it.

"Fair enough. I can understand that. I'm sorry you had to go through this.

"I told Pacey I wasn't interested and that I had a girlfriend. That should have been the end of things. I had no idea they were plotting to pull some bullshit."

The car falls silent, causing me to glance from the road to Zah. She's staring at me with a shocked expression on her face. I give her hand a gentle squeeze.

"What?"

"You have a girlfriend?"

"Yeah, I do. I want everyone to know you're mine and I'm not interested in anyone else. We need to tell everyone back home. Especially Erica."

Zahirah groans. "I can't believe she called you."

"She wanted to have your back. If you were seeing some other guy and he hurt you, I would have kicked his ass. You're important to us. You always will be. You have to know that. You're as good as a Coswell in our eyes."

I lift her hand to kiss it again as I come to the turn for our exit. I get excited as I pull onto the road to our cabin. I already have the key, so we can head right there.

"Where are we?"

"You're about to find out in just a second."

I park and hop out to round the car and open her door. She gets out with a smile on her face. I grab her backpack, small duffel, and teddy bear from the back seat, then lace our fingers together as we move for the front door of the cabin.

Unlocking the door, I let her in first and move in behind her. Placing her things down, I step behind her to wrap my arms around her waist. I nuzzle her neck and inhale.

"I'm so happy to have you in my arms. You want to eat first and then I can show you around? Or do you want to take the tour and eat after?"

Her stomach growls, answering for her. I laugh and lead her to the kitchen, where I have our dinner for the night. I can't cook for shit, but I know how to order and heat things up.

Tonight, I have some Chinese food I ordered. I pop it in the warmer and go to set the table, lighting the candle I placed there earlier.

When I look into Zah's face, my heart pangs. Her eyes are still a bit red and swollen. A reminder that because of me, she was hurt. I wish I never had anything to do with Carly.

I lean in and kiss her lips. She cups my face, causing me to deepen the kiss. I'm devouring her, for I don't know how long, when the timer chimes, signaling our food is ready.

I reluctantly break away to get our food so she can eat something. As we sit to eat by candlelight, I get some music going. Her face is now lit up with a smile.

"Bent?"

"Yeah, baby."

"What are we doing here?"

"I had planned for us to come here tomorrow and have our date night, then spend the night." I shrug. "I changed my mind and decided to bring you here a night sooner. If you want to go back, we can eat and go," I say as I realize she might not want to stay the night with me.

"I only have dirty clothes from my meet," she replies.

"You'll look adorable in my shirts. Arlene gave me something to bring for you to wear tomorrow night."

"You asked my roommate for help?"

"Yeah, I called in a ton of favors."

"The school's marching band though? That was smooth."

She gives me that special smile and I know we're all good. I sit happily as I watch her finally put something in her stomach. As we have dinner, I have her tell me all about her meet this weekend.

When we're finished, I take her on a tour of the cabin. Seeing her face light up when we get to the master bath and she sees the bathtub, gives me an idea. I take her back downstairs and light a fire, then tell her I'll be back in a minute.

Racing back upstairs, I run a bath and light a bunch of candles around the bathroom. I grab a few of the rose petals I have for tomorrow and sprinkle them in the water.

When I return to collect Zah, I'm not surprised to find her reading a textbook and making notes. My heart swells. This could be the rest of my life. I'm never allowing anyone to take her from me.

CHAPTER SIXTEEN

One Day

Zahirah

As we're lounging on the couch in the cabin, I can't stop laughing as Bentley tickles me. I have tears leaking from my eyes as I hold my teddy bear tightly to my chest, Bent's arms wrapped around me from behind. I haven't been this happy in a long time.

"Say you're sorry and I'll stop," Bentley growls into my neck.

"But I'm not sorry. You started it. Leave me and my bear alone and we won't attack you again," I say through my laughter.

"Fuck, I promised myself I wouldn't take you again before tonight, but you smell so good and feel even better," he groans in my ear as he creeps his hands under his T-shirt I'm wearing.

I moan as he palms my breasts in his hands and begins to roll my nipples between his fingertips. I drop the teddy bear and reach back for his hair as he sucks on my neck. He was right, sex is getting better each time we have it.

I love that he's taking the time to teach me how to please him as much as he pleases me. I don't think there is a place on my body he hasn't laid claim to. His mouth and tongue have been everywhere.

"Why make silly promises?" I moan as I push myself back into him.

"Zah, we've been having sex since last night. I don't want you to think that's all I brought you here for. I want to spend time with you."

"You are spending time with me. You just need to spend a little more inside me," I pant as he turns me to face him.

I lift my arms for him to peel his shirt off me yet again. He tosses it aside and pushes his basketball shorts down. He's already so hard.

A groan escapes his lips as I lick my hand, then wrap it around him to stroke his shaft. I keep stroking as he leans toward the table where he placed a few condoms just in case. Releasing him, I allow him to roll the condom on as I watch once again to learn how to do it for him.

I'm almost confident I can do it next time. Although I would be nervous. When he's done, he reaches for me and palms my ass as he tugs me into him.

I smile as he kisses me hungrily. I can still taste the apple juice he had a little while ago on his tongue. I suck his tongue into my mouth to get more of the flavor.

He breaks the kiss and places his forehead to mine. "I love you. You're so sexy. Just the way you smell turns me on. God, Zah, how am I supposed to keep my hands off you?"

"Who told you you have to? I'm all yours, remember?" I breathe.

He lifts me onto his waist and tugs my head closer to his so he can kiss me. I whimper as he guides his way inside me. My toes curl and I swear I just drooled into his mouth.

Bentley groans and keeps going as if nothing happened. I break the kiss and bury my face in his neck as he begins to rock into me while guiding me up and down. I claw my fingers against his neck and push them through his thick hair.

"You feel so amazing. Does it feel good for you? Do you want me to stop and eat your pussy?"

"No, please don't stop. I'm already so wet. You feel good too. I love you. Please don't stop."

"Fuck, Zah. I want you so much. I'm inside you and I still want you," he grunts.

I cry out as he places me on my back on the sofa. He doesn't miss a beat as he pounds down into me. I look down my body to watch our connection. He now has his arms wrapped around my thighs as he keeps thrusting.

His body looks so strong and powerful as he moves in and out of me. There is a bit of soreness from all this sex we've been having, but not enough for me to want this to end. I throw my head back and clench my walls around him.

"Fuck. Yes, baby. Just like that."

I repeat the action, and he hisses between his teeth. Bentley is gorgeous on any given day, but he's simply breathtaking during the throes of passion. My thighs begin to shake, and that telltale sign of my own climax begins to stir.

"I'm coming. Oh my God, Bent. I'm coming," I cry out.

He reaches for my clit and begins to rub it. The gesture only intensifies my building orgasm. I reach for his forearms and dig my nails in. He reaches to squeeze one of my breasts and bites his lip as he pumps harder and faster.

"So fucking good. You're so beautiful when you come for me. Don't hold back, baby. I want to watch you fall apart for me."

"Yes, Bent. Yes."

I come for him over and over again. By the time we are both spent, I need a nap and a good soak in the tub. Once he catches his breath, Bentley carries me to have both.

When he climbs into the bed to spoon me while dropping kisses all over my shoulder, face, and head, I feel the deeper connection growing between us. It's more than the sex. I can't describe it just yet, but it's kind of like our souls are locking together.

"One day I'm going to marry you," he breathes as my lids grow heavy with sleep.

"Don't make promises you can't keep."

"Zahirah?"

"Hmm?"

"One day you're going to be my wife. I'm going to marry you."

"Okay," I say with a smile on my face as I fall asleep.

I dream of the perfect life as his wife. A cute little house with kids and a dog. I dream of the future I've always wanted.

Bentley

As my words dance in my mind and I see the future I want, I can't get my mind to settle down so I can sleep. Having Zah in my arms, feeling her soft, warm body against mine, it all makes the dream seem more tangible.

As an hour goes by and then another, I give up on sleep and get out of bed to get something to drink. I grab my phone before jogging downstairs to the kitchen.

My mind begins to race even more. I have the option to declare for the draft this year. Depending on how well this season goes, it might be the right thing to do. Leave while my draft stock is high.

However, that would mean Zah and I will only get to have one year together at college. Reality hits hard as I take that option in. It hits harder as I realize we're only going to get two years tops.

I rub at my chest as a deep ache starts. I think I might be having a panic attack. I need someone to talk to so I can get my head around this.

"Hello. Bentley, is everything okay?"

"Yeah, Dad, sorry I woke you. I just really need to talk."

I can hear him moving around on the other end of the phone. Guilt fills me as I look at the time on the wall. I probably should have come up with another way to ground myself.

"Don't you worry about waking me. I'm here anytime you need me, son. What's up?"

I think over how to say this without revealing that I'm in a relationship with the girl next door. I'm not sure how our parents will take this or if his advice will change because of who I'm talking about. I need to vent and get some clear perspective, not a lecture and shutdown.

"Come on, son. This is me. You can talk to me."

"I'm seeing someone and we're getting serious. I … I love her. I think it's time I start thinking more about my future and what that means to her," I say cautiously.

"Ah, I see. Tell me exactly what your concern is," he says steadily.

"I didn't want to date before because I wanted to focus on the game. I didn't want to end up here. Needing to decide between her and the game.

"What if I can and should declare after this season? She's a freshman. She has three more years of school to go. What does that mean for us?"

"If she's the one and she cares about you, she's not going to make you decide. She'll support this dream you've had all your life. Your mother has never asked me to decide between my dreams and my love for her.

"She's supported me through the best of times and the worst. And, son, times have gotten really bad. I've always been able to lean on her love.

"If you can look at this young lady and see that type of love in her, she'll be there no matter what you choose. There will be a time when you'll know she has to come first.

"That one time when you're asking too much of her love and you have to be the one to make a sacrifice, but that's a different time and circumstance. You'll know what needs to be done when that day comes.

"For now, trust her to love you enough to support you. If she can't, she's not the one. You're growing into a good man, Bent," he says.

"But what if I don't make the right decision and I lose her? Where do I go from there? Nothing seems right without her anymore."

He chuckles and sighs. "Ah, you're definitely smitten. No matter what happens, son, you can always come home. Let that be your starting point.

"How you center yourself when you're feeling lost. Come home and ground yourself in the familiar.

"Meanwhile, I want you to trust your instincts. You've fallen for her for a reason. You're a QB for a reason. You're a born leader," he says.

I nod as if he can see me. I knew he would know just what to say. My dad has always been the voice of reason in my life. I have so many memories of him being in my corner. I don't know what I would do without him.

"Thanks, Dad. That all makes a lot of sense. I'll talk to you later. I think I should try to get some sleep. Thanks again."

"Good night, Bent. I love you, son."

"I love you too, Dad."

"Good night."

CHAPTER SEVENTEEN

The Family

Bentley

Zah has been busting ass all season. I'm so proud of her. She has a meet this morning and our entire family is here for the weekend.

They came for her and me. I have a spring practice game tonight. I'm so hyped. We plan to tell everyone about us this weekend. I mean, everyone on campus already knows she's my girl.

I made that very clear after that debacle with Pacey. Rumors had already gotten out fast about the band showing up to play for Zah for me. By the time we got back to campus the following Monday, it was pretty clear we were together.

I don't shy away from showing PDA anymore. I had wanted to give Zah time to make up her mind about us, but once she agreed to be mine, I pulled no punches. We still have our game going, but she's my girl no matter the outcome.

"She looks good," Mr. Nickels says as Zah and the other runners take their places.

"She's been working hard," I say proudly.

"The vibe here is great," Erica says excitedly beside me. "You both look so happy here. I'm not getting this on my campus. My school is so lame."

"You have options, sweetheart," my mother says.

"Quiet, they're about to start," my youngest brother, Eddy, says.

He's nine and has a thing for Zahirah. She babies him and protects him from the rest of us. In his eyes, Zah is a star. I can't blame the kid. She lights up my world too.

We all chuckle at him, but turn our focus on Zahirah and the track. I lift my hands to my lips and blow into them. I'm excited and nervous at the same time. This is a huge weekend for us.

I'm hoping our families will receive the news well. I don't know what I will do if they don't approve of us. Zahirah isn't one to defy her parents much.

Her decision to come here against their initial wishes is probably the most defiant she's ever been. If her parents don't agree, this could be the end of us. The thought makes me sick to my stomach.

"Come on, Zah, *go*," her dad bellows, pulling me from my thoughts.

I smile with pride as our family rises to their feet to cheer for her. I'm standing with my hair in my hands as I watch on. There's one girl ahead of her, but Zah is gliding as she stays on her heels.

"Come on, baby," I yell as she gets right up on the other runner.

Zah runs right by the other girl and leaves everyone in her dust. There's a clear gap between her and the others. There's no way they're catching her now.

My baby glides right across the finish line. I roar with excitement and rush down to the sideline. Zah races over to me and slams into me as she hops on my waist, wrapping her legs around me.

She had been worried all night that she would choke in front of our family. I told her she could do it. I knew she would crush it. When she picked up her hip number and was given eleven, I knew today would be epic.

"You did it, baby. I'm so proud of you," I croon as I hold her tight.

She cups my face and kisses me. I take the kiss a little further as I move one hand to her ass and grasp her face with the other. Whistles and catcalls ring out.

We're used to that around campus. It's not until throats are cleared that I remember where we are and break the kiss. I release Zah to allow her to slide down my front. Taking her hand in mine, I lace our fingers together as we turn to face our family.

Our dads are standing with expressionless faces and their arms across their chests. Our moms are on either side of them with smiles on their faces. I think we'll be fine with them.

"How long has this been going on?" Mr. Nickels asks.

"Since about two weeks after I arrived," Zah replies.

"Wait, you were the cheating boyfriend?" Erica says.

"I didn't cheat."

"He didn't cheat," Zah and I say at the same time.

"It was a misunderstanding. We cleared things up."

Someone calls Zah's name. She turns to find her coach waving for her to come over. Great, I'm going to be left to deal with this alone.

"I'll be back," she says to me as she grabs my bicep and lifts on her toes, puckering her lips.

I dip my head and peck her lips before she turns and runs off. Watching after her with a smile on my face, I take a deep breath. This isn't really how we planned to do this. I guess we both got caught up in the moment.

I turn back to our parents and groan. This is the moment of truth. I look to Mr. Nickels and stand up straighter.

"What are your intentions for my baby girl, Coswell?"

"I'm in love with your Zahirah, sir. In a year or two, I plan to propose. I should be settled and in the league by then. We can wait to get married after she graduates. Maybe plan the wedding for the spring or summer of the following year.

"I'll pay for grad school for both of us. I want to buy a house back home, but I understand we might have to move around for my team depending on where I get signed. I'm in full support of whatever Zah plans to do after school."

"Sounds like you've put a lot of thought into this," my father says.

My siblings are looking at me in shock, with the exception of Erica and Eddy; those two are scowling at me. I get that Erica is pissed we didn't tell her sooner. It's been eight months.

We've been home since we've been together, but there hasn't been a moment to come clean. Neither of us has been in Arizona at the same time. Between camps and training with specialty coaches, we've been missing each other when going back home.

"Unbelievable," Erica huffs.

Zahirah

Bentley pulls me into his arms and hugs me tightly as he kisses my lips a few times, then presses his forehead to mine. "I'll see you after the game," he murmurs against my lips.

"Have a good one."

He releases me and waves to everyone else before he takes off. Butterflies fill my belly as I think of later tonight. We plan to hang out and celebrate.

"This is all so weird. Why didn't you tell me?" Erica asks after Bentley is out of earshot.

I shrug my shoulders and bite my lip. "I don't know. It just never seemed like the right time."

"When you called crying to tell me a guy—my brother, who you slept with—cheated on you would have been a great time," she whisper-yells.

I grab her by the arm and tug her away from her other siblings before they overhear. The last thing I want is for everyone to know I'm having sex with Bentley. Although they might already assume we are.

"I was wrong. He didn't cheat. That girl who trashed his car set him up."

"But you were sleeping with him before that," she accuses.

"He took my virginity on my birthday. Things happened really fast, and I didn't know how you would feel. Please don't be mad at me," I plead.

"You're in love with him, aren't you?"

"Yeah, I am."

"So it's a mutual thing," she says as if speaking to herself. "I think it always has been. Now so much makes sense."

"Are you mad?"

"No. I don't think so. Will you be mad when I move here? Am I going to be a third wheel?"

I gasp. "What? You're coming here?" I say excitedly.

"That's the plan. I've been looking at new colleges, but you coming here made me miss you and Bent even more. I think this is where I want to be."

"Yay," I squeal and pull her into a hug.

"I want to see you this happy when I'm here getting all up in y'all's business. Bent is going to hate this."

I giggle at my best friend. "No, he's not, it's going to be like old times."

"Ugh, you two still study too much like little nerds?"

"Yup," I say, popping the *P*.

She groans and rolls her eyes. "You know that's the only reason our parents aren't freaking out. You two haven't dropped your grades in the last eight months, so you're getting a pass. If this was me and Jamie, it would be a whole different story."

I burst into laughter. "Jamie? As in my imaginary brother, Jamie?" I snort and laugh.

"Yes, he's hot now that he's older, you know," she says with a huge grin.

"I can't believe you remember that. Ugh, I wanted siblings so bad," I groan.

"That's why I shared mine. I wanted them to love you as much as I did. I didn't know one would fall *in* love with you. Scratch that. Make that two. Poor Eddy."

I turn to look over at Eddy talking to Garret and Baker. His little face is so long, like he just lost his best friend. He sees me looking at him and turns away quickly.

I catch Baker's eye, and he gives me a little grin. He's Bentley's best friend from back home. I'm not surprised he came in with the family. Baker is to Bentley as Erica is to me.

"My little buddy is mad at me. Do you think he's canceling all his plans to take me to senior prom?"

"Probably, but he'll be over it in nine years. You'll be married and having little nieces and nephews for us by then."

I laugh and tug her into a hug. I'm so relieved that she's okay with this. I was most worried about how she would feel.

"I should talk to him," I say.

"Nope, you should come with me to get something to eat. The parents are okay with it, but they still plan to drill you at dinner. You probably won't be able to eat a thing. It would be wise to get something down now."

I palm my face. I know she's right. My parents are just waiting to get me cornered.

"Fine, let's grab something now."

***

"Zah, I'm not going to lie and say I'm surprised about this," my mother says as we all sit at dinner.

The Coswell kids were all sent off to the Arcade next door, while Bentley and I were asked to stay to talk. Bentley reaches for my hand under the table and links our fingers together. His palm is sweaty, telling me he's as nervous as I am.

"I am," our dads say in unison.

"Bill, you mean to tell me you have never noticed the way Bentley looks at Zah or how he can't keep his foot out of his mouth around her?" Mrs. Coswell laughs.

"And Kerry, you have never seen how Zah gets stars in her eyes when she looks at Bent. We didn't even know she was applying to come here until the last minute. I saw this coming a mile away."

"Well, I'll be," Daddy says, dragging a hand down his face.

"I think what your fathers really want to say is we're happy for the both of you. Our main concern is whether or not the two of you are being safe," Mrs. Coswell says.

"And don't give us that look. We know you two are having sex. We saw that kiss and the way Bent couldn't keep his hands off you," my mother says as she gives us that knowing mom look.

"Just kill me now," I mutter as I try to shrink into myself.

Bentley chuckles and leans over to kiss the side of my head. I pinch him under the table. This is so embarrassing.

"We're always safe. Zah and I are both focused on school and our respective sports. We do have a sexual relationship, but we aren't indulging as much as you think."

"If your coach didn't rave about your grades and the increase in your film time this year, I wouldn't believe you," Mr. Coswell says.

"I really don't want to talk about you deflowering my baby girl," my father grumbles.

"Oh, get over it, honey. She's becoming a woman, and I couldn't be happier with her choice."

"I like Bent too, but they're still so young. So much can happen. Life hasn't begun to challenge them yet."

"That's why I love this for them. We will be here to guide them. They will always have us," Mom says with a smile.

Thank you, I mouth.

Bentley

My father pulls me into a hug as we stand outside the hotel my family is staying at for the weekend. Releasing me, he palms the side of my face. He looks into my eyes and smiles.

"Zah is the girl you called about, isn't she?" he says.

"Yeah, you remember that call?"

"Of course. My boy calls me in the middle of the night for advice; it sticks with me."

"That talk meant a lot to me. The thought of losing Zah causes me physical pain, but you were right. She supports whatever I plan to do."

"I love that girl like one of my own. If you ever need direction, come to me. I'll give you the best advice I have.

"Although I do believe the love you have for her will be your compass. I'm proud of you, son and I'm happy for the both of you. I truly believe in my heart you can be the man you promised me and Kerry you can be tonight.

"You always make good on your promises. You'll be everything Zah has dreamed of and what her father and I want for her. Really proud of you, son. We'll talk later. Go get some sleep."

I get choked up by his words. When he and Mr. Nickels pulled me aside, I hadn't known what to expect. The talk we had made me feel a greater responsibility to Zah and our love.

I meant every word I said. I'm going to love Zah with everything I am, and I plan to provide for her for the rest of my life. I want to be the man I've learned to be by watching my father and Mr. Nickels.

However, I don't tell him I don't plan on going to sleep anytime soon. Once I leave here, I'm meeting up with Zah. We're going to celebrate and hang out.

"Good night, Dad. It was good to see you," I say instead and pull him into a hug.

"Good to see you too. Even better to see you win. What a game. That's my son," he says proudly and cups the back of my head as he presses his forehead to mine.

I close my eyes and absorb the strength he's giving me. I don't know why, but it feels like we need this moment. He kisses my forehead and releases me, patting me on my shoulder before he turns to leave.

I turn and head for my car with a smile on my lips. This was a good day. A very good day.

CHAPTER EIGHTEEN

Put It Together

Zahirah

Four and a half months later …

"What?" I mumble into my pillow, confused and sleepy.

This week has been killer. I had two twenty-page papers due and mandatory evening lectures. It's only the beginning of the semester and I feel like I've been through finals week. I can barely lift my eyelids as it is.

"Wake up, sleepyhead," Bentley croons into my ear as he drops kisses on the side of my face.

"Why? I thought we agreed to sleep in today. Why are you here? How did you get in?"

He chuckles as he nuzzles my neck and breathes me in. I sigh and sink into my bed as he rubs my back. If he wants me to wake up, he needs to stop that.

"Your roommate let me in."

"Ugh, I miss Arlene. Why'd they split us up? I hate it already."

"She's not so bad. You're just being grumpy. I'm here because it's your birthday and our one-year anniversary. I told you to sleep in because I have a surprise planned for you," he breathes into my ear.

"No, not today. Go away. Surprise me tomorrow.

"If you want to give me something for my birthday, let me sleep. *Please*. I'm going back to sleep," I grumble and use all the energy I can muster to turn onto my side with my back to him.

"Fine, we can sleep in a little longer," he says with a smile in his voice.

The sound of his shoes thudding to the floor greets my ears before the bed dips under his weight. His heat warms my back, and his strong arm wraps around me.

"Happy birthday slash anniversary, baby. I love you," he croons into my ear.

I love you too. I think the words, not sure if my lips actually move to say them. I drift off to sleep as he cocoons me in his warmth.

***

I wake feeling like I'm in a sauna and wiggle around until I flip onto my other side. A smile comes to my lips as I find Bentley fast asleep behind me. I bounce my gaze across his face.

He's such a handsome man. I say man because the boy I used to stare at has vanished. The stubble on his chin says it all.

His lashes are so long and full as they rest against his cheeks. His thick hair falls onto his forehead as his natural curl fights against the style he forces it into each day.

I drop my gaze to his lips. His lips are so sensual looking under his straight nose. I can't help myself. I reach to brush my thumb across his brows.

"I can feel you staring at me," he murmurs.

"Is that a problem?"

He opens his eyes, and they sparkle back at me. He tightens his arm around me and tugs me into his chest. I bury my face into his chest as he kisses the top of my head.

"No problem at all. Have you rested enough? Can we get ready to leave?"

"What time is it?"

He reaches into his sweats for his phone. "Almost noon."

"Okay, okay, I'm up. Let me get up to shower," I yawn.

"You should pack an overnight bag."

I look at him through my lashes. "Oh really? What are you up to, Mr. Coswell? Where are you taking me?"

He turns onto his back and places his hands behind his head, showing off his muscled arms. I bite my lip as I look him over. Damn, this has been my boyfriend for a whole year.

"You'll just have to hurry up and find out."

"Ugh, give me about a half hour."

I rush to grab my things and head to the shower. Bentley remains in my bed like he owns the place. I'm grateful when there isn't a fight to get in a shower and get dressed.

My sophomore year has started off with way more challenges. I hate living in the dorms this year. Not only do I have a new roommate. I'm in a new dorm house. This one sucks.

Erica has mentioned getting our dads to get us a place off campus. She hates her dorm too. However, she's happy to be here with me and Bent so she's sucking it up for now.

Once I've showered, I head back to my room to get dressed. I find Bentley sitting on my bed with a frown on his face. My roommate is back and she's sitting on her bed staring at Bentley with stars in her eyes.

"I'm going to be in the car," Bentley says, standing.

He walks by me and presses a kiss to my forehead. I look up at him questioningly. He shakes his head and leaves without a word.

"Oh my God, I didn't realize who he was the first time we met. You're so lucky," Robin gushes once Bentley is gone.

"I've known him all my life. I don't see him the way everyone else does. He's just Bent to me." I shrug.

"Well, he totally made me nervous."

My mouth drops open, and I understand the look on Bentley's face. One of the first things Robin told me about herself is that she passes gas when she's nervous. In fact, within the first two minutes of meeting, she ripped a big one.

It was so loud there was no way we could ignore it like it didn't happen. Although I was going to try before she addressed it. I feel bad for her.

"Oh, you're going somewhere?" she asks as I begin to pack a bag after I've thrown on a pair of jeans and a sweatshirt.

"Yeah, it's my birthday and our one-year anniversary. Bent is taking me somewhere. Not sure where yet."

"Oh, you're always really busy. I thought I'd get a roommate with more time for me this year."

"My schedule is always crazy with track and classes. My best friend is here now, and I have a boyfriend. I'm sorry.

"Maybe you can hang out with us sometime. I will warn you, we've all grown up together and have our own vibe," I say.

"It's fine. I'll be okay."

I sort of feel bad. I made friends pretty fast, and I had Bentley my first year. Track went a long way to give me a friend group. I can't imagine how hard this would have been if I didn't have all of that working in my favor.

"I'll see you later, Robin. Coffee on me later this week?"

"Oh, okay. Yes, I'll be there."

I smile and wave. She's not so bad. I'm going to stop being so hung up on not rooming with Arlene this year.

Bentley

"This is so much fun," Zah squeals into the mic in our helmets.

She has her arms wrapped tightly around me as we ride on a snowmobile. It's the perfect day for this. We didn't get moving as early as I wanted to, but we arrived in time to still enjoy the day I had planned.

"Want to go around the mountain again?" I reply.

"*Please*," she drags out, sounding so adorable.

"Anything for my baby."

She squeezes her arms around me. I can feel her joy without having to see her face. I'm glad I went with this as our date.

I wanted to do something romantic but fun for our anniversary. I brought her here to the ski resort, knowing we could have the best of both worlds. In the last year, Zah and I have gotten so much closer.

I didn't enter the draft, as my coach convinced me to put in one more year. Zah had been all for me doing what I felt was right for me. In the end, I decided to stay because I know we have a shot at the championship this year and I have the potential to increase my draft stock.

The QB competition would have been stiff if I left my junior year. I have a better shot at the first round after this season as long as I remain healthy. My life feels like it's right on track right now.

I have a huge smile on my face as the sun beams down on us. Erica plans to come up tomorrow. When I told her my plan, she totally wanted to tag along. However, she does understand that this is a romantic occasion for us.

I caved and told her to give me this day and night before she joins us. We're all still getting used to this new dynamic now that Erica is a student here. It feels good to have them here with me.

"I don't want this to end, but I'm getting hungry," I say as we're halfway through another pass.

"You don't have to say that twice. I'm hungry and I have to go to the bathroom. Maybe we can come back out after," Zah replies.

"Yeah, that would be cool. It's sick out here at night with the lights and everything. Although you might change your mind once you see everything else I have planned."

"Oh, hurry. I know this is going to be amazing. I can't wait to see how you top last year."

"Nothing will ever top our first time, but I did my best."

"Fair point, but I'm looking forward to reminiscing on that night."

"You and me, baby," I croon and speed up to get to the rest of our date.

***

"That was delicious. A professional chef, I'm impressed, Bentley," Zah says with a smile on her pretty face.

We've been having such a good time. Snowboarding for a bit, riding the snowmobile, and now a candlelit dinner. I couldn't have asked for a better outcome.

The chef I've hired comes over with the strawberry shortcake I had him make for Zah. It's her favorite. I watch as her eyes light up.

"Go on, make a wish and blow out the candles," I say.

She looks up as if trying to think of a wish. I chuckle and reach into my pocket for the gift box inside. I wanted to give her something special.

"Oh," she gasps and then blows out the candles.

I place the box on the table, and her eyes go wide. I realize what this might look like and want to kick myself. Our fathers asked me not to propose just yet.

I agreed because Zah is only turning nineteen. I'll be twenty-one and I feel like that might be too soon. Although I know I will someday.

"It's not that. Not yet," I murmur.

"Oh, okay," she says and reaches for the box to open it.

Her face lights up all over again as she looks at the two-carat diamond earrings in the box. From the moment I saw them, I knew they should be hers. They're perfect for her ears.

"Bentley, I love them. Thank you so much," she sings.

"Happy birthday, baby."

"You say that like you got me something different for our anniversary," she says and looks across the table at me warily.

I shrug. "I couldn't do my girl like that. I do have something else for you."

"You really didn't have to. One gift would have been fine. I'm not expecting you to get me something for my birthday and anniversary every year."

"But you should, and I will. Let's eat your cake."

She shakes her head at me then cuts into the cake and slides a slice to me on one of the plates the chef brought over. He's cleaning up to leave.

Soon I'll have my girl all to myself. I spear my fork into the moist-looking slice of cake in front of me and lift it to her lips instead of taking the bite. Zah opens her mouth and takes the cake. I can't help smiling as she smiles back at me while chewing.

"Mm, wow, that's so delicious. It's so moist," she moans.

I can't take my eyes off her mouth. She's so adorable as she chews. I fork another bite and lift it to her lips once again, this time making sure to get more cream on the fork.

Zah's eyes sparkle as I place the fork before her mouth once again. She takes the sweet treat between her lips with a moan. Some of the whipped cream is resting on her lips, enticing me to stand from my seat and lean across the table. I capture her mouth in a passionate kiss as I suck, lick, and kiss the cream off.

"Mm, you're right, it is delicious," I say as I pull away.

"Are you talking about me or the cake?"

"Both. Are you up for a session in the hot tub?"

She tilts her head to the side and looks me over. I stare back at her with a smile on my lips. I know just how I want to end the night.

"Sure, why not?"

"Great. I did pack a swimsuit for you. Courtesy of Erica."

She rolls her eyes. "I should have known."

CHAPTER NINETEEN

Gift Exchange

Zahirah

I step out of the cabin we'll be staying at for the night and find Bentley already sitting in the Jacuzzi. The space is built to look like it's outdoors, but it's an enclosed space that's heated.

I pad over in the yellow bikini he handed to me while upstairs. It fits, but boy does it leave little to the imagination. Bentley drinks me in with his gaze as I place my towel and his gift down, then climb into the hot tub and sit across from him.

"Did you find everything you needed?"

"Yeah, I found a hair tie in my bag, and I had this scarf in there too," I say and finger the wrap on my head. "Do you want to exchange gifts now?"

He gives me a smile and reaches beneath the water to grab my ankle and lifts my foot to his chest. He then runs his palm up my leg and back down to my ankle. I smile at him as his touch brings a shiver with it.

"We can do whatever you like," he murmurs against my toes as he brings my foot to his lips.

"Okay, dry your hands. You can open your gift first since you already gave me my birthday gift," I say excitedly.

He laughs and reaches to dry his hands on his towel. I do note he doesn't lift it all the way to use it. However, I'm too excited to try to figure out why.

I hand him the gift envelope his present is in and hold my breath as he opens it. He tears it open and looks back at me with a bright smile on his face. I chew on my lip, waiting for him to say something, anything.

"Tickets to a hockey game," he says excitedly.

"Yeah, I know how much you love going to them. I thought you would like them. You and your dad can go," I ramble.

"I love them and you're coming with me. No question about that one. Do you remember that time our dads took us? You and Erica were so annoyed, but then you guys had a blast."

"Only because you and Garret made it fun."

"Garret is the best. I miss him," he says wistfully.

Garret is the third youngest in the Coswell family. Instead of starting college this year, he's off traveling and might join the military after he returns. When Garret and Bentley are together it's always a good time.

"Are you concerned about what he'll decide to do when he returns?"

He swallows hard and shakes his head. "No, he'll do what's right for him. I'm glad Dad talked him into waiting to make the decision. I'll be proud of him either way."

"Our dads have always been like the wise men on the block. Have you ever noticed how all the other kids would come to talk to them?"

"Yes, but I don't really want to talk about our dads right now. Come here, baby. You're too far away from me," he croons.

He turns to reach for his towel again. This time, his big body is blocking my view of what he's doing. When he does turn back to me, he lifts a brow as if to ask what I'm waiting for.

Leaning in and then reaching for my waist, he tugs me until I'm straddling his lap. I laugh and look down into his face as he runs his hands up my back. Suddenly, I feel something cold around my neck.

I look down as he's arranging a chain around my neck before he releases the chain to settle into place. I lift the necklace and smile. There are already three charms hanging from it.

A pair of track shoes, a football, and a teddy bear. I look up at him and smile. My heart is so full of love for him.

"The first time you said you loved me?"

"Yeah, I wasn't sure you would get it. I should have known you would."

I drop the chain back into place and cup his face between my hands. He glides his hands down my back and cradles my backside. I breathe him in as I feel the love pouring from him.

"I love you," I say against his lips.

"I love you too," he says before capturing my lips and devouring me.

I moan into his mouth as I allow him to dominate the kiss. The more we kiss, the more I can feel him growing hard beneath me. He groans and tightens his hold on my butt.

"Take your top off," he says in my ear, breaking the kiss.

I nod my head and reach to pop the clasp behind my neck. As the strips fall down, I feel him release the other clasp, causing the top to fall between us. Bent wastes no time; he palms my breast and brings my nipple to his mouth.

I close my eyes and throw my head back. The way he flicks his tongue against my hardened peak, then sucks on it, gives me a heartbeat between my legs. I can feel him twitching in his shorts beneath me.

Blindly, I reach to palm him and squeeze. He releases the strings on my bikini bottoms. Then he lifts his hips and begins to push his shorts down with my breast still in his mouth. I go to panic as we've never had unprotected sex before.

I stiffen and lock my body so he can't guide me down onto his lap. He allows my nipple to pop free from his mouth and taps my ass as he looks into my gaze. I widen my eyes at him.

"I put the condom on before you came out. I'd never break your trust like that. We're a team, we'll decide together when that's our next step. You can sit," he breathes.

I nod and begin to sink down on him. He groans and drops his head to my breast. I ride him slowly as he tightens his hold yet again.

"Bentley," I gasp as he begins to top from the bottom.

He feels so hard and good. I have way more experience than I did a year ago. Our connection has grown so much deeper.

"I love you so much, Zah. I love you more with each day. How can this pussy keep getting better? I want you more than anything," he groans.

I whimper and keep riding because I don't think anything I say right now will make sense. I only cry out loudly when he begins to stick his finger into my puckered hole. I come like he's pulled a trigger.

"Fuck, Bent," I keen.

This isn't the first time he's played back there, but it's always a shock when he does—in a good way. When he catches me off guard, I always have the most amazing orgasms, like now.

"Fuck, baby," he groans.

"Don't stop. I don't want to stop," I whimper.

He chuckles darkly before shifting our position until my back is to the wall of the hot tub and he's plowing down into me. My toes curl, my heart beating faster as my walls tighten around him as he hits my spot over and over.

By the time he's done wrecking my body, he has to carry me back inside. I fall fast asleep with a smile on my face. I love me some Bentley Coswell. Yup, I sure do.

Bentley

I love this girl so much. Never in a million years did I think this would be our life. Her gift was perfect. I love hockey almost as much as I love football.

Going to games is something I used to do with my dad all the time. My brother, Garret, and I lived for those games. When Zah mentioned Garret earlier, reality set in.

My life is about to change this year. It's my last college football season and my girl isn't leaving here with me. I'm nervous about everything coming my way: this season, the draft, and where I will land.

"You put my mind at ease, though," I murmur as I look down at Zah sleeping beside me. I lean in and place a kiss against her forehead.

As long as she's with me, everything is going to be okay. Zah is the light in my life. Things got so much better the moment she arrived on campus.

"I can do this."

CHAPTER TWENTY

Holidays at Home

Zahirah

Four months later ...

"Hey, Mrs. Fran, can I help you with anything?" I ask as I walk into the Coswell kitchen.

It's Christmas, and our families are having Christmas dinner together this year. Bentley and I were lucky to be able to come home. His team won their ball game just in time for him to be here.

It looks like they're going to the playoffs for sure. I'm so excited for him. This season has been everything he wanted and more. Bentley has balled out.

"Oh, yes, I was hoping you would offer. Your father and Bill had their hearts set on your mother's cornbread dressing and greens. She was supposed to make them before she hurt her wrist helping me with those stupid decorations. I feel so bad," she says with worry in her eyes.

"You want me to make them?"

"Yes, I have everything here already. The greens are already washed. You'll find everything else in the refrigerator and pantry. I know she taught you how to make them. She told me you've been cooking." She winks at me.

Mom did teach me, and the last two Thanksgivings, I secretly made both the collard greens and the stuffing for her. My dad was none the wiser. I have to say, I do make them both pretty damn well. I begin to roll my sleeves up.

"No problem. I've got you," I sing.

"Oh, thank you, honey. You're a lifesaver. I have a taste for the greens and the dressing myself."

I get to work gathering everything and begin to prep. There's Christmas music playing and laughter flowing through the house. I can hear the boisterous, booming voices of my dad and Bentley's father.

As I cut the greens and prep them to set aside while I get the neck bones seasoned in the pot, I begin to smile and wiggle my hips. Mrs. Fran looks up at me and smiles. We work in silence for the most part.

"The greens are in the pot, and the cornbread should be out in another fifteen minutes. I need to brown this meat and sweat these onions and green peppers down," I mumble to myself.

Suddenly, I'm wrapped in big, strong arms. I crane my neck to look up at Bentley. He dips his head and kisses my neck then pecks my lips.

"I was wondering what happened to you," he says as he searches my face with his gaze.

"I came to see if I could give your mom a hand."

"And she put you to work? Really, Mom?"

"You hush. You boys will eat up all the food, but you have no idea all the work that goes into prepping it. Zah is a good girl and she came to the rescue," Mrs. Fran says.

Bentley laughs as he begins to sway with me in his arms. He doesn't release me as his mom stares at us with a smile on her face. I begin to feel a little shy as I feel her gaze on us.

"You two are so adorable together. It warms my heart to see it. I don't think I've ever seen you like this, Bent," Mrs. Fran says.

"I've never been in love like this," he croons and kisses the top of my head.

"Aw, I love that, but you're going to have to let her go so she can finish those dishes. Now get," she laughs.

"Actually, I was looking for you for a reason. Baker, Gilbert, and the gang are all heading to the field for a game. Garret, Eddy, and I are riding over to join."

"Gilbert Manning? Wow, I haven't seen him since before I left for freshman year."

"So you want to come with us?"

"Yeah, but this is going to take some time to finish." I pout.

"Girl, you have it smelling like I'm in here," my mom says as she enters the kitchen.

"Hey, Mom. How's your wrist?"

"It's going to be fine enough for me to finish what you started. You go on and hang with your friends. I've got Fran, your father can help me lift a pan or pot or two."

"Are you sure, Mom?"

"You did most of the heavy lifting already. I can finish up. You kids just get back here before dinnertime."

I look up at Bentley. "You guys go ahead. I'll meet you there. I want to at least help and make sure this gets into the oven."

He pecks my lips. "Erica said she would meet us there too. She's talking to someone on the phone. You can come over with her," he says.

"Okay, cool. See you in a bit."

He leans into my ear. "I miss you already. Be safe."

"You too."

With that, he turns to leave. I look up and find my mother and Mrs. Fran watching me. I bite my lip and try not to roll my eyes.

"You see these two?" my mother teases.

"Aren't they the cutest?"

"Um-hm. Adorable and growing up too fast for my liking. It was just yesterday they were running around here playing with toys and fussing at each other.

"You really don't have to stay behind, Zah. What all haven't you done yet?"

"It's fine, Mom. I don't mind."

"Don't rush her away. I wanted to ask about the earrings and charm necklace he purchased a few months ago."

I reach for the necklace and bring it up to my lips. I love my necklace and the earrings. I haven't taken either of them off since he gave them to me.

"He gave me the earrings for my birthday and the necklace for our one-year anniversary," I gush.

"You had to see them," Erica says as she glides into the room. "They were both glowing and so stinking cute when I met them at the ski resort. I have to say, I was annoyed with them when they didn't tell me about their relationship, but seeing them together …" She shrugs.

Then she continues. "It all makes so much sense now. Like they've always been together or should have been."

"I have to say, I was tickled when he called to ask about my jeweler. I guess I took too long to get back to him because by the time I called him with the information, he informed me he had already made a purchase. He was so excited," Bentley's mom says.

"I'm just happy the two have been so responsible," my dad says as he comes into the kitchen.

"Can we talk about something else? There has to be something else of interest going on around here," I grumble as I chop at the ground meat in the pan.

"You're my baby, the most interesting topic in the world to me," my father says as he comes and wraps an arm around my shoulders.

"I doubt that, Daddy."

"Then you don't know my girl. Track star, straight-A student, most beautiful girl in the world, and my entire heart," he says and kisses my forehead as he gives me a squeeze.

"I think you're a little biased," I snicker.

"Nah, that's my baby. Why don't you come take a walk with me before you take off with the others. I wanted to talk with you, and I have a gift for you."

"Okay, let me get this all stirred up and in the oven."

"Didn't I tell you I had it? Girl, if you don't get your butt out of this kitchen."

"All right, all right," I relent.

My father leads me out of the Coswell home, and we begin to walk around our block. I've walked this path with my dad more times than I can remember. Memories of looking up at him as a little girl hit me hard suddenly.

He would hold my hand and look down at me with the biggest smile on his face. I think I've outgrown all of that. However, when he takes my hand in his, like he used to do when I was little, I begin to tear up.

I'm such a daddy's girl. My father has always been my hero. I've always had his support and words of wisdom to help guide me.

"I meant what I said, Zahirah. I'm so proud of you. You've turned into a beautiful young woman. Your grades have been outstanding, and I'm so damn proud of your track seasons. You're my little superstar, but you're not so little anymore," he chokes out.

"I'm still your little girl. That's never going to change."

"Oh, baby girl, I wish that were true. It's already changing. You're becoming an adult. You have adult situations coming your way. You know it's not going to be a walk in the park to be on Bentley's arm.

"I'm not going to sugarcoat it. You two are about to face a world of challenges. Starting with him entering the pros while you're still working on your degree and an Olympic spot. Do you think you're ready for this?"

"Yeah, Dad. I think I am. We've gotten stronger over the last year. Neither of us wants to bring the other drama.

"We're too focused on our sport and I'll be focused on my grades. Bent knows and respects that. I think I love him more because of it," I reply.

"I want you to remember you can always come home when life gets heavy and you need your mother and me. We're here and we'll support you in any way we can."

"I know, Daddy, but thank you for saying it out loud as a reminder. It makes me feel a whole lot better."

"You're my baby. I've always got your back. Oh, by the way, Bill and I can't wait for the spring to use those golf passes.

"That was a great gift, baby. Bill had to give up his membership when things were tight. I didn't see a reason to keep mine without him. We've been wanting to get back out there together. Thank you."

I give him a smile. "You're welcome. Speaking of Christmas gifts, what's this gift you have for me?" I ask as we make it back around the block to our house.

He stops in front of our driveway instead of continuing next door to the Coswells'. I look up at him expectantly. The sound of the garage door opening grabs my attention.

When I turn, there's a brand-new car sitting in the garage with a big red bow on it. I look back at my dad in disbelief. I had no idea my parents planned to gift me a new car.

The car I have is getting older and has had some trouble in the last few months, but I never expected this. I should have known when the state of my car became the first thing he would ask about during our weekly calls. My dad is a protector and provider.

"Oh my God, are you serious? This is mine?" I squeal.

I'm running in place because I don't know whether to hug the shit out of my dad, run to check out the car, or run to get Erica so she can see it with me. Someone pinch me. I jump into my dad's arms and hug him tight as I snap out of shock.

Erica, my mom, and Fran come out to see what's going on. Bill is standing on the porch with a big smile on his face. It's like the Christmas when Erica and I got new bikes and our dads stood outside to watch us ride them all day.

"Thank you, Daddy. Thank you," I sing happily.

"You're welcome, sweetheart."

"Oh my God. You have to drive us to the field. This car is so awesome. Way to go, Mr. Nickels," Erica croons.

"Only the best for my one and only baby."

"Can I take it for a spin?"

"Of course," Dad says as he hands me the key.

I hug him again. He gives me a big squeeze and kisses the top of my head. Releasing him, I then bounce happily in place.

"I love you guys," I say to my parents.

"We love you too. Drive safely," Mom says.

"I will," I call over my shoulder as I rush to the driver's side of my new car.

The chrome Mercedes screams fast and elegant. I couldn't have asked for a nicer car. When I get behind the wheel, I sigh.

"Wait until Bent sees this. I think it's nicer than his car," Erica snickers.

"Let's see what he thinks," I say as my father takes the bow off and I start the car.

The engine comes to life and we both squeal. This is the best Christmas ever. I pull off feeling like somehow I just became a real adult.

Bentley

We're in the middle of the game when a sleek, new-looking Mercedes pulls up to the field. When Erica pops out of the passenger side, I'm curious. However, when my girl hops out of the driver's side, I can't help but smile.

Zah looks good coming out of it. Her hair is in a ponytail and she has on a pair of jeans and one of my sweatshirts I shrunk in the wash. If you ask me, Zah is the reason it shrank. She had her eye on it and had worn it around my room a few times before it happened to become half its size.

"Is that Zah and Erica?" Gilbert Manning asks.

I look to him and frown. He's nearly drooling over himself. He's always had a thing for Zahirah.

I know that from high school. What he needs to remember is that she's off-limits, even more so now. Zah is mine.

To prove my point, I jog over and tug Zah into me for a passionate kiss. I devour her for everyone to see. A few whistles and cheering go up.

"I missed you too," she breathes when I break the kiss.

"You have no idea. Is this yours?"

"Yup, Daddy just gave it to me for Christmas."

"This is sick. How do you like the drive?"

"It's amazing. Drives like a dream. I can't wait to get it back on campus."

I lean into her ear and whisper. "We'll have to christen it later."

When I pull away, she's looking up at me with lust in her eyes as she bites down on her lower lip. I almost forget about the game I'm supposed to be playing and toss her over my shoulder so we can get out of here.

"You guys are together?" Gilbert asks from behind me.

I wrap my arm around Zah's waist and turn to face him. His eyes are wide, and he looks white as a sheet. Needless to say, he now knows he never has a chance with my girl.

"I thought I told you they were together," Baker says.

"I think I would have remembered that," Gilbert grumbles.

"Hey, I haven't seen you in how long, and that's all you have to say to me? I thought we were friends," Zah says to Gilbert as she tilts her head to the side.

"Oh, sorry. I guess I'm a little taken aback," Gilbert says then clears his throat. "You look good, Zah. It's good to see you. New car?"

"Yeah, my dad just gave it to me. How have you been? How's school and everything?"

"School is great. I'm about to graduate and start an internship with my uncle. I am going to take over and run the place, but it's protocol for me to intern and shadow him first," he rambles and begins to blush.

"I thought you wanted to start your own thing, move out to Silicon Valley and all that," I say as I furrow my brows.

Before we left for college, that had been his plan. I don't know if he's trying to show off for Zah or something else. The Manning family business is well known around here.

It's not like any of us can or have missed that Gilbert and his family are old money. The only reason he ended up in high school with us is because he was kicked out of more than one prep school. Our school was the next step down.

"I did, but some personal things got in the way, and I'll have to go to work for my family for now. When I take over, I can branch out then, I guess. I mean, if I do well," he says.

He shrugs then continues as he looks at Zah. "I mean, I'll be close to home, and I'll have stability. That's what really matters, right?"

"What matters is doing what's best for you. What makes you happy," Zah says as she looks up at me, totally oblivious to the fact that Gilbert is trying to throw shade and impress her all at once.

I palm her ass and dip my head to take her lips. She's all that matters to me. We're happy together.

"Are we going to finish this game or what?" Baker barks out.

"Yeah, hold on," I say before kissing Zah one more time.

"It was good to see you, Zah. I hope we get to hang a bit before the vacation is over," Gilbert says.

"Or maybe some other time since you'll be home when I come to visit."

"Yeah, sure."

I grit my teeth and hold in all the things I want to say. Knowing whenever she comes back home, he's going to try to hang out with her doesn't sit well with me.

Gilbert is in our friend group, but we do bump heads from time to time. I know the real him. He's not the guy he tries to pretend to be in public.

He's certainly never been the guy for Zah and never will be. As she cheers my name as I run back onto the field, I push it all aside. I have no reason to be jealous.

Zahirah and I are built to last. She's mine and I am hers. Nothing can tear us apart.

CHAPTER TWENTY-ONE

Dreams

Zahirah

"Done. It's official. I've declared for the draft, signed with my new agent, and booked my flight for the combine," Bentley croons in my ear as he walks up behind me and wraps his arms around me.

I just finished practice and came to the quad to meet him after he sent me a text that he wanted to hang out tonight. Bentley got his own place senior year to give us more privacy when we want and need it. I'm sure we're going to take advantage of that tonight.

I turn in his embrace and wrap my arms around his neck. He pecks my nose as he gives me a huge smile. He looks so happy.

"Oh my God, congratulations. Are you excited?"

"I think I am. Maybe a little overwhelmed at the moment. I mean, this is our future.

"I don't want to fuck this up. The wrong team, a slip in the draft, or the wrong city could fuck so much up for us."

"Bentley, I want you to breathe. It's all going to work out. I'm here no matter where you go," I say and lift on my toes to kiss him.

"Come on. Let's get out of here before the crew spots us and we can't get rid of them."

I snicker. "You want to order pizza?"

"Nah, I've got something planned already," he says.

"Oh really? Is this my romantic Bentley?"

"This is your man taking care of you. I want to spend some quality time with you. We've been so busy, I thought this would be the perfect time to kick back and chill."

"Sounds good to me."

We walk to his car hand in hand. As we ride to his apartment, we talk and laugh. I can't help but notice how happy I am.

My life is so perfect. My boyfriend is amazing. What more could I ask for?

When we get to the apartment, I double down on my thoughts of having the perfect boyfriend. He has string lights up around the living room. A bottle of champagne is chilling in a bucket, and it smells delicious.

"What's that smell?"

"I might have called your mom and asked for her recipe for chicken enchiladas," he says and blushes.

"You what? No way, those are my favorite."

"I know. I hope I got them somewhere close to hers."

"I'm yours for life if you did."

He tugs me into him and kisses me. We get lost in the kiss for a moment before he pulls away and kisses the tip of my nose. I smile up at him.

"I'm going to hold you to that."

"You're spoiling me. Whatever am I going to do when you're too busy winning championships?"

"I will always make time for you. Staycations during my bye weeks. Flying you out for dates during the season and trips all over the world during offseason. We'll make it work, I promise."

"I can't wait. All our dreams are coming true. You're going first round, you know that, right?"

He tugs me in closer and palms my ass. "I love your confidence in me."

"How could I not believe in my man? Besides, you played your ass off senior year. You earned this, babe."

"What's the first thing you want?"

"What do you mean?"

"Your dad already gave you a car for Christmas. I had been thinking about giving you one before that. Now I'm thinking maybe a house or a vacation between graduation and preseason. Anywhere you want to go," he croons.

"You are not buying me a house, Bentley," I scoff.

"Why not?"

"I'm your girlfriend, not your wife."

"Give it a year, two tops. I'm going to put a ring on your finger." He shrugs. "If we get the house now, you'll be settled by the time I do and you can focus on planning the wedding."

My stomach growls. "Let's eat. We can talk more about what our future looks like after I scarf down those enchiladas."

"As you wish," he says with a wink.

Bentley

I chuckle at Zahirah and turn to lie down across her lap. We've been sitting on the couch talking after finishing dinner. She runs her hand through the front of my hair, taking a lock to rub between her fingers.

I take her hand and kiss her fingers. I love this. It feels so right. I can see our future so clearly.

"We should have at least four kids. All after you win at least two gold medals, of course. I'll have two, maybe three rings by then," I say as I look up at the ceiling while playing with her fingertips.

She begins to giggle. "You want four kids?"

"Yeah, two boys, two girls."

"And if we have three boys first? Then what?"

"Baby number five it is." I can't help smiling at the thought.

Images of little ones who look like us fill my head. I know my parents will go nuts over them. I really don't care if we have boys or girls. I just want them with her.

"Ha! You'll be gone most of the year. Meanwhile, I'll be retired with four kids all by myself."

I look at her face to catch the amused smile on her lips. I lift up from lying across her lap. Then I place my forehead to hers.

"All I want is to have a family with you. I want to give them the perfect childhood we had. I want to be a great dad like mine and yours. As long as you all are happy, I'm good. One, two, or six." I crack a smile as I say six.

She gasps. "Oh no. I respect your mom, but I'm not following in her footsteps. Six, you're tripping."

I snake my hand under her shirt and palm her breast, flicking my finger over her nipple. I capture her lips and kiss her passionately. She moans into my mouth and runs her hand through my hair.

"We could get some practice in. All this talk of you having my babies has me so fucking hard right now."

She reaches into my sweats and grabs me. I twitch in her palm, causing her to give it a squeeze. I groan and tug the cup of her bra down to get access to her smooth skin.

"Oh fuck," I hiss and throw my head back as she leans in, pushing my sweats down, then takes me into her mouth.

Getting on her knees, she goes to work sucking and stroking me. I push my hand into her leggings and begin to finger her from behind. She's gotten so good at this.

I come after she gives me one of the best blow jobs of my life so far. However, I'm hard again almost instantly as she stands and begins to peel her clothes off.

When I catch my breath, I grab a condom from my wallet, shove my sweats down, and tear my T-shirt over my head, tossing it aside. I then roll the condom on and stroke myself as I look up at my sexy-ass girl.

Her toned body is amazing. Covered in all that gorgeous, silky dark-brown skin. I love how it glows with its own shine.

"Come here," I murmur as I stroke myself.

She comes to me and straddles my lap. I palm her ass and guide her to seat herself. A loud groan leaves my lips as her tight sheath sucks me in.

I go straight for her breasts and pull her nipple into my mouth. Zah rides me with so much pleasure in her voice and written all over her face. Releasing her hardened peak from my lips, I then look into her eyes.

She pushes her hands into my hair, pushing the long locks out of my face. As she tightens her grip, she begins to ride me harder. We're both panting and moaning.

"Oh fuck, yeah, Zah. Just like that, baby. Fuck, this cock was made for you."

"Bentley, damn, you feel good. I need more. I want you so much."

"You want more?"

"Yes, please. I need you so much."

I smile and tap her leg. She stands and looks down at me with so much lust in her eyes. I turn her and guide her back onto my lap.

Once she's seated on my length again, I reach for her legs and hold them open as I lean her back onto my chest while I thrust up into her. She begins to cream and scream.

It's so good my eyes roll back into my head. I angle my head and suck on the skin on her neck. The sweet scent of her skin makes my mouth water.

I could spend the night just tasting her and I'd be a happy man. Zah has brought new meaning to my desire for her. I push her to lean forward as I watch her ass bounce on me.

Biting my lip, I run my hands all over her smooth back and ass. She's so fucking sexy. The more I think of her becoming my wife and having my babies, the harder I get.

"Oh my God, you're so hard, babe. You're making me so wet," she cries out.

She's not lying. I'm super hard and her pussy is so wet it's singing back at me. She's dripping down my balls.

I roll my tongue inside my mouth as if I can taste her juices. She ripples and tightens around me, and I have to bite back my orgasm. I'm not ready to come yet. However, the sight before me alone is about to make me lose the battle.

"We're just getting started, Zah. I want to fuck you all night, baby. Let me show you what our future can feel like," I breathe against her skin.

I feel her about to come. I won't be far behind her. When she starts to grind her hips on me, we both surrender to our orgasms.

I roar her name as I spill into the condom. Pressing my sweaty forehead to her shoulder, I try to catch my breath. She turns to look back at me and smiles.

"We're going to need to head into my room for more condoms," I laugh.

"I'm going to need a minute to feel my legs."

"You and me both. I love you, baby," I say and peck her lips.

CHAPTER TWENTY-TWO

Torn

Bentley

"Come on, baby," I murmur as I sit in my seat in the bleachers watching my girl run.

She's behind at the moment, but I know that's not for long. I scoot to the edge of my seat, holding my breath. I want to be down there running with her to cheer her on.

I bite my fist as she gives it some gas and begins to move forward faster. Suddenly, she floats by everyone else and sails forward as if she's the only one out there. I get to my feet as my heart races.

"Come on, Zah, finish them," I bellow. "You've got this, baby. Come on."

"Yes, Zah, yes," Erica cheers as she stands beside me.

Robin is standing on the other side of Erica with wide eyes as she clutches her hands over her mouth. She's become like a little tagalong the last two semesters. She's grown on me. The crowd begins to roar like thunder as Zah takes the race, crossing the finish line.

"Yeah, baby. That's what the fuck I'm talking about. That's my girl," I roar as I fist pump.

Suddenly, the air is sucked out of the building. Zah drops to the ground, screaming as she holds her left knee. Before I know what I'm doing, I race down to where she's lying in tears.

I drop to my ass and pull her into my arms as I hold her between my legs. She looks up at me with tears swimming in her eyes. I don't know what to do, so I cup her forehead and hold her against my chest as I rock her soothingly.

"I'm here, baby. I've got you. Help is coming. It's okay, it's going to be okay. I'm right here."

"I think it's over," she sobs.

"Shh, don't do that. We don't know anything yet. Let them take care of you, baby. It's going to be okay."

I want to promise her it will all be all right, but I have this bad feeling in the pit of my stomach. All I can do is hold her and try to give her my strength. I'll be right here for her.

Zahirah

I have a torn ACL. Everything before the end of that race is now a blur to me. I wish I could start this day over. It's over, I don't think I will run the same again.

The doctor was positive and said I could make a full recovery, but I just have this feeling like running track has come to an end for me. I'm numb and don't want to think about what this all means. The reality that I may have won my last race today is a bitter pill I'm not ready to swallow.

"Can I get you anything?" Bentley murmurs as he holds me in his arms.

He's been the only thing holding me together all day. We've been in his apartment since I was released to go home. I couldn't be more grateful for him having his own place right now.

"No, I'm fine. I don't want you to move."

He tightens his arms around me and kisses the top of my head. I close my eyes and bask in his strength. It's all I can do not to fall completely apart.

"You have to think positive. You're going to come back from this."

"You don't know that."

"I do because you're the strongest person I know. If you put your mind to it, you can make it happen."

"I hope you're right."

He reaches under my chin to lift my head, so our eyes lock. There is so much concern in his gaze. I'm hit with a strong wave of emotion.

"I know I am, and even if I'm not, I'm here with you. Whatever happens, we'll get through it together. We can do anything together."

CHAPTER TWENTY-THREE

Losing Everything

Bentley

Two months later ...

There has been so much going on as I get prepared for the combine and the draft and get ready to graduate. When I'm not focused on training or my classes, I'm with Zah, trying to keep her spirits up.

My baby has been so depressed. The trainers have just started to work on restoring motion and strength to her knee. I think it's been weighing heavily on everyone's mind how long her injury will take to heal and allow her to return to the field, especially Zah's.

I'm doing my best to be present for her and remain focused on all the things I need to take care of. I know she's not leaning on me as much as she needs to because she doesn't want to be a bother.

That could have been me. I could be the one down with a torn ACL. There would be no draft and I'd be working on figuring out what the hell I plan to do with my life.

That's something I've thought about a lot. I'm trying to see this all through her eyes and feelings. To go from being on top to this, I feel so bad for her.

"Just a minute," I call out as my doorbell rings.

I just stepped out of the shower. I want to head over to see Zah and make sure she eats dinner. She's been studying and keeping to herself a lot. Sometimes, not even taking time to eat.

Wrapped in a towel, I jog to the front door and look out. Seeing it's Zah on her crutches, I quickly open the door. She has her hood up over her head and something is off about her posture that has nothing to do with the crutches.

"Baby?"

She looks up and that's when I can see the tears rushing down her face. I quickly move to lift her off her feet, catching her crutches to toss them into the apartment out of my way. She wraps her arms around my neck and buries her face into my shoulder as she sobs.

"Zah, baby, what's going on?"

"I'm losing my scholarship. Coach told me today after my session."

"Ah shit. I'm so sorry, Zahirah. We're going to figure this out, baby. I promise."

"There's nothing to figure out. My parents only allowed me to come here because of the scholarship. Now they'll surely want me to come home." She sniffles.

"Can you finish out the semester at least?"

"Coach said she's working on that, but it's not guaranteed."

I take a seat on the couch and place her on my lap. Pushing her hood back, I look into her face. My heart is breaking.

"If they won't cover the rest of the semester, I will. You don't have to go home in the middle of all the hard work you've already put in."

"I can't ask you to do that. This is all so messed up. I ... I don't know how to feel. It's like I'm losing everything I worked so hard for. Why is this happening?"

"I don't know, baby, but I'm here for whatever you need. You don't have to ask me. I'm going to take care of you. Besides, I'm sure if you tell your mom and dad what's going on, they're not going to allow your education to be interrupted," I say.

"Thanks, Bent. I just needed someone to talk to. It feels like the sky is falling and I don't know how to stop it.

"I mean, you always know something like this can happen, but when it does, it's like you're blindsided while watching the train run you over. None of the races, none of the wins make a difference. You can't perform, so you don't matter anymore."

"You matter, baby. You matter to me, and you matter to everyone back home. Track doesn't define anything about you.

"If they don't want to support the best runner on their team, fuck them. You still have tons of options. You're so smart and talented."

"I've always dreamed of going to the Olympics. I never thought of what I would do if I couldn't be a professional athlete. All I know is running."

"Remember in high school when you were on the media team? You were great at that. I know you had my attention every morning."

"Oh, please, you were a horny jock. I probably had all the teams' attention," she says with the first real smile I've seen in weeks.

"This is true, but it's not a bad idea. What about the summer you helped my mom out at the real estate office? You and Erica seemed to like that."

"I did. I really had a blast that summer, but I don't know if I could actually sell a house. That takes skill."

"I think Mom would love to show you the ropes."

"She's not even in the business anymore."

"That's what you think. She's still doing private sales here and there. She got back out there when Dad needed some help with the finances for a bit."

"I guess I have a lot of thinking to do. I mean, I won't know for sure for another ten or so months if I'll never compete again, but I don't want to sit around and wait. I want to have options. This is teaching me to keep options," she says.

"Speaking of options, have you eaten? What do you have a taste for? Let me feed you."

"No, I haven't eaten, but I'm not hungry for food right now. I miss you, Bent," she purrs as she runs her hands over my bare chest.

It's been two months since we've had sex. She hasn't really been in the mood, and for a while, she was in too much pain to think about sex. I'm hard instantly.

"Are you sure?"

She bites her lip and nods her head. Not willing to turn her down, I capture her lips and kiss her deeply. I stand with her in my arms, ready to carry her to my bedroom.

My towel falls to the floor, forgotten as I step over it and make my way to the bed, where I can take her with care for her knee. She moans in my mouth as I place her down on my mattress.

Zahirah

"I love you," Bentley groans into my mouth as he devours me.

"I love you too," I moan as he goes to pull away and reaches for the hem of my hoodie as I settle on the bed.

I'm nervous and excited at the same time. It's been too long since the last time we had sex. I miss him and want to feel him inside me, but I'm nervous about my leg.

However, sitting in his lap while he had nothing but a towel on made me throw all caution to the wind. I want him. I long to feel him making love to me.

"Bent, I want you so much," I whimper as he peels my sweats down my legs.

"I want you too, baby. Hold tight, I've got you."

Lust fills his eyes as he sees I'm not wearing underwear. I drop my gaze and see he's lost his towel somewhere along the way. He's already hard and waiting.

I squirm in place, wanting to push him onto his back and mount him. He reaches into his drawer for a condom and rolls it on as if reading my thoughts. However, he doesn't move to enter me as I thought he would. Instead, he gently pushes my legs open and flattens onto his belly.

"Oh my God, yes," I cry out.

He hums into my core as he demolishes my pussy. I mean, he's eating me like a meal he wants to savor. I rock my hips against his face, needing more.

It doesn't take long before he has me coming all over his face. I clench the sheets with one hand and his thick hair with the other. He has my left thigh cradled to the side of his face.

I want to try to bend my knee, but I don't want to do anything that will end this. As I come down from my orgasm, Bentley turns me onto my side and moves behind me. He then hooks my leg over his arm and thrusts into me from behind. I cry out his name and look back at him over my shoulder.

"Fuck, baby," he groans and captures my lips. He breaks the kiss and looks into my eyes. "Are you okay?"

"Yeah, keep going. I'm okay."

"If I hurt you, let me know. We can try another position."

"I'm good, babe. Please, I need you."

"Fuck, say that again."

"I need you, Bent. Please."

"I always want to give you what you need. You feel so good. I've missed being inside you so much."

He lifts my leg in the air and begins to fuck me harder. It's just what I need. I get so lost in us, all my stress and worries melt away.

I've thought about finishing the semester and going back home to finish up somewhere else. However, Erica is here. I'd be leaving her alone.

"Zah, baby, I need you here with me. I can feel your thoughts drifting," Bent groans into my ear.

He pulls out and rolls me onto my back. Pulling my right leg against his waist, he then settles between my legs and slides into me once again. We lock eyes as he rocks in and out.

He licks his lips, then leans in to take mine. I need more of him. I want to do my part.

I begin to rock my hips to meet his thrusts as best I can. He groans and his eyes roll back in his head. He's so deep and hard.

"Don't stop, I'm coming. Yes, yes, you feel so good," I whimper.

"Fuck, Zah, keep moving just like that, baby. I'm going to come so fucking hard. Oh my God, you feel good."

He begins to hit my spot, and my eyes roll back in my head. I don't think I'm going to last much longer without coming. I'm shaking and convulsing beneath him, ready to come apart.

"I'm coming. Oh God, I'm coming."

"Zah," he grunts as his hot seed spills into the barrier.

He rolls onto his back, breathing heavily. I look up at the ceiling and begin to think of all the things in my life I still have. Together, we can do anything.

"Zah—"

He doesn't get to finish his words as both our phones go off. I scoff a laugh and go to reach for my hoodie to grab mine. Seeing it's my mom, I grab the phone and sit up to answer.

Bentley gets up and heads into the bathroom, leaving me to be able to answer the call in private. I had tried to call my mom earlier when I first got the news, but it went to voicemail. I have a smile on my face as I pick up the call and lift the phone to my ear.

"Hey, Mom," I sing into the phone.

"Zahirah, where are you, baby? Are you sitting down?"

"I'm at Bent's. Yeah, I'm sitting."

The smile falls from my face. A strangled sound comes from the bathroom, almost like a mix between a sob and something soul torturing.

My blood runs cold. I turn to look at the bathroom door, but I can't move. My crutches are still by the door where Bentley threw them.

"Mom, what's going on?"

"It's your father and Bill. They were killed in an accident. Baby, you kids all need to come home."

"*No*," I scream. "*Daddy, no.*"

I try to stand but fall right onto my butt, sobbing. Bentley appears and wraps himself around me as he sobs with me. I hold on to him tightly, as it feels like my entire world has just imploded.

"We're going to get through this together. I'm so sorry, baby. I'm so sorry."

"This isn't real. They can't be gone. No. This isn't real. Not my daddy. Why?"

"I don't know, baby. I don't want it to be real either. I just talked to him this morning before I left for training.

"We said we would talk again tonight. He was going to come to the combine. This was his dream.

"He was so excited. Now he's gone. I'm doing all of this on my own now. He's gone," he sobs.

I'm so confused and numb. I don't know how long we sit on the floor naked and sobbing. My world just ended. My daddy is gone, and my second father is gone with him.

This can't be real.

CHAPTER TWENTY-FOUR

Empty Hearts

Zahirah

"How are you girls holding up?" Mrs. Gunderson asks as Erica and I sit on the couch in the Coswell home.

Our moms decided to do a joint funeral and repass. We've been asked the same question more times than I can count. I'm still trying to make sense of what's even happening.

Everything feels empty: our home, these people's words, everything. I don't want to be here because I don't want this to be real.

How can the two men who raised and looked out for me all my life just be gone? That stupid truck driver took them from us. Why didn't he pull over?

Why didn't he get more rest before getting out on the road? Now two of the most important men in my life are gone. I'll never hear my daddy's voice again, I'll never see his smile or have a talk with him.

"We're not," Erica chokes out beside me, pulling me from my thoughts. "We're not holding up. In one single moment, our fathers have been taken from us.

"Holding up? I don't know if my family will ever be the same again. We're not holding up at all. We're barely breathing.

"I get it. You're all trying to be kind and don't know what to say. Guess what?

"We have no words. Our hearts are broken, and we're all lost as fuck. Excuse my language.

"My father wouldn't have liked that, but ma'am. We're not holding up and if one more person asks that question ..." Erica shakes her head and gets up to run off.

"I'm sorry. I didn't mean—"

"It's okay. She's right. We're not okay. Thank you for being here," I say and push up to get up and grab my crutches.

I do my best to hobble after Erica. It looks like she raced out the back door. I get to the sliding doors and see her sitting in the grass with Tara and Lauren. My heart breaks a little more when I spot Bentley sitting on the swing set, not that far from them. His head is hung, and his shoulders are slumped.

We haven't had much alone time since arriving back home to support our moms. Being an only child, I've spent most of my time with my mother helping her make the arrangements. Mom, being Mom, has tried to be strong for everyone.

However, I've heard her breaking down at night. The sobs have been tearing me apart. This all hurts so bad.

"Hey, you need some help?" Garret asks as he appears.

Bentley lifts his head and turns in my direction. In the next breath, he's on his feet, rushing to help me off mine. He lifts me into his arms as Garret takes my crutches.

Returning to the swing with me in his embrace, he then retakes his seat and places me on his lap. Tightening his hold around me, he buries his face in my neck and inhales deeply.

"I'm sorry I haven't been there for you. I've just—"

"Bentley, don't. I understand. You lost your father too. This isn't just happening to me."

"It shouldn't be happening to anyone. This is so wrong. They were going to the golf course. Two friends going to have a good time and a few laughs.

"Two fathers wanting to unwind after a week of providing for their families. Two best friends." He pauses and swallows hard. "Two best friends spending their last moments together."

"This hurts so bad. I don't know what to do," I breathe.

"Me either, baby. Me either."

***

"Hey, Mom. Can I help you with anything?" I ask as I enter the kitchen.

"Uh, no. I have everything covered. Fran needed a break, so she went upstairs. I'm just trying to get all this food put away.

"You get off that leg and have a seat. Hearing your voice will do a whole lot for me right now."

I move over to take a seat. Everyone else went for a walk, not wanting to come back into the house. Bentley offered to give me a ride on his back, but I didn't want to be a bother. The last thing we need is for him to get injured trying to take care of me. Besides, I thought they could all use some time as siblings.

Not that they don't treat me as one, but this is different. I belong here with my mom. I can see the cracks she's trying to glue together by sheer will.

"What do you want to talk about?"

"How's school?"

"Oh, that's not a great topic," I snort.

"What? What's going on, Zah?"

I sigh. "I'll only tell you if you promise not to worry about it."

"Now I'm worried about it. Talk to me, girl."

I purse my lips. I hadn't planned to tell her about this, but it's happening, so I might as well. I'm going to need to make a decision.

"I'm losing my scholarship because of my injury. I've been in touch with Coach to see if she could pull some strings to at least cover the rest of the semester.

"I got a text this morning that there may be a way. However, next semester I'm on my own. I can apply for an academic scholarship, or I could come home and go somewhere else." I shrug.

"What would you like to do?"

"I don't know. Erica transferred to be there with me and Bent. He's graduating and I'm losing my scholarship. Where does that leave her?"

"Erica will be fine. I'm asking you what you want to do. If you want to continue there and finish your degree, we'll make it happen. Scholarship or not."

"I can't ask you for that."

"I'm your mother. You're not asking me for anything I'm not going to do for my baby. I know your father and I didn't want you to leave, but we were proud of you. I know he would want you to do whatever your heart tells you."

"Can I think about it. I kind of don't know what's up or down at the moment and I don't think I should be making any decisions about anything until my head clears a bit."

"Oh, I understand. I still have a lot to figure out. My best friend is gone, and I don't know what to do without him.

"I just have to keep moving for now. If I stop, I'm going to fall apart. I need to be doing something," she says sadly.

"I saw that fabric in your craft room. You want to make a day of it tomorrow?"

"I would love that. It's been so long since we've spent the day crafting together. That's a great idea."

Bentley

"Someone tell me this is going to get better," Lauren says somberly.

"I don't know that any of us can," Garret replies.

"Hey, at least we all have each other. Zah has no one. We're lucky to have each other to help support Mom," Erica says.

My heart tightens. She's right. I have five siblings I can lean on and who can lean on me.

However, I've been feeling too lost to be there for Zah or anyone else. I don't know what to do for anyone. The pain is searing so deep I can't think at times.

"I hate this. I hate that I can't fix this for her. I hate that I can't be what she needs.

"I hate that she was robbed of her father and our dad. I want to make this go away for her, but I don't know how to fix it for me. I feel so fucking guilty for not being what she needs right now.

"It's making me sick, but I'm so fucking broken. I can't fucking breathe," I sob.

My brother, Garret, pulls me into a hug and my sisters and little brother join in as I cry. Garret tightens his hold on me. It's like he's the only thing holding me together.

"It's going to be all right. Zahirah is strong. She knows you're hurting as much as she is. Don't be so hard on yourself," he says into my ear.

"I'm supposed to be strong for her. She has so much shit on her shoulders right now."

"And so do you, Bent. We'll all try harder to be there for her, but you can't put all this on yourself," Erica says.

"Dad would say the best way to help someone else is to get right with yourself," Tara says.

"I know that's right," Lauren says. "You have a dream to catch, big bro. We'll look after your girl. We're going to stick together."

"I miss him so fucking much already." I blow out a breath.

"You know he's probably watching us right now, fussing that we're avoiding the house while Mom probably needs us," Garret scoffs.

"Tell me about it. I'm going to head back before he haunts me in my sleep," Eddy says.

We all give a light chuckle and turn back for home. My heart is still heavy and feels like something is missing, but I'm glad to have my siblings. Erica takes my hand and gives it a squeeze.

The next thing I know we're all holding hands, swinging our arms like we used to when walking with our dad. Lauren begins to sing one of the songs we would sing with him, and the next thing I know, we're all singing with her as we make our way home.

CHAPTER TWENTY-FIVE
Different People

Zahirah

"Wait, wait. Stop. Just stop. Bentley, what are we even arguing about?" I yell as my head spins.

After spending a few days with our families, Bentley, Erica, and I all returned to school. I learned my mother had paid this semester's tuition before I even touched back down on campus. To save money, Bentley said I should move in with him instead of living in the dorms.

It seemed like a great idea back then. Now I wish I never had. All we do is fight.

It's never over anything that makes sense. Bentley has been picking fights and it's driving me crazy. It's like we're not even the same people anymore.

It's only been a little over a month since our fathers' funerals but there is so much going on that hasn't been said or addressed. I'm tired. We're both still grieving and this is just too much.

"What do you mean, what are we arguing about? Have you been listening to me?"

"Yes, I have and nothing makes sense. You never say what you really mean."

"Zahirah—"

"No, Bentley, I don't want to do this anymore. I'm leaving."

The scowl falls from his face and then the blood drains from it. He looks at me like he's lost or lost for words. I'm so drained I can't think about his feelings and mine anymore, or which he's settling on.

"What do you mean you're leaving?"

"Things haven't been right. I talked to my adviser, and we spoke with my professors. Given the circumstances, most of my professors agreed to allow me to take my exams early.

"I'm just going to take whatever grade I get for the class I was denied a final for. I'm going home. My mother needs me and you and I need to take a step back before we ruin the friendship we have," I say.

"Friendship," he scoffs. "I thought this was more than a friendship."

"It is, but is it worth losing everything we are if we keep going like this?"

"How is this not ruining us?"

"Bent, you have your team. You're moving soon. You wouldn't be here with me anyway."

He stumbles over to flop down on the couch beside me. Dropping his head in his hands, he sits silently for a few beats. I swipe at my tears as my heart slowly crumbles.

"What happened to us getting through anything together?" he chokes out.

"You're not allowing me to be in this with you. The more I try, the more you push me away. I'm tired, Bent.

"You're not the only one hurting. I think … I think I'm saving us. We can't keep going like this."

"So you're abandoning me?"

"What? I'm not ... how could you say that? I lost my father too. Have I forced you to only see my loss? No, I've been here for you.

"Draft day, I was by your side. When I saw the look on your face as your name was called and you looked to those two empty seats, I held my shit together and poured everything I had left into you.

"Then I cried that night because I not only missed my dad but yours too. I cried into my palms while hiding in the bathroom, so I didn't steal your night. Bentley, I lost my career, my scholarship, and my father in what feels like one breath.

"I'm not abandoning you. I'm trying to save what's left of myself. Leaving you is taking from me the only thing I have left.

"I have nothing," I sob-yell. "But I refuse to be nothing. If I stay, that's what I'll be. Nothing but your emotional whipping post."

"Zah, baby, I'm sorry. I know I'm not handling this right. I ... where are you going?"

I shake my head and limp to the door. I've made up my mind. My mother needs me, and I deserve better.

This isn't the man I love right now. I can only hope he heals and returns, but this toxic loop we're in, it's not for me.

"We both have a lot we need to work through. I don't think that can happen while we're together. As your friend, I'm always a call away. As your girlfriend, I hope we can find our way back someday.

"I love you, Bent. You go make your dream happen. You give them hell. I'll be watching."

With that, I leave before I'm not able to. This is the second hardest thing I've had to do. Burying my father was the first.

It feels like nothing will ever be the same. I make it to my car and fall apart behind the wheel. I sob so hard I think I'm going to throw up.

Bentley

The door clicks shut, and I feel like my life has just walked out of that door. I want to be angry at her, but I can't be. Everything she said was true.

"I'm sorry," I sob into the empty space.

It's happening again. I can't say a word to Zah without putting my foot in my mouth. I never mean for us to get into fights, but I just can't find the words for what I'm really trying to say.

I want to ask her if she's okay. If there's anything I can do. I want to talk about how we're both feeling and how we can help each other through it.

I'm frustrated because I want to be there for her. I want to stop the nightmares that wake her up at night. The nightmares she's not talking to me about, but I know about because I'm up all night trying to avoid my own.

We're both fucked up and probably should take some time apart, but I miss her already. I was going to ask her to come with me. Finish her degree while we start fresh.

Now I'm stuck here staring into my palms, wondering what I'm going to do next as tears stream down my face. Grabbing one of the throw pillows to scream into, I then bring it to my face. Her scent hits me in the face immediately.

I didn't even sob this hard after losing my father. She's gone. Zah left me.

"I'm sorry, baby. I didn't know what to do. I'm so fucking sorry," I sob.

CHAPTER TWENTY-SIX

Not Alone

Zahirah

Two months later …

"Hey, Mom. I'm going to grab a bite and a milkshake. You want anything?" I call through the house as I grab my car key.

I need some fresh air. Today has been rough. I've been torturing myself watching clips of Bentley during OTAs. He looks good but distracted at times.

In the last two months, he's been one of the main stories on rotation. How he lost his father and a close family friend only a month before being drafted in the first round. They've been questioning his mental ability to be ready for this.

I want to tell them all to shut the fuck up and allow him to do his job. Throwing a ball is like breathing for Bentley. When it's time to show up, he will. I know he will.

He's going to do this for his dad. They don't know him like I do. I've picked up the phone to call him a million times, but I know neither of us is ready.

"I'm fine. You go and enjoy yourself. Don't rush back," Mom calls back to me.

"Okay, you sure I can't bring you anything back?"

"No, I'm headed next door in a bit to sit with Fran for a little while."

"All right, love you. Tell Mrs. Fran I said hello."

"Um-hm. She told me you've been avoiding her. You need to go over there and tell her hello yourself. She'd love to see you."

"Yeah, I know. I will," I say quickly and dip out the door.

I haven't been able to face Bentley's mother. It's hard enough to see the sadness in my own mother's eyes. Eddy comes over almost every day looking for me. He's such a sweet kid.

Other than that, I've been avoiding all the Coswells. Lauren and Tara have invited me to hang out, but I just don't feel right. There's a part of me that wonders if Bentley was right.

Did I abandon him? Maybe there was another way to do this. I shake those thoughts off as I head for my car.

"I had to come all the way home to get you to talk to me."

I turn to find Erica glaring at me. I gasp and rush to tug her into a hug. I don't even bother to think about it. I miss her so much.

"I should push you on your ass, but I've missed you too much," she grumbles as we embrace tightly.

"I've missed you too."

"Then why haven't you been answering my calls?"

"I don't know. Things ended so messed up with your brother. I was trying to make a clean break."

"By dumping my entire family and holing up in your mother's house, not willing to talk to anyone?"

"It's not like that. I have my reasons for staying in the house. This is my first real venture outside.

"I need to get away for a little while. I need out of my head," I say.

"Okay, so where are we going?"

"Wait, what are you doing here? I thought you planned to take summer classes."

"Nope. I hate it there without you guys. I dropped out. I'm thinking this college thing might not be for me. Garret had a great idea. I might travel for a bit."

"Really?"

"Yup. Mom is warming up to the idea. She wasn't as pissed as I thought she would be when I told her I dropped out. Actually, it seemed like she was waiting for me to."

"I'm heading to get something to eat. Maybe a burger and fries and a milkshake."

She gasps. "Oh, you dirty brat. You were going to go to our spot without me."

I snicker. "I was going to think about you while there. You would have been in my heart."

"You look good, Zah. I saw you walking and shit. Have you spoken to Bent?" she asks as we climb into my car.

I take a deep breath and shake my head. I knew this was coming. Today of all days, I don't want to talk about this.

"I figured. He's still a mess about you two. He misses you."

"He hasn't called me either," I mutter.

"He's trying to give you space. He knows he fucked up. Listen, babe. All of us are still fucked up. This is all still so fresh."

"Above Baker and Garret, Dad was Bentley's best friend. I think he's a little lost for wise counsel. Especially when it comes to you.

"Add to that being a rookie QB while the world is watching and waiting for him to fall apart. I remember what you told me before you broke up with him and how you felt. I'm not saying to ignore that. I'm saying this is Bentley, at least reach out so he knows he didn't fuck this up as badly as he thinks he has," she pleads.

"Can we talk about something else?"

"Sure, I want you to come travel with me."

***

An hour later and my head is still buzzing from Erica's words. *I want you to come travel with me.* I came back home to be close to my mom.

I don't know that I want to go running off when she needs me. However, I still haven't figured things out. Traveling the world has a nice ring to it.

My father left me a nice trust fund that would allow me to go without having to worry about my finances. I had been looking at a few online courses that would allow me to finish my degree.

Maybe some time out of the country will allow me to heal instead of sitting in a house full of haunting memories.

"Hey, I didn't know you two were back in town. How's it going?" Gilbert Manning comes over to our table and breaks into my thoughts.

Erica and I had fallen silent for the millionth time since we've been sitting here eating and having milkshakes. I think we've both been getting lost in our thoughts and memories. There are so many here.

"Hey, Gilbert," we say in unison.

"I was just about to get a bite to eat. You ladies mind if I join you?"

"Have a seat. You're the first person who hasn't looked at us with pity in their eyes. Of course you're welcome," Erica says.

She's right. Everyone has been gawking at us like two helpless puppies. I'm not sure how much more of it I can take.

"In that case, you guys want to get out of here? We can go sit at the old hangout," Gilbert offers.

"That doesn't sound like a bad idea," I say.

"Cool, give me a minute to order and get my food."

"Cool." I shrug. Gilbert turns and heads over to get his food while we finish up ours. Erica pulls out her phone and frowns.

"What's up?" I ask.

She looks at me and schools her features. "Nothing. Boys are stupid is all. Maybe they're smarter in Italy or France."

"Doubt it," I chuckle.

"What do you know? You were giving your cookie to my idiot brother."

"Ha. That idiot knows his way around a bag of cookies."

"Ew, TMI. I don't want to hear that crap. Bad enough I once walked in on him naked.

"Now I get so disappointed when a guy has a little dick. Like, what the fuck? Why am I related to the biggest dick I've ever seen? Just saying that shit out loud makes me sick." She pouts.

I'm now laughing so hard I have tears. Bentley is kind of huge. I squeeze my thighs just thinking about it. Boy, do I miss sex.

"You're nasty. You're thinking about him, aren't you?" Erica hisses as she narrows her eyes at me.

I hadn't realized that I started to bite my lip as images of Bentley going down on me floated through my head. I groan and shake my thoughts off. That man turned me into a sex addict and now I don't have a dealer anymore.

"Call him, Zah."

"Nope. We're not ready."

She sighs. "Then at least come with me."

"That I'm thinking about. Let me talk to Mom. If she's cool with it, I'll go."

Bentley

I kneel before the toilet, emptying my stomach. I'm not purging, this isn't a hangover, and I don't have a stomach bug. What I am is drowning.

Every time I step up to a podium, they ask me the same thing. How do I feel to be here after losing my father a month before the draft? I purposely had them call Kerry, a close friend of the family.

If they knew he was going to be my father-in-law someday, they would be after Zah relentlessly. I want them to leave her alone. They've asked about the young lady who was at the draft with me.

I brushed it off and said she's my sister's best friend and a longtime friend of the family. They weren't going to leave that one alone until I hired a team. I now have a publicist, a personal assistant, and security.

The only reason they backed off my love life is that Zah is no longer in my life. I've had Jerome make sure the focus remains on anything but Zah. In turn, the media has homed in on my dad and his death.

They're waiting for me to break. This is way more pressure than I thought it would be. I need Zah so much.

"Hey, bro, you all right in there?" Garret calls through the door.

He's been here for the last week, checking in on me. I think I need him here. I almost fucked up and did something stupid.

"Yeah, I'll be all right," I choke out.

"I'll be right here if you need me."

It sounds like he slides down the wall to sit outside the door. I begin to sob. His presence only reminds me that I'm not being strong for everyone who needs me.

He's my little brother. I should be taking care of him, not the other way around. Just like I should have taken care of Zah before I lost her.

I'm failing and not just at keeping my girl. I don't know if I can handle this spotlight while I'm trying to breathe enough to pull it together. I lie on my side on the cold floor and curl into a ball.

"I want to go home, man," I sob. "I need to go home, but I can't give up. Dad wouldn't want me to give up."

"I know, Bent. I know. That's why I'm here. We all see you hurting. The world doesn't know you like we do.

"They're not giving you the space you need to get right, but you have us. We're going to cover you as much as we can, bro."

"I want Zariah back. I want her here with me. I need to fix this."

"Okay, so we fix you first. That's not going to work until you deal and can see her needs too. I heard what happened.

"She's not wrong. I know you and I'm sure I can tell you how you fucked things up. I promise, you pull it together, I'll help you get her back," he replies.

"He was my best friend, my dad. This shit fucking hurts. I'm trying to see past that, man. I'm trying real hard, but all I can see right now is how I'm fucking everything up. I just don't know how to stop."

"You breathe, big bro. You breathe. You're not alone. You can do this, breathe."

I cling to his words. He isn't wrong. I'm not going to keep shitting on Zah's feelings just for my own comfort.

I'm bleeding out, and when she's around, I seem to keep bleeding all over her. I need her, but I love her more than myself. I want to be whole for her so I can be there when she needs me. This reminds me of what my father once said.

There will be a time when you'll know she has to come first. That one time when you're asking too much of her love and you have to be the one to make a sacrifice ... You'll know what needs to be done when that day comes.

This is it. It's that moment. It's time for me to make a sacrifice.

So I breathe just like Garret is telling me to. I breathe and promise myself that I'm not going to go after Zah until I'm ready to be the man she deserves.

CHAPTER TWENTY-SEVEN

Reunion

Zahirah

Eight years and four months later …

"You look hot as fuck. My brother is going to lose his shit."

"Are you sure this isn't doing too much? I mean, I don't want to send any mixed signals."

I wasn't going to come out for this game at all. However, Bentley called and asked me to come. I was surprised to hear from him. We haven't spoken in almost eight and a half years.

I'll admit, hearing his voice rumble through the line did something to me. I've missed him so much. It has taken everything in me to keep my distance.

However, mid-season of his second season, he started to look more like himself. Healthier mentally and physically. I hadn't wanted to get in the way of that progress, so I was extremely happy when he reached out first.

Now here we are in Vegas for one of his away games. I'm so nervous and don't know what to expect. Because he has a bye week next weekend, he doesn't plan to return with the team after.

We're spending the weekend here. Bentley, his older siblings, his best friend, Baker, and me. I nervously fidget with the hem of my dress, then reach for the teddy bear charm on my necklace and bring it to my lips.

"No, you're not doing too much. I think it's just enough to remind him what he's missing and keep him on his toes."

"But I'm not trying to do any of that."

"Why not? The man is still crazy about you and you're both miserable without each other."

"Whatever, fine. We're going to be late."

I grab my little purse and fur and head out with my best friend to meet the rest of her siblings and Baker in the lobby so we can head to the stadium. Yes, a fur. It was waiting for me when we arrived at our suite.

A late birthday gift from Bentley. I've been trying not to read too much into that. The card was sweet.

Something to keep you warm. Thank you for coming.
Happy belated birthday.

Love,
Bent

I smile as I think about finding the gift waiting for me. Erica packed this minidress and heels for me. I had jeans and a jersey prepared to wear tonight.

Now looking around at everyone else, I see I would have been out of place. All the Coswells have dressed up for this. Eddy and Tara are the only ones not here as they're still not old enough.

When we get to our box at the arena, I get the dress code. There's a little party happening. Garret and Baker remain close to my side the entire game. There's this one guy who's been trying to get a little too close.

I blame Erica and this tight little dress with the fuck-me patent leather heels. The right side of the dress, under my arm and across my stomach, is bare. I had to be out of my mind to agree to wear this.

The champagne has been flowing, loosening my nerves a bit. I can't help but wonder what Bentley is going to say when he sees me. We have so much we should say to one another.

I'm pulled from my thoughts as Bentley throws a game-winning touchdown, and the people in the box go wild. I'm so happy for him I can't stop smiling.

The family passes hugs around and the girls and I have some more champagne. I really should stop drinking. I've been too nervous all day to eat.

I'm already a bit tipsy. I have so many things I want to say to Bentley. It's been almost nine years. I would like to think we're both in different places in our lives.

We've been like ships passing in the night. While I've been traveling the world with Erica, Bentley has had a stellar career playing professional football.

They call him the touchdown king. If there's a way for one to be made, Bentley is going to do it. His arms, his legs, whatever it takes. I'm so proud of him.

"Mr. Coswell wanted Miss Nickels to come with me," Sarah, Bentley's assistant, says.

"I've got her," Garret says quickly. "I know where he wants her to go."

I look to Erica, and she has a shit-eating grin on her face. I narrow my eyes, wondering what they're up to. We were all supposed to go out to dinner and dancing after the game.

"Yes, but I—"

"I've got it, Sarah. Don't worry about it. See you tomorrow," Garret says firmly.

Sarah gives a tight smile then looks me over before turning to leave. I shrug her look off and follow Garret. He leads me back to the car from earlier. It takes forever, but I'm taken back to the hotel we're staying in.

However, he doesn't take me back to my room. He takes me to a presidential suite, opens the door, then tells me to head in and make myself comfortable. I look up at him in confusion, but after a moment, I step inside.

The door clicks shut behind me, and I'm left alone. At least I think I'm alone. I take off my coat and drape it on the back of an accent chair.

"Sarah, what's the ETA on Erica and Zah making it to the restaurant? Are they there yet? Shit, I'm going to be late. Why didn't you bring Zahirah to the waiting area I told you to?" Bentley's voice booms through the room, sending a chill down my spine.

I begin to walk toward his voice. When I get to the room he's in, I find him in a pair of slacks with no shirt on. His ass looks great. He turns at the sound of my heels and freezes.

"Hey," I say and wave.

He furrows his brows one second and rushes across the room in the next. Before I know what's happening, he has my face between his hands as he devours my mouth. I whimper and lock my arms around his neck.

"You look fucking amazing. I've missed you so much, baby. I can't believe you're here," he groans into my mouth.

"Bent, wait, I … oh my God," I cry out as he lifts me onto his waist and pulls the front of my dress down to expose my breasts, then pulls my nipple into his mouth.

All my thoughts are scrambled. He continues to suck on my breast as he reaches to tug my dress up over my ass to gain access to my seam. A growl leaves his lips as he finds me wet for him.

In the next motion, he shoves his fingers into me as he moves across the room. I'm confused as he doesn't move to the bed but over to an accent chair. However, I'm too busy coming all over his hand to think clearly about what's happening.

He places me on my feet and bends me over the chair. In the next motion, he's on his knees eating my pussy from behind. I can only grab the arms of the chair and hold on.

"God, I've missed this pussy so much. You taste so amazing. Come for me, baby.

"Show me this body still knows me. I want you to come all over my face. Can you do that for me?"

He slaps my ass, causing me to cry out. This is not my Bentley, but I'm not about to complain or stop to think too hard about that. I crave him something awful.

"Yes, Bentley, yes," I scream as my legs shake, and I come.

"That's my girl. I want you so bad, Zah. Do you want me to fuck you? Are you ready to have me inside you?"

"Yes, please."

He chuckles darkly and stands to his feet. The sound of his belt clinking fills the room. The next thing I know, I'm so full my eyes cross.

Bentley has a tight hold of my waist as he fucks me hard and deep. I bite my lip as my eyes roll back. He begins to slap my ass, alternating from one cheek to the other while he continues to thrust.

"So fucking good. So wet and tight. Oh my God, I want you so much.

"You feel how hard you make me? I hate being without you. I love you so much, baby," he hisses through his teeth.

"I love you too. Oh my God, I'm coming again. I've missed you *soooo* much." I drag out the word so.

If the hardness of his dick were any indication as to how much he's missed me, I'd say it's a hell of a lot. Damn, I don't think he's ever fucked me like this before.

He lifts my leg over his arm and shifts his angle. I begin to scream my head off. He's hitting my spot like it's a bull's-eye. I think I might black out if he continues like this.

"We're not going to make the dinner or the party. I can't stop fucking you. I want to take you all night.

"You think you can handle that, baby? Me fucking this tight little pussy all night? Oh my God, I'm going to come," he growls the last part.

I'm already coming so hard I actually do pass out. All I know is that something warm fills me and then my legs give out. What the fuck just happened?

Bentley

When I turned to find Zah standing there, I thought I was dreaming. She looked like a goddess. I hadn't planned to have sex with her.

However, one look at her in that sexy-ass dress and those heels and I had to have her. I was already coming off a high from winning and throwing the game-winning touchdown. Having her in my arms felt so right.

My plan had been to get her here so we could talk. I want her back. I want us back. Now I can't keep my dick out of her.

"Yes, baby, keep coming for me," I growl as I rock in and out of her as she matches me thrust for thrust.

"Bentley, I can't."

"Yes, you can, baby," I croon before I dip my head and take her nipple into my mouth.

I almost lost my shit when I found her pantyless and braless. I mean, I sort of wondered how she could have on either with that dress, but damn, I was turned on when I pulled her dress down and exposed her full breasts. Finding her uncovered wet seam is what pushed me over the brink of sanity.

Now I'm balls deep inside her once again and I still don't think my sanity has returned. I tighten my hands on hers as I look her in the eyes. I want her to come for me before I come inside her.

My heart swells at the thought of having her in my bed and back in my life. I can't wait for her to see the house I've bought and the life I've been setting up for us. I've been working toward our dream for the last eight years.

"Yeah, that's my good girl. Let me feel you. Come all over me."

As I pump my seed deep inside her, Zah blinks up at me. Her eyes clear, as if in this moment she's sobering up. I could taste the alcohol on her breath from the first kiss.

I'll admit, I had a few drinks after the game before heading over to shower and get ready. I'd been nervous about how things would go with Zah and might have overdone it.

I kiss her hard as I shudder with my orgasm and growl. I think my climax helps to clear my head as well. I break the kiss and look down into Zah's eyes, searching. Her eyes grow wide, and she begins to wiggle away from me.

"What's wrong? Where are you going?"

"You promised we would decide together. Fuck, what was I thinking? How could I do something so stupid?"

"Zah, I got caught up. I wasn't thinking. I've never had unprotected sex with anyone else."

"I'm not worried about an STD, Bentley. Do you understand what this could mean?"

"Come on. I'm not an idiot. Of course, I know. Why are you making this a big deal?

"If you're pregnant, we'll get married. I'll take care of you both."

"Just like that? We haven't talked through any of our problems."

"You weren't saying that a few minutes ago," I mutter.

I regret the words the moment they're out of my mouth. Zah's mouth falls open, then rage fills her eyes. I groan and pull a hand down my face.

"Fuck you, Bentley. You're an asshole. This was such a big mistake."

"Baby, wait. I didn't mean that. All right, all right, that was a dick thing to say. I'm an asshole for sure.

"Don't leave. You're right, we do need to talk. I'm sorry," I plead.

"Save it. This is my fault; I had all that alcohol on an empty stomach. I walked in here and saw you and lost my damn mind.

"I need to stay away from you. I've just started to get my life together and now here I am doing dumb shit."

"I didn't know making love to someone who loves you counts as dumb shit. Good to know."

"It is when you allow said person to nut up in you all night. Oh my gosh, how many times was that? This is Vegas, I'm sure I can find a Plan B."

"You would do that?" I ask, sounding hurt to my own ears.

"To keep us from hurting an innocent kid with our bullshit, yes."

"Our bullshit?" I explode.

I know I need to walk away and take a beat, but I keep going. It's like I unravel all the work I've done on myself. Watching her try to walk away from me again and hearing her say she doesn't want our baby cuts me to my core.

I think what sets me off is the fact that I realized rounds ago that we were having unprotected sex. For a fleeting moment, my drunken mind had thought that maybe a baby would make her stay.

"Whatever, Zahirah. I'm used to you abandoning me. Go ahead and walk out.

"I can't make you love me. I can't make you stay. All I seem to be able to do is make you come."

"If that's all I am to you, then you should go. It's best you get rid of the baby now, that way they don't have to learn what it's like to love you and lose you over and over again. It's not like I'll do right by either of you.

"Get the fuck out. You only remind me of everything I've lost. I—"

"Bent, you better stop now if you ever want to say another word to me again. Stop now because if you cross that line, I'm done.

"I don't have that kind of forgiveness. Right now, I don't know if I'll ever forgive you for what's already been said, but if you keep talking, there's no friendship, no relationship, nothing," she chokes out with tears in her eyes.

I turn without a word and storm into the bathroom for a shower. I try my best to wash away the regret and the stupid shit I've said.

My mind races with so many things at once. Why can't I ever get it right when it comes to her? I love her more than anything, but I keep fucking this up.

Dad, how do I make this right? I'm so lost without you.

CHAPTER TWENTY-EIGHT

New Beginnings

Zahirah

"Ugh, a part of me is super happy my brother fucked up again and got you on that plane with me. Then there's the part of me that hates seeing you like this and who's tired of looking at his sorry, sad face on FaceTime," Erica whines as she comes and pushes my legs out of the way so she can sit on the window seat beside me.

I've been sitting here contemplating my life. For a month and a half, Bentley continued to send sorries and apologetic gifts. Then he started to make trips home, trying to see me. Those visits made the decision for me.

I stopped putting Erica off and took her up on her offer to come to Spain with her. I had wanted to take a break from traveling and work on some things. I sort of feel bad; she believes I'm avoiding her brother.

In truth, I don't know how to tell my mother I'm having a baby by my neighbor, whom I refuse to speak to. I spend three months of every year with my mother. That was her only ask when I was nineteen.

I love those three months a year. Eventually, I built my bond with the Coswell family back up. Now, everything back home is up in the air for me.

"You haven't told him I'm here with you, have you?"

"No, I always keep my promises."

With her words, the seed of guilt only digs deeper. I'll have to come clean soon. She's already been concerned about me not feeling well all the time.

"He did mention the PI again."

I groan. "Oh no, why?"

"Don't worry. He said he's going to call him off. Something about knowing he messed up and needing to come to grips with it," she says with a somber look on her face.

"Good for him," I say and fold my arms over my breasts.

I whimper as I put a little too much emphasis into the gesture and rub my sore breasts the wrong way. Erica narrows her eyes at me. I look away and try to ignore her gaze.

She gasps. "Oh my God, now it all makes sense. You're preggers.

"Bentley knocked you up that night. Way to go, bro. I'm going to be an auntie. Yay," she squeals excitedly.

"No, no, no. No way to go. I couldn't force myself to take that stupid Plan B. I had hoped that maybe ... ugh, all we do is fight.

"It's not like when we started. I have never loved and hated someone so much in my life. How am I supposed to raise a baby with someone who makes me so angry?"

"Well, you two should have thought about that before making a baby," she says pointedly.

"Don't you think I know that? My mother is going to kill me."

"I doubt that. You're twenty-seven. She'll get over it. Mom is going to love this."

"Erica, no. You can't tell anyone who the father is. Not until I figure out how to tell him.

"We said some really fucked-up shit to each other. Bentley said most of it. I don't know if we can come back from any of it. I swear he was on the verge of telling me he hates me."

I pause and shake my head. "Until we learn to communicate and not through our grief, we can't move forward. He makes me feel like you guys losing your dad was my fault or something.

"Yeah, the passes they used that weekend were my Christmas gift, but they used to go all the time. I feel bad enough as it is. Garret once told me Bentley felt guilty because he wasn't able to deal with his grief and support me through mine. What if the real reason is because he blames me?" I sob.

"Oh, honey. I don't know what's going on in my brother's head, but I'm just about certain he's not blaming you or those passes. No one is. The same thing could have happened on a store run for the moms."

"But it didn't, and if he does blame me, what does that say for this baby and its future? Will he continue to resent me and the baby every time he looks at us?"

"Oh, Zah, this is so much deeper than we all thought. We thought we were helping that night in Vegas. Garret and I had no idea you felt like this.

"Bentley doesn't know this is how you feel either. I wish you two would just have a conversation. I get it.

"I've seen how he is with you and how those dumb fights start. That's what's so frustrating. I know he doesn't mean it.

"He just gets all tied up when it comes to you. Almost like he's watching himself fuck up, but he can't stop before he does."

"That's toxic, Erica. This child doesn't deserve that."

"So what are you going to do?"

I shrug. "I'm going to hide out here and work on my vlog and company for as long as I can. When I go back, I'll get a new place for me and the baby.

"To be honest, I don't think I'm going to date for a while. As mad as I am at Bentley, there's still a part of me that's in love with him. I don't think that's fair to anyone else. That's why I've never dated since we broke up."

"You're not going to tell him?"

"I don't think he cares. He told me to go through with the Plan B."

"Are you fucking kidding me? He didn't. Why the fuck would he say that?"

"I told you, we said a lot of things."

"Okay, okay. I'll keep your secret under one condition. I get to be in the baby's life and we're doing this together," she says and places a hand over my stomach.

I lean my head on her shoulder. "I was hoping you would say that."

She kisses the top of my head. We fall silent for a beat. I wish I could call Bentley and have a conversation like we used to before it all fell to shit.

Things were once so easy. Our lives were all planned out. Now everything seems broken and irreparable.

"Zah?"

"Yeah?"

"He's going to be pissed. When he finds out, you guys are going to have another blowup. Are you sure this is how you want to play it?"

"I know, but I don't know what to do. Do you remember how we used to be so attuned and he would come running when I needed him, not knowing that I did?"

"Yeah, that has always been so crazy to me," she says.

"I'm hoping he'll know, and he'll come home when we need him. If he does, I'll tell him. If he doesn't, this is it. We aren't meant to be together. It's the end of our story."

Bentley

"Did you hear me, Mr. Coswell?"

"Sorry, no. I didn't hear any of that. I have a lot on my mind," I say as I look at Sarah and knit my brows.

"Should I start from the top?"

I frown and shake my head. It will only be a waste of time. I haven't heard a word she's said in the last thirty minutes.

I keep playing that night with Zah over in my head. I said some really fucked-up shit. She had every right to be angry with me.

I did make her that promise. I've been loaded down with guilt since. I keep thinking about her taking that pill and flushing away our future.

I want to be a father. I want to be Zahirah's husband. Eight years and she's still the fire that burns my soul.

I've been thinking about what my dad would say. I fucked up. However, it's not that I've fucked up, it's what I've learned from it all.

Zahirah and I were so young when all that tragedy struck. I can't blame her for walking away. I wasn't handling my shit well.

I should have tucked some of that away like she was doing for me. That's where I failed. I couldn't find the words to tell her I was hurting too much to be the man she needed, and that was scaring the shit out of me.

My compass was gone, and I was dragging us both down, looking for a new direction. In Vegas, I fucked up because I tried to move forward without showing her I'm not the same man.

I've grown. The alcohol didn't allow me to prove that. However, I know I'm a different man than the broken one she walked out on in college.

"I'm going to go, but there is something I thought I should tell you. It's about the PI."

This gets my full attention. I had told her to terminate his services. If Zahirah doesn't want to be found, I'm going to respect that.

"What about him?"

"He wanted you to know there's another PI looking into her. He said he did track down who the guy is and who he's working for, if you want to know.

"Boss, none of this is any of my business, but my gut isn't sitting right with this. Please contact him and get all the information. I personally don't know how I feel about Miss Nickels because I've come to see you like a brother.

"I can be a little overprotective of you at times, but you're clearly in love with her. From the sound of Fred's voice, you're going to want whatever information he has. Call him." With that, she stands and leaves.

Sarah has been one of the best things to happen to me since my rookie year. She keeps me and my life going. I trust her.

That's why I pull my phone and dial Fred right away. My mind is racing. Who else could be looking into Zah and why?

"Fred here, talk to me," my PI answers the phone.

"Hey, this is Coswell."

"Hey, buddy. I'm glad you called. You know us PIs have a certain way we move. If you've been in the business long enough or if you're any good, you can spot another investigator without a problem.

"I noticed the guy my first week in. Naturally, I was curious about him. I also wanted to keep an eye on him to see if he could lead me to Miss Nickels and cut out some of the work.

"His name is Hudson Willis. He works for the Manning family. You and Miss Nickels went to school with Gilbert Manning, am I right?"

"Yeah, we did. He was a buddy of mine once."

Fred gives a long whistle. "Glad you moved on to better friends. Listen, from what I gather, Manning is trying to find Miss Nickels himself. I had been working on finding out why, but then your assistant called to cancel the job.

"I can back off if you like. However, after digging into Manning, I see he's a piece of work. I wouldn't want him sniffing around anyone I care about."

I bite my fist. I should let this go. Zahirah is a grown woman. I have no right to interfere in her life.

"Fuck that. Keep an eye on them. If you find her, it's not my business where she is. The new priority is her safety. If that's not your thing, I'll hire someone else."

"Anything can be my thing for the right price. I'll even give you a discount because my Spidey senses have been going off with this one."

I snort. "Name your price," I say and hang up.

It only takes a few minutes for him to text me his number. I make the wire transfer and scrub a hand up and down my face. I've been away from home for too long.

"Garret," I call through the house, knowing he's somewhere around.

He comes into my office, stuffing his face with a sandwich. I shake my head. Dad would be happy Garret ended up with me instead of going into the military. Turns out my brother makes one hell of an agent.

That was money well spent. My mom is happy, my business is always looked after, and I have a constant voice of reason. I know I've loved having him by my side.

"What's up?" he asks through a mouth full of food.

"I think it's time we start looking into going home. I'll be a free agent going into season after next. See if you can quietly put out some feelers, nothing official, just bullshit talk with your buddies for now."

"This have anything to do with Zah? I thought you were walking away," he says and lifts a brow.

"I was." I take a pause and sigh. "I just have this feeling. I'm not going to do anything to close that door yet. If we can get me home, I want to at least consider it."

"A lot can happen in two years."

"Exactly," I say as I think about all that needs to be done to go back home.

Two years is plenty of time for Zah to have the space to forgive me. Heck, I could be back home within a year and a half, to be honest.

Maybe in two years, we can sit down and have a real conversation. For now, I'm going to keep my eye on Gilbert. I never did trust him around Zah.

CHAPTER TWENTY-NINE

A Coincidence

Zahirah

Two months later ...

"Oh my God, you're not going to believe who I ran into in town," Erica gushes as she rushes into our apartment.

I snap my eyes open as I realize that once again I was nodding off. At four months pregnant, I tend to do that a lot. I've been editing this travel vlog for the new channel for hours now because I can't seem to keep my eyes open.

I started the new channel and stopped showing my face and using my voice after we left Arizona. I figured if I want to stay hidden and keep my pregnancy to myself, I need to start fresh.

"Oh, I'm sorry. You and baby Coswell were sleeping." Erica pouts.

"Will you stop calling him that?" I hiss.

"It's not like we know for sure it's a boy, and you haven't given him or her a name, so what else should I call the little love bug?"

"I know it's a boy. I don't need anyone to tell me that. I wanted his name to be a surprise, but you're getting on my nerves," I snap.

"Okay, Mommy is cranky today. Got it. Wait, you named the baby?"

"Sort of."

"Sort of? What does that mean? Does my nephew have a name or not?"

"For now, you can call him AC," I mutter.

She looks at me and begins to tear up. I groan, knowing she's figured his name out already. I cover my belly and give her a small smile.

"Aaron Christopher," she chokes out.

"Yeah, it feels right, you know?"

She nods her head and begins to wipe at her tears. "I should have known when you asked for Dad's middle name. I love it. My dad's middle name and your dad's middle name. It's perfect."

"I couldn't remember what the *A* stood for at first. I didn't want to ask, but it was going to drive me crazy. Anyway, who did you run into?"

"Oh, um, right," she sniffles. "I was in town to get you those peaches and I ran right into Gilbert Manning. Isn't this such a small world?"

"Oh wow, yes. It is. That's so crazy."

"He said he's here on vacation with some family. His grandma or something. They have a boat docked at the port.

"He invited us to dinner. I kind of think the invitation was meant for you more than me, but I want to see this yacht."

"Why would you say that?"

"Come on, Zah. I know you've only ever had eyes for Bentley. Don't ask me why or how I didn't see it sooner, but Gilbert has always had a crush on you."

"We're just friends. I really don't see him like that. He's not bad looking, but he's not my type."

"Yeah, I know what you mean. Decent guy, but I think his money does a lot of talking for him. Rumor is, he's not packing either."

"What is it with you? Why are you so obsessed with penis size?" I burst out laughing.

She scoffs. "I've had way more experience than you, but not with the luxury you've had. Trust me, size matters and some of us aren't receiving the gift you are … were."

"Why do I bother?" I giggle. "I don't really care what Gilbert is packing. I'll never see it. That just sounds weird to even think about."

"I'm not telling you to jump his bones, but it might be nice to get out for more than footage. Let's go and have some fun."

"Do I get a nap before we leave?"

"Yes, you and AC can have a nap." She runs over and places her hand on my bump. "Auntie E loves you, Aaron. I can't wait to meet you."

She then kisses my cheek. "I love you too. I'll wake you up to get ready."

Bentley

"Hello," I say into the phone as I sit at my locker.

"Great fucking game, man. You're amazing, brother."

"What's up, Fred? You don't call me to congratulate me on games. How is she? Is she in trouble?"

He pauses for a moment. "I know where she is. I know you said you didn't want to know, but I thought I'd call anyway."

"Thanks, man. Just keep her safe. Whatever it costs, I'll pay. Call me if she needs me."

"Coswell, I—"

"I don't want to know. Later, Fred."

I hang up and close my eyes. I do want to know. I want to know so fucking bad.

Every time I talk to Erica, I hope that miraculously Zah will appear behind her. Erica swears she's traveling alone this time. Zah doesn't post those cute little video vlogs to her channel anymore.

I miss seeing her face. I'll admit that I watch the old videos every night before bed just to hear her voice. Maybe it's good she doesn't post anymore for me to know where she is.

"Fuck, I could go to her. The season is almost over," I murmur to myself.

Let it go, Bent. You don't have the time.

CHAPTER THIRTY

Old Friends

Zahirah

"Thanks for coming to hang out with me," Gilbert says with a smile.

"No problem. Dinner on the yacht was fun. Although I didn't know you would be here this long."

"My grandmother wanted to stay a bit longer. Her yacht, her decision." He shrugs.

"That's cool. How are things going with the family business? You running things yet?"

"Not yet." He chuckles. "I sort of hit a snag. My family would prefer me to be married before I'm handed everything."

"Oh, that must suck. What are you, twenty-nine? That has to be a lot of pressure."

He shrugs again. "Notice I said would prefer. The real pressure comes from my grandmother. No one is good enough for her. My fiancée has to have her approval."

"And she doesn't like your girlfriends?"

"None that she has met. She's a romantic. She has this great love story in her head for me.

"I'll see it in your eyes when she's the one, Gilly," he mocks.

I snicker and take a sip of my water. This is such a lovely house he's renting for the week. He said his grandmother needed some time on land.

"Are you sure I can't get you something stronger than water?"

"Oh, um, no. That's fine. Water is perfect," I say with a smile.

The last thing I need is for him to run back to Bentley to tell him I'm pregnant. I get a little nervous and begin to fidget. I'm saved as an older woman enters the room.

"Grandmother, I would like you to meet Zahirah," Gilbert says as the woman takes a seat.

She looks me over with a warm smile. I return the smile as I take her in. She has all the markings of a woman of wealth.

The Chanel suit, the pearls, the diamonds. Her perfectly coiffed hair. There's a regal air about her.

"Aren't you lovely. Very pretty indeed. Do you live here?"

"I'm visiting for a bit. To be honest, I'm getting a bit homesick," I reply.

"Where is home, dear?"

"Arizona, Grand. We went to school together. She's from our hometown."

"Oh, this is the young lady you used to talk about. Uh, Zahirah Nickels, the track star, yes?" she says excitedly.

I look to Gilbert and knit my brows. His cheeks blush and his blue eyes widen. I watch as his mouth flaps open and closed a few times.

"Grand, I … uh … yeah. That Zahirah. I didn't know you remembered any of that."

"How could I not? She was all you talked about in high school. I've been waiting for years to meet her.

"Have you eaten, dear? Would you like some lunch?"

"I don't want to be a bother. I should probably be going soon."

"Nonsense. It's not every day I finally get to meet Gilbert's girlfriend. I'll go to the kitchen and have them prepare something for us," she says happily.

"Oh, ma'am, I'm not—"

Gilbert reaches for my hand and squeezes it. I look to him, and he shakes his head at me. I search his face and take in his tight expression.

I fall silent and allow his grandmother to leave the room. Once she's gone, he stands and gently tugs my hand for me to follow him. I do so with furrowed brows.

"Oh my God, I've never seen her so happy to meet a girl in my life before. I don't want to break her heart. We leave in a few days.

"Could you do me a favor and just go with it? She has more days behind her than in front of her. Who knows if she'll make it back home? Please, Zah.

"I'll give you anything you want. Name it. Just pretend to be my girlfriend for her sake," he pleads.

I look up into his eyes, searching. He's serious. I take a step back. This is all a bit too much. My stomach decides this is the moment it's going to act up.

Covering my mouth, I race back inside for the powder room I used when I first arrived. Thank God I make it and am able to empty my stomach in private. Once I'm done, I wish I could hide out in here forever.

"Zah, are you all right in there?"

"I'll be out in a second," I call.

Splashing water on my face, I then take a deep, calming breath. I can do this. I'm going to go out there and tell Gilbert and his sweet little grandmother I need to go home.

I nod at my reflection and turn to do just that. However, that's not what happens at all. I step out of the bathroom, and they are both standing there, looking concerned.

Suddenly, Mrs. Manning's eyes light up. She pulls me into a surprisingly strong hug. I return the embrace as I look up at

Gilbert with wide eyes. He looks back at me pleadingly as he mouths, *please*.

"Oh, this is wonderful news. You're expecting, aren't you? Gilbert has a little one of his own on the way. When are you due, dear?"

"Uh, um. July, ma'am. The baby is due in July," I reply, too shocked to say anything else.

"None of this ma'am business. You will call me Grandmother Christen or Grandma Christen. You are family now."

Gilbert gets this grin on his face. "We were waiting to say anything about the baby. Zah plans to finish up her work here and we'll be able to finalize our plans stateside when she returns home."

"Oh, we have so much planning to do. An engagement party, a baby shower, I think a year is a long enough time to plan a proper wedding. Depending on whether we can get a suitable venue. No worries, dear. We'll take care of everything," she chortles.

Gilbert wraps an arm around me and tugs me into his side. Then he places a kiss on my forehead. I try my best not to cringe.

"Thank you," he whispers in my ear. "I take it the father and your mother aren't aware of any of this? There isn't anyone who could expose us?"

I shake my head. Then I pause. "Erica," I breathe.

He nods slightly. "Will she talk? Do you think she will take a million for her silence?" he murmurs.

"She won't say anything."

"Is it Coswell?"

I remain silent. Who the father is is my business. He doesn't need to know.

"Your silence is answer enough. I will be here for whatever you need. Ask and it's yours. Thank you for doing this. You're a great friend."

I relax just a little. I'm doing this for a friend. As we sit down and his grandmother begins to speak excitedly, I can't bring myself to tear this hope away from her. I also feel guilty as hell for lying.

What am I doing?

CHAPTER THIRTY-ONE

Heads-up

Bentley

A month later ...

I'm jogging to blow off some steam. My team has been playing like shit in OTAs. The rookies are trash, and the vets act like they don't care.

I'm ready to go. As the QB, it's my job to motivate my team, but I don't want to be here. My heart is already gone.

That's a first for me. However, I just have this feeling, like this isn't where I need to be. One more season.

I've been in talks to go home. They want me bad enough. I think this deal is in the bag.

The problem is, I don't know how Zah is going to feel. I don't even know where in the world she is.

My phone rings, pulling me out of my thoughts. I look to see it's Fred and pick up right away. My heart is racing.

I told him not to call unless Zah needs me. The thought of something happening to her leaves a sour taste in my mouth. I'm already planning how to get to her.

"Is she in danger?"

"I don't know his endgame, but Manning is up to something."

"What do you mean?" I bite out.

"I know you don't want to know where she is, fine, but he does, and he's conveniently placed his ass right into her life. They've been hanging out.

"Nothing wrong with that, but he's a different guy when she's not around. He's a church boy tending to his dear old grandma during the day and a wild animal at night.

"I'm still digging into what his intentions are here. He shouldn't have been here as long as he has."

"What's making you call me now?"

"I got a hit for a plane ticket booked in her name. It seems she's going home. They're engaged."

I stumble to a stop. My ears are ringing. He couldn't have just said what I think he did.

"What? Come again. What did you say?" I grind out.

I feel sick to my stomach. I have to drop to my ass to catch my bearings. Did I hurt my girl that badly? What the fuck is she thinking?

"They're engaged. I couldn't believe it myself."

"That's bullshit. She would never."

"I'm only telling you what I know. No disrespect. She's a damn pretty woman.

"He's not the best-looking guy. Why the hell would he be engaged to her and out fucking everything that breathes every chance he gets?

"My gut is telling me some bullshit is going down. I'm going to keep on it. Something is bound to come up."

"If he's who she wants, that's her business," I say brokenly. "Send me your final invoice. We're done."

I hang up and sit staring into space. I have no answers for what to do next. At this point, I don't think I want to go back to Arizona ever. She gave up on me.

I don't know what hurts more, that it's over or that she's choosing that asshole to move on with.

"Damnit, Zah. We weren't meant to end this way. I still love you."

Zahirah

"How long are you supposed to pretend to be engaged to him?" Erica asks as I pack my bags.

"I don't know," I groan.

I already want it to be over. I'm getting more frustrated with each day. The sooner this is over, the better.

"I don't like this. Something feels off about it."

"I know. Once I'm home, I'll be able to think things through."

I've been hiding out long enough. It's time I head home and start to build a life for me and my baby. Oh, and there's the engagement party my fake grandmother-in-law has planned for me. I'm exhausted from the pretending.

Grandma Christen decided to extend their stay once again to be here with me and the baby. All of this has become so disruptive to my life. I've been to tea every day with Gilbert's grandmother.

If I don't show, he blows my text messages up. It's annoying, to be honest. I had three more weeks here, but Erica and I decided to just cut this one short and head home.

"Hey, remember when our dads built that fort in the backyard for us?" Erica says out of the blue.

"Yeah, I remember. They climbed in there with you, me, Bent, and Garret. That was so much fun."

"Stupid sandstorm. They had to tear it down the next year."

"Yeah, but Bent and Garret had outgrown it anyway, remember?"

"I guess. What I remember most is how much time Dad spent with us in there. I think Bentley is going to be that type of dad.

"Hearing the doctor today say that it's a boy made me think of how he's going to feel to find out he has a son. Dad would be so proud."

I swipe my forearm across my cheeks. "I'm going to tell him. I almost called him after the appointment."

I don't tell her that I opened my phone to, but got sidetracked and opened a post about Bentley and his new rumored girlfriend. I ended up sobbing instead. I'll tell him.

For now, I need to go home. Everything will get better when we go home. That's what I need to hold on to for now.

CHAPTER THIRTY-TWO

The Whole Truth

Zahirah

A year and three months later … Back to the present

I release a heavy breath and lift my gaze back to my mother's. I'm surprised when I don't see disappointment in her eyes but understanding. I've been holding on to all this confusion, hurt, and guilt for so long; it feels good to say it all out loud.

"And you know the rest. Gilbert has pushed his way into every part of my life like he's my real fiancé. Even Aaron's birth.

"I hadn't planned for him to be there. I've been trying to find a way out, but here we are, the day before my wedding," I grumble.

"Not if I have anything to say about it. I knew from the time that little boy was born, he didn't belong to that … that. Lord, I'm trying to be nice.

"The boy is good to you and Aaron. He has never done anything to make me want to hurt him other than pushing you into this wedding. I knew with everything in me that something wasn't right and you didn't want this. But my grandson looks like his father, not that waterhead snob trying to trap my baby."

I burst into laughter. "I've never even slept with him. Not that he hasn't tried. He kind of gives me the ick when he does.

"I can't explain it. I'm so relieved that it's all over," I say and roll my eyes.

"Now is it? You have a whole family you owe an apology to. All the Coswells deserve the truth, not just Erica. Wait until Fran and I get our hands on her.

"You also need to talk to the father of that child. At first, Fran and I were giving you time to come clean and break off this charade. When we saw you weren't going to handle it yourself, we made the call.

"When we called Bentley to tell him to get his butt home before he lost you forever, that boy was on the first thing smoking. He's here, Zah. That has to speak for something," she says.

"It does, but what about all the things we said? We still haven't dealt with how this all started," I say.

"Then you get to work. I know Bentley. He's a good man. Did you know he calls me every Sunday to check in?"

"On game day?" I ask with my brows furrowed.

"Yes, no matter what's going on, he makes that call. Has since your father died. He has a good heart, Zahirah. He just gets twisted and tangled up when it comes to you.

"We all say things when we're passionate about something. The more passionate we are, the stronger our words can seem. Let me ask you something," Mom says.

"Okay."

"Did he say anything worth keeping his son away from him?"

"No."

"Did his words really hurt you enough to close the door on a love you were once willing to do anything for?"

"No."

"Did Bentley Coswell truly shatter all the trust you had in him?"

"No, but Mom—"

"Zah, he hurt your feelings. However, that's not enough to keep that adorable, brilliant little boy away from his father. What you've been doing to Fran has me so furious with you, but I understand. I get it now.

"I can tell you one thing. We're all going to stop playing these little games today. Aaron will meet his father. You're going to tell Fran to her face that baby is her grandson by blood and not just in her heart.

"He's going to be one next month and I'm tired of this. I'm tired of seeing my baby hurt. It's so nice of you to care about Mrs. Christen, but them folks ain't my people.

"Fran, that's my friend. Bentley is like a son. You can't keep hurting people who love you for folks trying to manipulate you. I promise you, Gilbert is up to no good. I'm not entirely convinced his grandmother doesn't know it either," she says and rolls her eyes.

"Really? You think she knows?"

"Girl, please. Now hand me my clothes and go get Denzel to give you my discharge papers. I left Aaron with Tara. The boy will be full of sugar and swearing like a sailor if we don't hurry up."

"Oh my God. Tara, Mom, really?"

"Well, my options were limited since his father doesn't know about him."

I roll my eyes. "I'll get your paperwork."

Bentley

I'm sitting in the waiting room with Erica. My knee bouncing as I send up a prayer that Mrs. Nickels is okay. I think of her words on our last Sunday call and smile.

"Bentley Coswell, it's time to stop running. You are always welcome to come home. Maybe it's time that's exactly what you do. You never know what could be waiting here for you," she said.

"Yes, ma'am. You might be right."

"Then what's stopping you, honey?"

"Daddy told me while I was in college that I could always come home. You know, home would always be my place to reset. He's not there anymore.

"I don't know if his words still apply and I'm terrified of finding out they don't. Coming home is my final play. At least that feels like what it is, ma'am," I replied.

"Then do what you do best, baby. If this is the final play, you go for the touchdown, Bent. We're here to cheer you on. I promise. You hear me?"

"Yes, ma'am. I do."

I think harder on our last few calls, wondering if I missed something in her voice. Was she feeling unwell then? Lately, when we talked, I've been feeling like she's been trying to tell me something.

Then she and my mom called to tell me to get my ass home before Zah ended up married to Gilbert. I've been so focused on that, I haven't thought about much else. I guess she didn't want to come out and tell me up front about Zah and Gilbert, but have I been missing something else?

Could she have been sick, and I missed being able to say or do something? Mrs. Nickels has been a big part of my growing up and working on myself.

While I did the work, she's been in my ear every Sunday. No matter where in the world Zah has been, her mother has been a constant in my ear. I don't miss a call with her.

If I know I'm going to have a late game, she's the first call I make when I wake. She's always there and ready to talk. I don't know what I'll do if I lose her too.

I pull a hand down my face as my thoughts go to Zahirah. I'll be a better man for her this time. Losing her mother would be devastating.

I'm mature enough this time to see her through this, I know I am. That's why I'm not moving until I know Zah and Mrs. Nickels are okay.

"Oh shit," Erica mumbles, pulling me from my musing.

She stands quickly, looking like a bandit on the run. She heads for the nurses' station, leaving me sitting here confused. I've been so deep in thought, I don't know what I missed.

"Auntie E," a little voice squeals.

I turn toward the voice and find Garret with a little boy in his arms. The boy has little black and white low-top Chucks on his feet and khaki shorts, with a yellow T-shirt. From here, I can see his shiny-looking, little toffee-colored brown legs and his head full of thick brown ringlets.

I get to my feet with my brows knit. When I lock eyes with the kid as he turns toward me, my stomach tightens. He gives me a huge smile, showing off his tiny teeth.

"Uncle ..." He knits his brows as if not sure how to finish. Then he turns to look up at Garret, who's smiling back at him. The little guy points back at me behind him. "Uncle?"

"Not Uncle, sweety. That's Dada," my mother coos as she stops beside the two and begins to rub the boy's back.

He whips his head back in my direction. "Dada," he squeals and holds his arms out.

I stand there in shock for a moment, not knowing what to say or do. His eyes are so big and bright, not quite the same hazel as mine, but a really light brown. I move forward and take him from my brother's hold.

He wraps his arms around me and places his head on my shoulder with a sigh. As if this is where he belongs, or as if he's been waiting to find me. Feeling his weight against my chest makes this all so real.

"You knew about this?" I growl at Garret as I squeeze my son in my embrace.

"Not until I arrived at the house, while you guys went to the stadium. Bro, I had no idea."

"She has tried to deny it, but I've known from the day he was born. He has your nose and your little smile," Mom chokes out.

"I think we should take a pause and allow Zah to—" Erica cuts off as I spin on her and glare.

I have so many emotions as she looks back at me. A million thoughts and questions are running through my mind. I land on complete devastation.

I always knew Erica and Zahirah were tight, but I never thought my sister would choose her over me. Especially not to keep something like this from me.

"You knew the entire time. You lied to me. When I asked you repeatedly if you knew where she was or if she was with you, you lied. She was standing right next to you every time, wasn't she?"

"No. She was in Spain with me, but never around when I took your calls or called. I always left the flat to avoid the risk of you seeing or hearing her in the background."

"Why, Erica? You're my little sister."

"She's my best friend. She needed space."

"I have a son," I bark, my voice breaking with emotion.

"You told her to get the fudge out," she bites out, making air quotes as she says the word fudge and looks pointedly at my son, "and to go take a Plan B. So excuse me if I sided with my best friend when my big brother was being a butthole," Erica hisses.

"He did what?" my mother gasps.

I close my eyes and press my nose to my son's head. I have to count to ten to reel it in. I have a son. She didn't take that pill.

"Wait, he's really ours? I mean, Zah is family. She's like my sister, so of course he's like my nephew. But ... the baby is my real nephew, like my nephew by blood?" Eddy says, sounding as surprised as I feel.

"You couldn't have thought a kid that cute or smart belonged to Manning," Erica huffs.

"Why would you say those things? No wonder she's been freezing us out," my mother says as if she's in sheer disbelief.

"I said a lot of things, but I didn't mean any of them. I was hurt and angry. We both said things," I mutter.

"Dada," my son coos and cups my face to kiss my cheek.

"Hey, buddy. That's right, I'm your dada. You're so handsome. What's your name?"

"Me Aaron. I big boy. Smart and strong. *Grr,*" he growls at the end and makes a muscle with his little arm.

I chuckle and kiss his forehead. I never knew I could love someone so fast and completely. *Aaron.* Did Zah name him after my dad?

"Aaron Christopher Nickels," Erica says as she comes over and ruffles his hair.

"Mommy, Nana," Aaron squeals as he tries to jump out of my arms.

I turn to find Mrs. Nickels and Zahirah. I've never seen Zah look so pale in my life. She's standing with her mouth hanging open as I hold my son in my arms.

I glare at her as the situation begins to set in. Quickly, she snaps out of it and rushes over to take Aaron from my arms. He wraps his arms around her neck and hugs her tightly.

"Before you try to verbally take my head off, for once, listen to me and hear me," Zah says, holding a hand up as I open my mouth.

"First, I was going to tell you. Second, hold on." She pauses as Aaron gets fussy in her arms.

She places him on his feet and takes his little hand in hers. I take a step back as the wind is knocked out of me. He's so tall standing on his own two feet.

He takes a few steps forward and holds out his tiny free hand for mine. I take his hand and look down at him in awe.

"When was he born?" I ask tightly.

"His birthday is next month. July."

"He can walk and talk?" I knit my brows.

"He's been walking since he was eight months old. And he's been making noises—as if he could talk and hold conversations— since Erica started asking him for dating and shopping advice," she says and snickers lightly.

"Yeah, so about since he was five months," Erica says.

"No one else is pissed off about this?" Eddy growls.

"Will you chill?" Erica snaps. "The only people here who have a right to be seriously pissed are Bentley and Garret. The rest of us have been in Aaron's life one way or another since the day he was born."

"Um, guys, we're starting to draw a crowd. Mom has been cleared to head home. I'd like to talk and explain if you will listen," Zah says.

"Rice and nuggies, Mommy," Aaron pleads, looking up at his mother.

I dip to scoop him back up into my arms. "You like rice and chicken nuggets?"

"Yes, yum. *Please.*"

"Anything you want, buddy. I'll make them myself," I promise.

"Bent—"

"A year, Zah. My son is going to be a whole year old."

I hear her sigh behind me as I walk off with Aaron in my arms. I never want to let him go. Now that feeling I've been having for months makes sense.

So many times I wanted to come home. It's like I knew I needed to be here. The only reason I didn't was because I was waiting out the season and my contract.

I didn't know if Zah and I would ever be a thing again, so I didn't rush back. Then there was the root of it all. I didn't know if this was home anymore.

I couldn't bear to know that without Dad, I didn't belong. A whole year. When was she going to tell me?

CHAPTER THIRTY-THREE

Broken Plans

Gilbert

I've been pacing since I arrived here at Hamilton's apartment as I try to wrap my head around the shitshow today has been. My plan is broken.

I'll have to rethink everything. Zah is still mine. I'm not giving up that easily. Coswell has another think coming if he thinks he's just going to walk in and fuck everything up for me.

"What are you going to do now? This project falls apart without your money. No wedding, no money, Gilbert. That's a huge problem for me.

"I stuck my neck out and vouched for you. You have to get that money and make good on this. You hear me, bro?"

"I hear you," I bellow.

I glare at Hamilton as he tells me something I already know. I started to make some investments because I was so sure I was going to seal the deal.

I had no idea that motherfucker was coming back. He hasn't been here for twenty-four hours and she's shutting me out. I can't believe this is happening.

So what, her mother fainted. We should still be getting married tomorrow evening. Old bitch ruined everything. My mind goes back to the moment when I was so sure nothing could get in my way.

The wind blew through my hair, the salty sea air filled my lungs, and the feeling of success buzzed through my veins. The day couldn't have gone better. I played my part perfectly.

"So, how is everything going?" Hamilton crooned on the other end of the phone.

"It's going better than I could have asked for. She was here today, and get this ... she's pregnant. I was right, something did happen in Vegas.

"My intel was spot on. Either that little pill she bought didn't work, or she didn't take it. Coswell dropped her right into my arms with this one," I crooned.

"Wait, pregnant? How does that work for you? Your grandmother will never accept another man's bastard child."

"She'll never know the child isn't mine. She assumed the kid was mine without even asking questions. I went with it, so did Zahirah."

"I'm going to get the girl, the money, and the empire. The little brat will be the cherry on top to burn Coswell to his core. His brat will call me Daddy while I fuck his girl every night."

"You're sure she's going to marry you?"

"Zah's a sweetheart. She'll do anything for a friend. Once I get the engagement ring on her finger, Grand will help me get to the finish line.

"Zah won't know how to break her heart. Once we're married, she's mine, no turning back. Coswell will have to watch me take care of his little family and there isn't shit he can do about it. Who's the loser now?"

I'll never forget how he spat those words in my face after breaking my jaw and telling me to stay away from Zahirah. It killed me to pretend that I was over it to remain connected to his circle. Zahirah never knew why I disappeared for the two months it took for my jaw to heal.

"Remind me never to piss you off. Dude, you've been playing the long game since he kicked your ass and told you to stay away from Zah in high school," Hamilton chuckled.

He's the only one I've ever told my plan to. I couldn't trust anyone else like I could trust him. He knows some of my darkest secrets.

"I knew back then he wanted to fuck her himself. Acting all high and mighty like they were too good for any of us. As if she were too good for me to touch."

I had a feeling Coswell was going to end up with Zahirah. It was the way he looked at her. The two never could stay away from each other.

When Zah told me she was going to Vegas for that asshat's game, I knew I had my shot. Those two were going to fall in together and I'd be able to take her.

I've been working my way in as her friend for years now. She's never responded to my flirting, but I haven't allowed that to deter me. All I needed was the right opportunity.

"I thought you liked her. This is really only about revenge?"

"Oh, I like her all right, that's what's going to make taking her from him so much sweeter. I bet she fucks like a slut. I can't wait to destroy that fat ass."

"Well, good luck. See you when you get back. Glad your trip was worth it," he said.

I grinned and ended the call as I looked out at the sea. The trip had gone very well. It had been more than worth it.

I knew my grandmother would approve of Zahirah. It doesn't hurt that I've wanted her for years. I've always shown Zah the sweet boy my grandmother believes me to be.

Not the bastard my father disowned and walked away from. I got lucky that I killed him before he could breathe a word of all the things I'd done to get expelled and disowned.

I lifted my glass of champagne into the air and gave a toast to my success. Patience gets you everything. I'd have Zah and my revenge.

"To the life I was always meant to have and my gorgeous fiancée. I'm going to be a dad," I muttered to myself and grinned.

"Don't worry about the money. I'll come up with something. Just buy me a little more time," I say to Hamilton as my thoughts come back to the present.

"Are you sure about this?"

"I never fail. You know this."

"If you say so. I'm not helping you bury anymore bodies, so leave me out of any of that."

"Remember, I have no problem collecting or disposing of the bodies all by myself," I say and give him a grin.

I'm sure he has read between the lines when his face turns pale as a sheet. Now is not the time to overestimate one's value. I shrug and turn to leave his apartment. I have a plan to save.

Zahirah

"Thank you," Aaron sings as Bentley hands him his plate of nuggies and rice.

I can't help smiling as Bentley palms Aaron's little head between his hands and kisses the top. My son looks up at his father with a big smile on his face.

"Good manners, buddy. Nice job," Bent praises.

"Nice job," Aaron repeats.

He picks up his fork and begins to eat his rice. "Hot sauce, Dada. You forgot Aaron's hot sauce."

Bentley looks up at me. I shrug and get up to get the hot sauce for my baby. He won't eat rice without it.

"Oh, he's serious."

"Yeah," I snicker. "I put a little water in a bowl and mix it in before pouring it on his rice."

"He, um, hangs with Eddy a lot?"

"Is that where he gets it from?"

"I think so. Your dad gave him hot sauce once when he was little and he had to have it on everything after that."

"Oh my God, I totally forgot about that."

"Eddy loves him. He offers to babysit for me all the time."

I wish I could take the words back the moment they are out of my mouth. Bentley's face clouds over with anger and silence falls over the room. Aaron humming as he eats is all you can hear.

"These are his cups? Does he drink juice or water with his meals?"

"Water please. Thank you," Aaron answers for himself.

"You can use the blue sippy cup. The yellow one is his morning cup for milk."

"Nuggie, Dada?" Aaron asks as he holds up one of his nuggets.

"You would share with me?"

"Yes. Good job, Aaron. Good boys share."

"Thank you, buddy. You eat your food. I'm not hungry this time."

"Okay. Eat-eat, Mommy?"

"Mommy is going to have a sandwich."

"PBJ, yum."

"He's so smart. I mean, he's not even one," Bentley chokes out.

"He gets a lot of attention and modeling." I shrug.

"What happened, Zah? If I'm doing the math right, you were pregnant when I found out you were first engaged. Gilbert Manning? Really?"

"It's more complicated than that."

"Not too complicated to come to me. You were having my baby."

"You were seeing someone. I didn't want to get in the way," I snap back.

"What? What are you talking about?"

"That influencer. The one you were dating last year."

"Baby, I don't know where you're getting your information from, but I haven't been dating anyone. And even if I was that's no excuse for you not telling me about my son."

"I … it was all over the internet. I thought."

"You thought wrong. Shit, you're talking about that crazy chick, aren't you?"

He groans and pulls a hand down his face. Aaron looks up at him; I can see the wheels turning in his little head. He then looks at me.

"Shit. Shit."

"Aaron, no. That's a never word."

"Oh, wow. I'm sorry. Buddy, Daddy didn't mean to say that. Zah, I'm going to go for a walk. I need some air."

"Aaron walk with Daddy?"

Bentley looks at me, his expression conflicted. I can see he doesn't want to say no. I nod, and he lifts Aaron into his arms.

I stand staring after them as I rub the back of my neck. This has been a long-ass day. I feel like I've just lived the last ten years in one day.

I knit my brows as Bentley's words sink in. I grab my phone and begin to Google. The more I read, the dumber I feel.

None of it was real. That woman had made up the entire relationship and the rumors. Bentley had to press charges and get a restraining order.

I'd never dug too deep into their relationship because it hurt too much. If I had known the truth, I would have told him about Aaron sooner. It didn't help that Gilbert always cautioned me against reaching out to Bentley.

"Shit," I mutter.

Bentley

My son is adorable and so smart. I need space from Zah, not him. So when he asked to walk with me, I couldn't say no. He made it half a block before he wanted me to pick him up.

I could only laugh and lift him into my arms. By the next block, he was fast asleep. I don't mind, having him in my arms is enough for me.

"Where should I put him?" I ask as I enter Zahirah's house once again and find her sitting on the couch.

"I'll show you to his room," she says and stands.

She's changed out of that sexy-ass dress since we've been gone. I might be mad as hell at her, but she's still gorgeous as ever. I still can't believe she was going to marry Gilbert.

"Do you want to put him in his PJs?"

"Yes, please."

She nods and goes to collect his little pajamas. I move to the little bed and sit down on the floor beside it. I then pull his shoes from his feet.

My boy is knocked out. I stare down at his face and smile. I can see so much of Zah, but there's a ton of me.

"He's so beautiful," I murmur.

"He is. Best thing I've ever done."

I look up into her eyes. Hearing her say that answers a number of my questions. I take the little train pajamas she's handing me.

Gently, I remove his T-shirt and then his shorts. I chuckle at his tan lines. I have a son.

His little toes are so cute. Once I dress him in his nightclothes, I turn with him in my arms and place him in his little bed. I kiss his head and stand to leave.

I wait out in the hall, staring up at the ceiling. This has been unreal. The tiny human in there is my son.

"Do you want to talk?"

I turn to find Zah peering up at me. I move to crowd her space and pin her to the wall. She places her hands on my chest as I lean my arm over her head and look down into her eyes.

"I want what I came here for," I say.

"What did you come here for?"

"You. You're not his. You shouldn't be marrying him."

"That's our son, my son. I'm here for you both. He can't have you, Zah. He doesn't deserve you."

"I've never been his."

"Tell me something I don't know. No matter how he touched you, you have always been mine."

She shakes her head. I get ready to set her straight, but she reaches to cup my face. I turn my head and kiss her palm.

"No, Bent. You don't understand. It was all fake. We were never really engaged.

"We were friends. He asked me to come over to hang out one day in Spain. Long story short, his grandmother thought I was his girlfriend, and he asked me to play along.

"Then I got sick while there and she realized I was pregnant, and she assumed the baby was his. The whole crazy situation spiraled out from there.

"It was never supposed to get to the wedding. I don't know how things got so far, but that's over now. I don't owe him anything. I want my life back. I'm tired of pret—"

She moans into my mouth as I cut her words off with a passionate kiss. I have my hand down the front of her sleep pants and my fingers in her pussy before I can think about what I'm doing.

"Tell me you don't want me, and I'll leave," I breathe into her ear.

"Bentley, I … I don't want you to go, but I don't think—"

"Don't think, baby. Just feel. Let me make you come.

"This night is going to get ugly once we get to the real shit, so let me give this to you."

She lifts on her toes as she whimpers, and I continue to finger her. I cover her mouth with mine once again, kissing her deeper. I miss her so much.

I'm still angry, but I need this as much as I need air. I can't help but groan as it sinks in that she never allowed that bastard to touch her. This pussy is still mine.

Her legs begin to shake, and she comes all over my hand. I look down into her eyes and grin as I pull my hand from her pants and stick my fingers into my mouth.

"Where do we go from here?" she pants.

"I have a lot I want to say to you. A few sorries and a lot of groveling and explaining. You didn't deserve Vegas, and I probably deserve the last year.

"You and I need to communicate more. I don't want to lose you. I don't want to be apart.

"You and Aaron are my world. I thought you were done with me and that you moved on. Honestly, hearing that you thought I did too ..." I shake my head.

"I get it. I understand why you didn't come to me. I had planned to let you go, but I couldn't without hearing from your mouth that you don't want me anymore. I came to hear you say it."

"Bentley, my heart has always belonged to you. I came to Vegas because I missed you. I thought we could at least start to be friends again and take things from there."

"That's exactly what I wanted. Then I had too much to drink before getting back to my room and you appeared like an angel in that dress. I lost my shit, and everything went to hell from there."

"You might want to work on not using that word."

I snort and lean in to kiss her. "I'm so sorry. I wasn't thinking. He's so smart, baby. You're doing an amazing job," I say against her lips.

"He is pretty amazing. I love him so much. Thank you."

"Thank you for what?"

"Giving me our son. The best sex of my life turned into my greatest blessing. I love being a mom."

"Best sex of your life?" I scoff and lift a brow.

She bites her lip and nods. I palm her ass and drag her body into mine. I'm so hard, but we should take our time and talk a whole lot more.

"Come on. Show me the rest of your house and Aaron's morning routine."

"You say that like you plan to be here in the morning."

"Zah, I'm home, baby. You know you're all I've wanted. Having you in my life has always been my endgame. I'm so sorry I didn't handle things better."

"We all did the best we knew how."

"We have time to get into that. Come on, it's been a long-ass day."

CHAPTER THIRTY-FOUR

We're Back

Bentley

"Higher, Dada, higher," Aaron squeals as I push him on the swing in the backyard of Zahirah's house.

This place is nice, but I'm going to give them something nicer. I already have Garret narrowing down our options. I plan to sign my new contract on Monday.

It was rough and a ton of emotions came up, but Zah and I spent the night talking and saying what we felt. I think we made a lot of progress.

There's still something she held back, I could feel it, but time got away from us and we both passed out. I'm letting her sleep in this morning. I brought Aaron out here to play.

I love the sound of his voice and laughter. He's been proving all morning how smart he is. He's so polite and sweet.

I'm going to find a football to toss around with him as soon as I can. There's so much I want to do with him. I still have so much to learn about him.

"Hey, there you two are. I thought I heard squealing," Erica says as she comes around the side of the house.

"Hey, what are you doing here?"

"I came to make sure my favorite boy wasn't standing over two bodies crying," she taunts. "Good to see you made it through the night. Where's Zah?"

"I'm letting her sleep in."

"Cool. Are we good, bro?"

I tug my sister into a hug. "Yeah, we're good. Just don't ever do anything like that to me ever again."

"I won't. I hated every minute of it."

"Come on. Let's go inside. I'll wake Zah and make her breakfast."

I grab Aaron from the swing and toss him up into the air. He squeals happily and begins to giggle as I tickle his stomach. His little giggles make my heart swell with pride.

"You're great with him already," Erica says.

"I love him already."

We walk into the house as Zah comes out looking like she had a fight with the bed. I bite my lip to hold my laughter in. She looks at me and rolls her eyes.

"I need coffee. Lots of coffee."

"Mommy. We play. Come back outside, Dada."

I laugh. "I've got you, buddy. Let's feed Mommy first. You want an apple?"

"No. Raisins, please."

"He's talking about granola," Erica says.

"I know, Zah already gave me a crash course in Aaron speak."

The doorbell rings as we all head to the kitchen. Zah frowns and turns to answer it. I stop her and hand Aaron over.

"I'll get it."

She shrugs. "It's probably one of the moms."

I peck her lips and go to get the door. I have a huge grin on my face until I open the door and find none other than Gilbert standing on the other side. I fold my arms over my chest and glare down at him.

"You need something?"

"I'm here to see my fiancée," he growls.

"I don't know why. No one by that title lives here."

"Where is Zahirah? I'm here for her, not you."

"Dada, up up," Aaron comes running to my side with his arms held up.

"Hey, buddy. What happened to your snack?"

"Hey, son. I haven't seen you in a few days. Come here, little guy," Gilbert croons as he holds his hands out.

"*No*," Aaron whines and hides his face in my neck.

The shit-eating grin I have on my face right now has to speak volumes. I couldn't have asked for a better reaction. I rub my son's back as I sway him in my arms.

"Where's my fucking fiancée? I want you away from my family. You need to go," he snarls.

"Watch your mouth around my son before I shove my fist down your throat. I already told you, you don't have a fiancée at this residence. I know it was all BS.

"Zahirah is over it. It's done. Stop pretending and leave my woman alone," I bite out.

"What's going on?" Zah asks as she and Erica come rushing to the door.

"We need to talk," Gilbert snarls.

"You will never talk to her like that. Watch your tone."

"Coswell, everything between us was fine before you showed up. Zahirah, I heard your mother was discharged from the hospital last night. That gives us plenty of time to get ready for the ceremony this evening."

"Oh my God, what aren't you hearing? Erica, can you please take Aaron back into the kitchen?" Zah says.

Erica takes Aaron from me and leaves with him. I pull Zah to my side, then fold my arms across my chest. Gilbert looks like his head is going to explode.

"Listen, you asked me to do you a favor. That favor blew up into way more than I bargained for. There never should have been a wedding planned with all those people you invited.

"None of this was ever what I wanted. I'm not marrying you today or any other day. I'm sorry and I'll be happy to talk to your grandmother if you want me to, but this is over. I have my own life to get back to," Zah says in frustration.

"I've been here for you and Aaron this entire time. Where has he been? How has he shown you he cares?"

"That's none of your business. You've shoved your way into situations I really didn't want you to be a part of more times than not. This isn't a real relationship, you know that, right?"

"What does he have that I don't?"

"Gilbert, please leave while we're still friends. You're making this really awkward. Tell your grandmother I'm very sorry."

"In other words, we're back and you don't need to come back."

"Bent," Zah snorts.

I shrug as I give this asshole a warning glare. I told him a long time ago to stay away from Zahirah. Maybe his jaw needs a reminder.

Gilbert balls his fists at his sides, but he nods his head and turns to leave. Zah wraps her arms around my waist and sags into me. I wrap my arms around her and give her a squeeze before I close the door and lead her to the kitchen.

My sister is having a full-blown conversation with Aaron. Talking about a pair of shoes she's thinking of buying off her phone, while he kicks his feet happily in his high chair. Eating granola and apple slices from his little bowl.

"So what's the plan for today? We hanging out, or do you two need some alone time?" Erica says and wiggles her brows at me.

I rub the back of my neck. "I promised Mom I'd go change the flowers at the cemetery. I haven't been since we buried Dad."

"Oh, would you mind if I went along? I'd like to take some flowers to my dad. I'd also like to finish our talk," Zah says.

She has that same hesitant look from last night, so I agree. The sooner we get through our shit, the sooner we can move forward with our lives. I need her to know I'm fully here this time.

"I've got the kid. I was supposed to have him for the weekend anyway. You two do whatever you need to do. Just promise me one of you will keep a level head and call for a moderator if things go south."

I snort. "I think we can handle things like adults."

Erica purses her lips and gives me a look. "Yet you're the one always with your foot in your mouth."

"Don't you have a pair of shoes to buy? I'll pay for them. Now get lost."

"Love you," she sings.

"Yeah, I love you too."

Zahirah

"Hey, Mr. Coswell, it's me, Zah. It's been a while. There's something I always wanted to say.

"I'm so sorry. I wish I never gave you and Daddy those stupid passes. I'm sorry, all of this is my fault. If it weren't for me, you two would still be here.

"I didn't mean to take you from everyone. I miss you guys so much. I wish you both could be here to meet AC.

"I named him Aaron Christopher after you and my dad. He's such a good boy. I'm so sorry," I sob.

"Zah, what are you talking about?" Bentley says from beside me.

I turn to look up at him. He's looking down at me in confusion. I wrap my arms around my middle and shake my head. I've been wanting to get this off my chest since last night.

"It was my fault. I bought them those passes for Christmas. That's why you couldn't stand being around me. I'm so sorry."

"What the hell? Shit, baby, are you serious?"

I nod, not able to speak. I have a lump in my throat that feels the size of a watermelon. When I look up through my lashes, he's searching my face with his gaze.

"I never blamed you for anything. That's not—"

"You may not have consciously blamed me, but I think subconsciously that has always been an issue."

He opens his mouth to speak, then closes it and purses his lips. I put my head down, no longer able to look at him. A chill runs through me and I shiver.

"Are you done here?" he asks.

I already placed fresh flowers on my father's grave. This was our last stop. I nod once again.

Bentley wraps his arm around me and leads me to the car. We climb in and ride back to the house in silence. I think I'm going to be sick.

Once we get back to my place, he parks in my garage, and we go into the house. I'm trying to think of the right thing to say, but my guilt is consuming me.

"I would like us to go to counseling as a couple and maybe even individually. I've already been seeing someone. I'll get a recommendation for someone new here.

"It helped me a lot. It's your choice. All expenses on me," he says as we sit down on my couch.

I look down into my hands as I think his words over. I've been avoiding this topic and living my life without opening those wounds for so long.

"Okay," I murmur.

"And for the record, I've never thought about those passes or placed any of the blame on you. Zah, you were never my issue.

"I was hurting so much, and I didn't know how to be the man I promised your daddy and mine I would be. Every time I tried, I said the wrong thing or did the wrong thing. And I'd start a fight, it was my childish way of trying to pull my foot out of my mouth.

"Baby, none of that was on you. That was some shit I spent eight years working on. First alone, then I got some help—Garret, your mother, mine, and my therapist. They were there for me to work through my shit.

"I never even thought about those passes if I'm being honest. I can't believe you've thought all this time that I was angry with you. I'm so sorry, Zah."

"For what?"

"I'm sorry I wasn't what you needed when you needed it. I'm sorry I couldn't see past myself. I'm sorry that after doing all the work, I fell back into my own bullshit and fucked us up all over again."

"I could have stayed," I murmur.

"No, you were right to leave me. I'm questioning now if I deserve you. That's why I want us to go to counseling.

"I can want you, but that doesn't mean I deserve you. I'm here to do the work with you this time. We got a hell of a bad hand. We were kids and had the rug pulled out from under us."

"You can say that again."

"It feels like I've spent more of my life grieving than anything else. First, the loss of our dads, then the loss of you. I'm thirty-one, Zah.

"I want to stop hurting. I want you. I can't have you thinking that the moment something gets hard between us, I'm going to bail or make shit weird.

"I also want to free you of this guilt. It's not real. It has no root."

"But—"

"No, baby. Our dads could have been going anywhere together. You remember how they would sneak out together for ice cream or milkshakes when our moms were on diets?"

I nod and smile. The memory hits so hard I almost gasp. We used to tease them about it all the time.

"See? The only person I used to blame was that trucker and I had to let that go and forgive him. That shit was eating me alive.

"Baby, I was a twenty-one-year-old kid watching his girlfriend's world crumble around her, while losing his dad, his best friend. My dad meant so much to me. I felt guilty for not knowing how to be a shoulder for you to lean on when you were losing way more than I had.

"You're so strong, Zah. I may not even deserve you today, but I'm going to make myself worthy if you will have me. And once we've done the work—and we both know I'm worthy of your time, heart, and love—then I'll do everything in my power to make the dreams we used to talk about come true," he says like a promise.

"You know what's crazy? In hindsight, I can see everything we did wrong. It's like watching your favorite movie and yelling at them to get their shit together, but they can't hear you," I say into my lap.

"I know exactly what you mean. So many times, I've wanted to come back to you and say so much, but I knew I wasn't ready. I didn't have the right words."

"Do you think we'll find those words now?"

"Yeah, Zah, we'll find them because I'm not whole without you. We have so much to fight for this time."

I scoot closer to him and push my hand through the front of his thick locks. It all falls right back into place, bringing a smile to my face. He cups the side of my head and leans in to capture my lips.

I moan into his mouth and wrap my arms around his neck. It feels like coming home. This is where I've always belonged.

"I want you so much right now. If you want to wait, say the word. It's your decision."

"Thank you for acknowledging my feelings, but I've wanted you since you showed up. I've missed you so much, babe," I say.

"Thank God," he groans.

He stands with me in his arms, and I wrap my legs around him. Bentley continues to devour my mouth as he carries me to my bedroom.

It's as if my soul sighs in relief as he kisses his way down my body. When he pops the button on my jeans, I start to panic. I've put in a lot of work to get my body back after having our son, but nothing is the same.

Bentley doesn't miss a beat. He peels my jeans down my legs and kisses all over my skin. I sit up and lift my arms when he goes to peel my shirt off.

Unfastening my bra, he allows the fabric to fall into my lap, where I push it away. He eats me up with his gaze. I go to cover my breasts, feeling all types of self-conscious.

He shakes his head. "You never need to hide from me. You're so fucking beautiful. I can see all the signs of you carrying my son.

"Thank you, Zahirah. Thank you for not—"

I cover his lips with my finger. "I couldn't bear the thought of destroying something we created together. You don't have to thank me.

"We made him together. I'm sorry—"

He takes my lips, cutting my words off. I'm breathless when he breaks the seal of our lips. He looks me deep in the eyes.

"No more sorries. Let's reset the clock from this moment. We're here, we have our son, and we're going to spend the rest of our lives together."

He drops his gaze to my neck. "You still wear it?"

I reach for the charm necklace and bring the bear to my lips. "I never take it off."

"I have a ton of charms to add. Come here, beautiful. I want to make love to the love of my life."

CHAPTER THIRTY-FIVE

A Fresh Start

Zahirah

"Come on, baby. You know that was funny. I had the hardest time of my life trying not to laugh," Bentley croons.

"Okay, okay, you're not wrong, but you're not going to do my buddy like that."

My laughter fills the air as Bentley and I ride in his new sports car. We're on our way to another date. This is our fifth date in the last two weeks.

"Eddy is a big boy; he can handle a little teasing. I'm still trying to figure out what he was thinking. Mom has always been sharp," he says through his own laughter.

"He wasn't thinking. I mean, come on. How much did you think things through when you were his age, wanting to impress the girls?"

He gives a small chuckle. "You were the only girl I was trying to impress, Zah. Remember? I had to think before I did everything."

We've been to see a counselor, and we do a lot of talking and even journaling together. Bentley wants me to see he's a changed man. He's doing an amazing job.

I've seen it not only in his words but also in his actions. He's an amazing father and a better boyfriend than I remember. It's hard not to fall in love with him all over again.

I find myself smiling and laughing a lot these days. He reaches over and places his hand on my thigh. I look at the side of his face and smile, reaching to run my hand through his hair. He still keeps it long, the longest length reaching just past his shoulders.

Erica has been calling him John Wick. I've gotten a kick out of that. Yeah, Bentley's haircut does come close, but that's about it.

The one thing that has changed, which I noticed in Vegas two years ago, Bentley's body is, hands down, crazy in shape. I mean, straight insane since college.

I thought he was fit back then. It is so different now. He has that grown-ass man weight and muscle. He carries it all so well too.

He's also become a beast in the sheets. I have zero complaints there. Not that he hasn't always been amazing in bed.

My nights are filled with more orgasms than I can count. Waking to him and going to bed in his arms at night has been heaven. Our connection has become deeper than it has ever been.

"Were you really going to kiss me that one time?"

"You mean the summer before I left for college?"

"Yeah," I say with a smile.

"I was. I know I shouldn't have, but I was. If not for that call, I would have."

"Do you regret the time we lost?"

The car falls silent. I bite my lip, wondering if this is when he'll shutdown on me. He gives my thigh a gentle squeeze.

"Every day, but living in my regrets only robs us of our now. Can I ask you something?"

"Yes."

"Are you happy now?"

"Yes, very."

"Good. Do you think we're moving forward?"

"It feels like it. Aaron loves having you around."

"I'll always be here for my son, but I don't want you to take that as an obligation to have to stay with me."

I sit and think his words over. Do I think I have to stay with him for my son? No, I want Aaron to have his father in his life, but I don't need to have Bentley in my life for that to happen.

"I don't feel obligated. Yes, I want Aaron to have a whole family. However, I don't want him to grow up in a family that's broken from within.

"I feel like we're in a good place. We're already moving forward. I believe if we continue on this path, we'll get to what we've always wanted," I reply.

"Then I'm right where I'm supposed to be, Zahirah. Not a step out of place. This is our fresh start."

I smile and settle in my seat. That was a great answer. I feel the same way.

We fall into a light banter for the rest of the ride. When we pull up to the Japanese Friendship Garden, I get excited. I've heard so much about this place, but I've never been. Bentley asked if I had and when I said no, he got to planning.

I can't wait to see what all he has planned. It's early evening. The sun hasn't set yet, but it will soon.

Bentley takes my hand and leads me inside. Once we are walking in the garden, it oddly seems like not many others are around. I look up at Bentley curiously, but he only smiles back at me.

I shrug it off and go with the flow. The place is so tranquil and romantic. The sound of the flowing ponds and Bentley's rumbling voice brings a sense of ease and peace.

"I have something for you," he murmurs in the middle of our conversation when we come to a little area with rocks that look like we can perch on the edge of them.

I take a seat, and he sits beside me. I look at him expectantly, wondering what he's up to. He pulls a gift-wrapped box from his pocket and places it into my hand.

"What's this?"

"Open it. I want to see the surprise on your face," he replies.

"Okay, let's see," I sing.

Tearing the paper away excitedly, I hold my breath with anticipation. I reveal a jewelry box and open the lid. I tear up as I find a new charm for my necklace. It's a tiny baby shoe with Aaron's birthstone in it.

"Oh, wow. This is adorable," I coo.

"I thought it was fitting for your next charm. Although I might need to get you a matching bracelet for all the charms you'll need for those six kids you promised me," he says while clearly trying to stifle a laugh.

"Bullshit," I gasp out, causing him to lose his battle with his laughter.

"You can't renege now. We already started."

"Bent, I'm willing to have three more, tops. I'm not having five more babies."

He presses his lips to mine and kisses me firmly. "I just wanted to get you to agree to have more with me," he says against my lips.

"All you had to do was ask. You have a better shot asking than trying to make me commit bodily harm," I tease.

"Good to know. We'll have that talk soon. Come, dinner is waiting."

"You rented the place out, didn't you?"

He shrugs his shoulders. "I might have."

I smile and hand him my new charm. "Will you put it on for me first?"

He takes it and hooks it on the chain for me, then pecks my lips. Not only do I feel loved, but I can also see it in his eyes. This date moves to the top of my fave list.

Bentley

We walk into the house hand in hand. Aaron is fast asleep on my shoulder. We stopped to pick him up from my mom's when we got back.

That date was amazing. Anytime I get with Zah is more than I can ask for. The look in her eyes when I gave her that charm was worth a million dollars.

Something so simple means so much to her. I think that's what I love about her so much. Zahirah isn't afraid to laugh at herself or to dance in the rain.

It makes me want to give her the world. Something I plan to give her and my son. There isn't anything I wouldn't do for these two.

"I'll put him to bed. You want to go take a bath? I'll join you in a bit."

"No, I'll help. We've been gone all day. I missed him."

I nod and squeeze her fingers. We make our way to Aaron's room and Zah gets his PJs as I get him undressed and use the baby wipes to wipe him down.

When I'm done and go to throw out the wipes, Zah gets him into his pajamas. My boy is knocked out. He looks like a sleeping angel.

"He sleeps just like you."

I scoff. "I wish I could sleep that hard. The kid would sleep through a tornado."

"Bent, when you fall out, your ass is out for the count. You sleep like the dead."

I bury my face in her neck and laugh. I do tend to sleep hard. Inhaling deeply, I count my blessings.

"I'm not ready to be out for the count tonight. Come dance with me."

"Dance with you?"

"Yeah, like we used to do in college after we got our grades back. Come on, it will be fun. The perfect ending to the perfect day."

"Okay, let's go."

We both kiss our boy good night and head out to the living room. I pull my phone out and find a song that speaks to how I'm feeling. "So Easy" by Olivia Dean fills the room.

I tug Zah into my embrace and begin to sway with her in my arms. She reaches up and cups my face as we lock eyes. In this moment, I see my past, present, and future all rolled into one.

It's not pretty. In fact, it's pretty damn ugly in some parts. However, it's mine.

"I love you," we say at the same time.

We start to laugh. I tug her into me and capture her lips. I kiss her hungrily.

"Is a year and nine months enough time between babies? I'm asking for a friend."

"I have a bet for you. If you win the championship this season, I'll allow you to get me pregnant again. Deal?"

"Oh, baby, you have a deal. I'll even throw the game-winning touchdown for you and Aaron," I say as I rub her back.

"Okay, Bentley. Okay."

CHAPTER THIRTY-SIX

Birthday Boy

Zahirah

"Aaron birthday. I big boy. Happy birthday, me. Yay," Aaron squeals and claps as his eyes light up with joy.

He has frosting on his face from his first cupcake ever that his grandmothers fought for him to have. I only caved because Bentley joined in with puppy eyes to help the moms and his son to win me over.

Since it's his birthday and Bentley promised to deal with the fallout of the sugar rush, I figured I'd let him have it. As I watch my son sitting in his high chair, happy as ever, surrounded by all the people who love him, I can't imagine my life without him. He's safe and happy and he brings more joy to my life with each day.

"Now this is the smile your father would want to see on your face every day," my mother whispers in my ear.

I turn to look at her, my smile faltering just a little. I would have loved for my father to be here for this. Aaron's party has turned out so cute and there's so much love here.

The entire Coswell family is here, my mom, and a few of the moms from the playgroup I joined for Aaron to have some little friends. My home is filled with more laughter and happiness than I can take.

I glance back at my son, and my smile returns as I watch him and his father interact. Bentley is whispering something in Aaron's ear as he tickles him, pulling that adorable squeal from our boy's lips.

"I have a lot to smile about these days," I reply.

"That you do. It's good to see you both happy. That's all I ever truly wanted."

I turn to look at her again and pull her into a hug. I hold on a little longer than necessary. I've learned to cherish moments like this, not knowing when I won't be able to have them any longer.

"You do know they are both here, don't you? You might not be able to see them, but I can feel them. Your father and Bill will always be here to look over him," she says as she gives me a tight squeeze.

"Yeah, I know," I choke out.

"I'm so proud of you. You, my baby, are lemonade personified. All you have accomplished has left me in awe."

"Thanks, Mom. Although I do need to figure out what's going to be next."

"You'll figure it out. How much time do you still have using your savings?"

"If I live frugally, I can stretch out five or six more years, but I don't want to wait until it's all gone."

It's actually more than that, but I like to aim low and reach higher. I honestly could probably hold off until Aaron goes off to college. However, that's not my style. Even with all my travels, I still have some of my trust left, but I'm not going to rely solely on that or get complacent.

"If you need anything, you know you can ask me."

"I'm a long way off from needing help, Mom. Aaron and I will be just fine."

"I'm just saying. You don't have to deny yourself or my grandson anything."

"Thanks, Mom."

"Should we get started on his gifts?" Bentley croons into my ear as he comes up behind me and wraps me in his arms.

I crane my neck to look up at him. His hazel eyes are sparkling back at me. Dipping his head, he pecks my lips and then my nose.

"Sure, if we get started now, we might get to all of them," I tease.

"I'll admit, I might have gone overboard. We can start with all the ones from the guests." He laughs and kisses me again.

I can't help but laugh. Overboard would be an understatement. Bentley purchased every learning game he could find and the toys ... Oh my God, Aaron doesn't have enough time in a day to play with everything his father bought him.

He could play with a toy a day for a year and still not play with them all. Mind you, I'm only speaking of the things he allowed me to see. I get it.

Bentley is still trying to make up for the time he lost with our son. I'm still working through a bit of my guilt about that. However, I do believe Bentley would have spoiled Aaron either way.

"Uncle Eddy," Aaron squeals and laughs.

I turn to find Eddy tossing Aaron in the air, causing his little nephew to laugh with joy. Garret is standing nearby with a smile on his face. Erica and Lauren have their phones out, taking pictures and recording.

Tara is standing by the gift table with her hands on her hips as if she's trying to figure out how to tackle the mountain that is our son's birthday gifts.

"I think I'm winning life," I murmur.

"What's that?" Bentley asks.

"Nothing. Come on, we can help him open them together. It looks like Tara is coming up with a plan for the order," I chuckle.

"I bet she has a clipboard and checklist somewhere," he grumbles and shakes his head.

Yup, I'm winning at life. I couldn't ask for better family and friends. All it takes is a single moment to change everything.

The moment Bentley appeared at my rehearsal dinner and my mother fainted will forever be the moment that changed my life for the better.

Now that Aaron's birthday party is out of the way, I can lock in and get some other things in my life on track to ensure that change continues to bring joy like this.

Gilbert

That fucking bitch. I didn't even get an invite to her brat's birthday party. I should be there.

I can't believe how everything changed in the blink of an eye. One minute, I was engaged and about to get married to the one woman I've obsessed over since high school. The next, I'm left holding my dick, wondering how the fuck I got here.

No wife, no family fortune, no fucking empire, no revenge. Instead, it's like that son of a bitch broke my jaw all over again. He's back here in Arizona, living with my woman, being idolized by the entire state like some immortal hero.

I fucking loathe Coswell. However, killing him would be so unsatisfying. I want him to suffer.

Coswell is going to pay. Zahirah will too. I've been patient before. I can do it again.

The only thing getting in my way is Hamilton and those fucking partners of his. They are rushing me to do something I can't right now. I need time to think and come up with a plan *B*.

"You're running out of time," Hamilton says as if I don't already know this.

"Aren't you getting tired of telling me things I already know?"

"Honest? Yeah, I am. However, I like my life. If I don't make sure you keep your word, I'm fucked. Bro, what are you going to do?"

I sigh and drag a hand down my face. Words aren't going to fix this. I resent him thinking if he keeps talking, it's going to change something.

"I need some time to think without everyone in my ear. If it's not you, it's my grandmother," I bite out.

"Is she considering giving you the money without the marriage?"

"No, she's still trying to figure out how I fucked things up with Zahirah. She wants her grandson back. She's been talking about counseling and lawyers."

"Dude, the moment your lawyers try to serve Zah to take her son, she and Coswell are going to blow all your shit up."

"No fucking duh, Captain Obvious."

"Listen, maybe it's time to come up with another plan. These people mean business and when they find out we've been bullshitting, they're going to come to collect whether we have it or not."

"*We* weren't going to have anything from the beginning. You were just the middleman. It's always been my money, my investment."

"Bro, this isn't just about you. Yeah, you were putting up the majority of the funds, but this is my name and reputation on the line. Don't be an asshole."

I glare at him, tired of hearing his voice. My grandmother, for now, isn't a voice I can silence. She won't tell me if I'll inherit everything upon her demise.

I'm not ready to take that risk. I need to acquire the money while she's still alive and I'm in her good graces. However, Hamilton is a buzzing I can do without.

"Listen, Gilbert, I'm your friend. I want this to work out for you as much as I want to be clear of getting my head chopped off."

"I have a question for you. Do your partners know anything about me?"

"No, not much. Remember, I'm vouching for you, so my name and head are on the—"

I don't give him a chance to finish. I've heard all I want to hear from him. Standing from my seat with the smoking gun still in my hand, I mutter to myself about having to clean up this mess.

"At least now there's silence, and the deal dies with you. If they don't know me, they won't be looking for me. One problem solved.

"Plan *B* is already working in my favor. Now, to get you cleaned up, or should I leave you for your housekeeper to find? Yes, I'll wipe all your cams and leave. That sounds best," I croon.

With that, I get to erasing all traces of my visit tonight. My phone pings in my pocket. I take it out and smile when I see the notification to let me know my gift for Aaron will arrive first thing in the morning.

I'm not going to punish the brat for his mother not inviting me to the party. She can't erase me from the boy's life. I was there from the beginning, no matter how hard Zah tried to make that.

"Don't worry, son. Daddy isn't going to let them take you from me. We'll be together."

Bentley

I lean in the entryway of the living room with a smile on my face and my arms folded across my chest, watching my little family. Zahirah and Aaron are knocked out. They're on the couch, fast asleep, Aaron resting on his mother's chest.

I guess the party wore them both out. My heart swells from the perfect picture they make. I've been in my feelings all day.

Watching my son's happiness brought me a kind of joy I can't even explain. Seeing all our friends and family who love him celebrating with him was another level of joy.

"That has to feel good," Garret murmurs as he appears at my side and nods his head toward my girl and my son.

"Yeah, it does," I say then gesture with my head for him to follow me.

Aaron might not wake, but we could wake Zah. I don't want to disturb them. Zah deserves the rest. That was one hell of a kiddie party.

"This all looks good on you. Are you ready for this new team?"

"Yeah, I'm going to dig into this new playbook first thing tomorrow. How's the house hunting going?"

"I'll have a few lots for you to check out this week. A new build seems like your best option. I know you want to be settled before the season starts, but nothing out there fits the checklist you gave me.

"Between me and Sarah, we'll make sure the house is done. I mean, it will give Zah a chance to give her input and put her stamp on it since you are technically buying it for her."

"Fair point. Speaking of Sarah—"

"She arrives in the morning. The movers already took care of her place. She just has to turn the key and enter. She'll be back to work by Tuesday."

"Thanks for all you do, man. I couldn't have done any of this without you."

"Are you kidding me? My big brother is Bentley Coswell. Bro, I have the best job in the world and got a degree out of it."

I breathe a quick chuckle. "But I still want to say thanks. I appreciate you."

"I appreciate you more. You know, I didn't want to go to college because I had no idea what I wanted to do. Enlisting seemed like I wouldn't have to make a choice.

"Losing Dad and seeing that you needed me changed all that. It gave me purpose. I'm meant to have your back.

"You don't need to thank me. There's nowhere else and nothing else I'd rather be doing," he says and pats me on the back.

"I love you, man."

"I love you too. I'm glad I showed up when I did. I needed you as much as you needed me."

"Yeah." I nod my head as I think on that. "You want a beer?"

"Sure. You want me to help you get them to bed first?"

"Yeah, that would be cool. Thanks."

"Anytime. I've got you."

CHAPTER THIRTY-SEVEN

What I do

Bentley

I find Zah sitting on the couch in her little office. I walk over with my tablet in my hand and place my free hand on her shoulder. She looks up from her laptop and smiles.

I gesture with my head for her to scoot out of the way so I can climb behind her to sit with her. She makes room for me, and I settle into place. I've been going through the new playbook and some film Coach wants me to look over.

"Where's Aaron?" I ask as she gets comfortable between my legs with her back pressed against my chest.

"Tara and Eddy came by to pick him up. Something about a movie date. Code for they and your mother want to spoil him some more and my mom most likely will be there to help," she laughs.

I join her laughter as I glance at her computer screen. She has a few tabs open to what look like bank accounts and social media dashboards. Seeing the balance in the accounts, my brows shoot up.

"What are you up to?"

"Just looking through my finances to see what's happening and trying to figure out my next pivot. The travel vlogs are drying up without new content.

"It's not as easy to up and go with a baby. I had enough in the bank to take a break after having Aaron, but I think it's time I get back at it. Not travel vlogging, but I need to find something else to do to keep my income flowing," she replies.

"Wait, that's from your vlogs?"

"Yeah, my channels were pretty popular. I did well for myself."

I snort. "Well for yourself? Baby, I'm taking Aaron, and I want child support. I can stop punishing my body," I tease.

"Ha, you're not even built like that." She laughs.

"Have you thought about getting back into sports?"

"Sometimes. The stats on sports channels have been enticing. I would love to start a sports podcast. I just haven't come up with an angle or concept yet."

"How about a podcast with your professional QB boyfriend? We could name it something corny but catchy, like Running the Touchdown. We could give advice on how to stay in a competitive space, working through the challenges of injuries, tell old college competition stories. I don't know, we can brainstorm a bunch of shit," I offer.

"Really? Do you have time for that?"

"I'll make time. You can work with Sarah to sync our schedules. It will be fun."

"You know, I wasn't sure about her when I first met her. She's growing on me though."

I kiss the top of her head. I've noticed that the two have been cautious around each other. I trust Sarah. Garret trusts her too.

Give it some time, I think the two will be good friends. Sarah already knows Zah and my son come first. She's not going to do anything to ruin this for me.

"What makes you say that?"

"She didn't give off vibes like she wanted me around in Vegas," she says.

"I think she was being protective of me. We've developed a brother-sister relationship over the years. I'm glad Garret brought her onto the team."

"Why a female? If you don't mind me asking."

"I had a male first. One of the tasks I ask of my assistant is to keep the groupies away and make sure no one breaches security to hide in my hotel rooms and shit like that. Dude was allowing girls to get right by him in hopes he could get the leftovers when I turned them down.

"He was a liability. I fired him and told Garret to find someone who could do the job properly. That's when he found Sarah. She's been with me ever since. Never a problem out of her."

"That makes sense. I'm glad Garret has been there for you. Sounds like he's really had your back."

"He has. So, Running the Touchdown? You and me, a podcast?"

"I like the name, by the way. Let me do some research and think about it. I'll have my people call your people."

I laugh. "Or you could be a stay-at-home mom. That way, you can sit on that fortune you have there, and I'll handle everything you need.

"I've been meaning to add you to my accounts. We can log in and see if we can do that now. Take all the time you want on what you want to do next."

"Now that sounds like the Bentley Coswell I know. Child support," she snorts and laughs at my earlier joke.

She cranes her neck to look back at me and pulls a face. I lean in and capture her lips. She and Aaron are already set for life, even if she didn't have all that money of her own.

My little family will never want for anything. However, I have to admit, I love the idea of us having a podcast together. I think it's going to be fun.

Zahirah

Standing in the kitchen, the aroma of sautéing onions and peppers fills the air. I'm getting dinner ready for tonight. I've been in my thoughts all day after Bentley offered to start a podcast with me.

I love the idea. It's pure gold. The only reason I didn't say yes right away is because I don't want to do anything that will cause conflict in our relationship.

Couples who open their lives to social media usually open themselves up to a whole lot of madness. People feel entitled to the details of their lives. I don't know if I want that.

"You've been lost in thought since I arrived here. What's going on with you?" Erica asks from her perch at the kitchen island.

She dropped in as Bentley was heading out to the gym. It feels like forever since the last time the two of us hung out. Although I know it was sometime last week.

"Just thinking about a talk I had with your brother."

She groans. "What did Big Head do now? Do I need to kick his ass?"

I laugh and shake my head. I love how hard Erica is always willing to go for me. It warms my heart to know she always has my back, no matter what.

"No. He didn't do anything bad. He actually made a really sweet offer."

"Oh yeah? Is he trying to knock you up again?"

I snort and roll my eyes. "Not that kind of offer. I think it's time I get back to work. I was thinking about my options since I'm not going to be traveling like I used to anytime soon. Bent offered to do a sports podcast with me."

Her face lights up and I can feel the excitement that bursts from her. I think I felt the same way when he made me the offer. I shouldn't be surprised, but it's such an amazing and thoughtful offer—I'm still a little stunned.

"Oh my God. I would freaking love that. You two can be so funny to listen to at times and your chemistry is amazing.

"I think that's a great idea. What's holding you back? I would totally come on to produce the show if you guys need help," she gushes.

I have to admit, her excitement is making me more excited about the idea. I'm truly considering whether we should and could pull this off.

However, I pump my brakes as my reasons for being reluctant begin to push their way to the surface. I have to remain grounded when it comes to the repercussions that could come from this. Our real lives come first and so does our son.

"I don't know. Look at all the content creators who have been couples. It rarely ends well for their relationships.

"How do we do this and not risk our relationship? Let's be honest, Bentley Coswell is a huge household name. This is going to blow up if we do this."

"All the more reason to do it," Erica says as she looks at me pointedly.

"I love him for making the offer, but will it work out? The last thing we need is more drama. I don't want to lose any more time with him."

Erica sighs and combs her hand through the front of her hair. She takes a moment as if she's thinking over what I've said. I begin to add the meat to the pan with the onions and peppers as I wait for her to say what's on her mind.

"First, since when do you ever do anything scared? Second, the way my brother loves you, that podcast would be canceled and forgotten before you could think about packing your bags or breaking up with him.

"Besides, you have me. I'm not allowing some trolls who don't know a thing about my brother or my bestie to break them up with comments, DMs, or gossip-rag bullshit. Do the podcast, Zah.

"Fuck them people. Get your money and allow my brother to do something totally cute and romantic for you. So what's our new podcast called?"

I laugh and smile at her. She's made a ton of good points. I do want to do this.

"He suggested Running the Touchdown. So stinking cute if you ask me," I say excitedly.

"Oh, I love that." She clicks away at her phone for a few moments then looks up at me and smiles. "Done, I bought the domain name. Let's get this thing started."

I clap my hands and lift my shoulders to my ears happily. This is really happening. I'm going to start a podcast with Bentley Coswell.

We'll have something new to build together. I already have so many ideas. This is going to be awesome.

I love my life.

CHAPTER THIRTY-EIGHT

Episode One

Zahirah

Six months later ...

"How's it going, everyone? I'm Bentley Coswell and I'm here on this podcast with my beautiful partner in life, former all-American track star and swimmer, Zahirah Nickels. If you don't already know, I'm the starting QB for—"

"Bent, I don't think there's a person in the world who doesn't know who you are or what team you play for," I laugh.

He gives me an adorable smile. I'm excited and super nervous. I can't believe we're recording our first episode. Erica did her thing on marketing and promoting and helping me to get everything set up for audio and visual.

"I never assume people know who I am. I'm trying to remain humble, baby," he chuckles.

"Babe, the last time you tried to come grocery shopping with me, I had to finish shopping alone, pay for everything, and still ended up waiting in the car for like an hour while you were signing autographs.

"The only reason we left when we did is because the baby started to scream his head off because he was over it. Who doesn't know who?"

"Fair point. Sometimes it's hard to get fans to understand you're with your family, trying to do the everyday stuff they're doing without being stopped for pics and autographs."

"This is true. I honestly believe they're too excited to think about that in the presence of their idols or someone they respect and look up to."

"I get that. That's why I try to be polite and honor their requests."

"Have you found a way to create balance?"

"Ten years in and I'm still learning. Nowadays, you and our son come first. It broke my heart when I saw our son crying because he had to wait.

"I vowed then and there to find a way to create boundaries. So guys, if I beg off and can't take a pic or sign something, just know my little guy is probably nearby waiting for me. All I ask is that the fans respect that, you know?"

"Yeah, I get it. I also love that your assistant started to give out cards with an email address to request signed photos when you can't take the time. That's so cool."

"She also keeps a stash of autographed photos to hand out. Sometimes there's time for her and Garret to take care of you guys while I keep moving and sometimes there isn't. We do try."

"Speaking of signed things. I thought it would be cool to do a giveaway with some signed swag from you. If you're watching or listening to this, go on and like, share, comment, and subscribe. We're going to pick a few lucky winners."

"Baby, do you miss it? I know I miss being at your meets watching you compete. Guys, look up Zahirah Nickels and track. My girl was something else.

"I was there when a knee injury ended her career after an epic finish for the win." He releases a whistle. "Pure magic. If I had your speed, I'd be a running back or something."

"Nah, you were meant to be a QB. As for missing the track. Yeah, I do. I miss being able to compete most of all. I thought about getting back into competitive swimming when I realized I wouldn't be able to run anymore."

"Really? I didn't know that."

"You weren't really around during that time. You might have been ... I don't know, starting your rookie season and all that."

"Why didn't you follow through?"

"My bestie asked me to travel the world with her. At the time, that felt like the right thing to do. One thing led to another, and I began a travel vlog. Turned out to be the thing for me."

"My girl might be the go-to when it comes to planning a vacation and getting the hookup on all the best spots. We'll link the channel and all her info for you guys to check out," he says.

I lift a brow at him. He returns the look with a smile and a shrug. I hadn't planned to mention the other platform.

"I don't think I was supposed to say that, guys, but I believe if you work hard, you play harder. Those of you out there working hard at your sport should take the time to kick back and have fun. Zah can help you do that with her travel vlog.

"It used to ground me during the season after a game. I would watch and feel like I was right there with her. Football can get intense. Being able to get away in my head like that did a lot for me," he says.

I sit with my mouth hanging open. I didn't know he used to watch my vlogs. Bentley takes in my surprised look and winks at me.

"The season is almost over. Do you want to take the baby and head out somewhere? You can get some new content for the channel."

"Are you serious?"

"Yeah, start planning something. I'm open to wherever you want to go. AC can go on his first trip out of the country."

"Auntie E is coming," Erica sings from behind the scenes, causing me and Bentley to laugh.

"That's my little sister, Erica, guys. She and Zah have been best friends since they were little. We all grew up together. I couldn't have chosen to do this with two better people.

"I remember being six and these two on the sideline wearing jerseys with my number. Our dads had them on their shoulders while they were cheering me on."

"You remember that?"

"Yeah, of course. I remember because our dads had to hold on to you because you would run the sideline like you and me were racing. I'd get so pissed and be focused on trying to beat you instead of playing the game."

I burst into laughter. "Okay, I do remember that. I also remember standing down by the end zone waiting for you after I beat you there."

"Doing that stupid little dance. God, I hated your little ass," he teases.

I laugh so hard I'm in tears. Bentley looks at me lovingly and shakes his head. I wipe away my tears and smile at him.

"I made you a better running quarterback. I think I deserve some type of gratitude, buddy."

"You know, I knew you were my biggest cheerleader when you ran onto the field to chest bump me at my first junior varsity game in junior high. I think that was when I started falling in love with you," he says.

"I knew I loved you long before that, but you completely stole my heart when you got the entire football team to show up for my first junior high track meet to cheer me on."

"Oh," he croons and pulls a hand down his face. "I totally remember that one. I did it because of that junior varsity game.

"I wanted you to feel how I felt when you ran out on that field. You were like a bullet. You have no idea how many of the guys on the team I had to threaten after that.

"They all wanted to ask you out. I wasn't having it. Damn, I got into a lot of fights over you."

"Seriously?"

"Zah, you have no clue how long I had a thing for you."

I blush and duck my head. I'm learning a lot today. Remembering this isn't just an video recording, I clear my throat and think fast so we don't have dead air.

"I think this would be a great time to take a few calls," I say.

"Let's go. I'm here for it. Come on, guys, call in. I want to hear from you. Arizona, we're on our way to the championship.

"Hopefully by the next episode, I'll have that ring with my home team."

I can't help smiling as I think of his reason for playing his ass off this season. He's been killing it in the playoffs. I'm so proud of him.

"We have Amy on the line," Erica says.

"Hello, Amy," Bentley and I say.

"Hey, guys. First, I want to say I'm loving this. I'm a huge Bentley Coswell fan. I've been following him since his college career.

"This is so cool because other than that psycho who was lying about her relationship with Bent, we've never heard anything about his love life. Bent, you've always been so private.

"I love hearing about your family and you two are so stinking cute. Bent, you sound like you're totally in love. No wonder we're about to win the championship."

"Thanks for the support, Amy. That means a lot to me," Bentley says.

"I do have a question for you. Do you feel like Zah and your son are the reason for this season's amazing success, or does it have something to do with coming home?"

"It has everything to do with Zah and my boy. It also has a lot to do with coming home because this is where my family is. I couldn't do this without them. This ring will mean so much more than any of the others."

"I love it. Keep it coming, guys. Zahirah, I'm going to look up your tape as soon as I get home."

"Thanks, Amy," I sing.

"Don't forget to like and subscribe, sweetheart," Bentley says.

"I already have. Thanks, guys. Love you, Bent, bring it home."

"We have JoAnn next," Erica says.

"Hey, JoAnn," we greet.

"Hey, guys. So I actually know of Zahirah. She kicked my sister's ass a few times back in the day. I mean, damn, honey. You're fast as hell."

"I'm so sorry to hear about your injury. You had so much potential to go so far. It's good to see you've landed on your feet.

"I did want to ask, how old is you guys' little one?"

"He's one," Bentley says.

"Going on thirty," I add.

"Oh, they are so sweet at this age. Bless you guys."

"Thanks for checking in, JoAnn."

"Anytime, guys. You have a fan in me. Good luck, Bent. My household is rooting for you."

"We have Haydon and Litia calling in as a couple," Erica says.

"Hey guys, what's up?" Bentley says.

"Hey there. This is so cute. I wanted to say thank you, Bentley. Haydon and I have gotten things signed by you a few times and a few pics. You were so kind each time," Litia says.

"Man, Coswell. You got a pretty little thing there. Do you guys work out together as a couple?"

Bentley scoffs, trying and almost failing to school his face. I run my finger down my nose, giving him the signal we came up with to let the other know to be patient.

"Nah, I get my workout in at the facility. Zah has her own routine."

"Yeah, it's called running after a one-year-old," I laugh.

"I hear you there, honey," Litia says. "You guys said your trip will be the little guy's first trip out of the country. Does that mean he goes with Daddy to away games?"

Bentley looks at me apologetically. I think we said too much. We both agreed not to mention Aaron's real name or reveal any images of him.

We also want to limit the information we share about him. Those are our hard limits for this. I guess we both got a little too comfortable talking to each other.

I wink at Bentley to let him know I'm okay. We'll just have to be more careful in the future. Bentley nods and returns the wink.

"Right now, he's still so young and gets fussy when we travel. Going with Bent to away games is a huge challenge. His dad is usually focused on the game and doing his job anyway.

"Besides, he loves watching the game from home with his aunts and uncles. He doesn't quite understand what all the excitement is about, but he loves being a part of it," I reply.

Bentley mouths *thank you*. I smile and we finish the call with Haydon and Litia. Bentley signals to Erica that we'll take one more call.

"We have GM," she says as she queues the next call.

"Hey, GM," I say and make a face at Bentley.

He shrugs his shoulders and sits back in his chair. I grab my water bottle to take a sip as we wait for GM to reply. I'm not expecting the voice that comes through.

"Zah, Coswell. I find your little podcast to be so funny. Aren't you a cute little family now. Why not tell your new listeners and viewers all about how you two just got back together since Zah was already engaged to another man last year?"

Bentley holds his hand up as I go to reply. My nostrils flare as I feel like steam is coming out of my ears. I can't believe Gilbert is doing this.

"Ah, Gilbert. I thought you were smarter than this. Do you really want to have this out over a recorded medium?"

"I only want the truth to be out there."

"The truth? Whose truth? The actual truth or your delusion. I'm only asking so I know where we're going here? I want to make sure my lawyers hit you for the right offense."

"You can't come for me for the truth. Zahirah was engaged. In fact, you showed up the day before her wedding and crashed her wedding rehearsal dinner."

"Bro, you trapped her into a fake engagement to help you secure your inheritance. She thought she was helping a friend," Bentley explodes.

"So you admit it. That's all I needed."

"Fuck you."

"We should talk sometime, Zah. I have a lot more I'd like to say. I'd also love to see Aaron. I miss him."

"Stay. The. Fuck. Away. From my family. I'm warning you, Manning," Bentley growls.

Erica cuts the call. I feel like I'm going to be sick. What the fuck just happened?

"So that was a fun episode," I joke.

"I'm sorry, guys. I don't play about my woman or my family. I will go through the proper channels to deal with that asshole.

"Zah is an amazing mother and partner. She has a huge heart and tried to help someone she thought was a friend. He took advantage and now we're here."

"I'm sorry, guys. I'll do better at screening the calls," Erica says.

"It's not your fault. Thank you, everyone, for listening and watching. We hope you come back and join us in the future.

"Hug your loved ones and be good to them. From Zah and me, y'all be blessed," Bentley says, ending the podcast.

I sit with my palms flat against the table as I try to wrap my head around what just happened. That's exactly what I didn't want. That asshole even said my son's name, which I know he did on purpose.

I have no idea what his endgame is. I don't want him and never did. He's acting like we were in a real relationship.

"I tried to drop him; the controls locked up on me. Sorry, guys," Erica says, breaking into my spiraling thoughts.

"Don't worry about it. I'll take care of him."

"Yeah, but what did that just do to our podcast? Erica and I put in so much work to do this," I say as I snap out of shock.

"I'll work on damage control," Garret says as he enters the studio we're in.

"I'm not going to lie. He might have done you guys a favor," Erica says. "People love drama."

I groan. "Ugh, that's not what we wanted. That's exactly what we didn't want."

Bentley stands and comes to pull me up from my chair. He hugs me tight and kisses the top of my head. I wrap my arms around him and melt into the comfort of his embrace.

"Babe, we did good. That might have been a tiny setback, but we'll roll with it, together. I'm here, you're here.

"We're going to make this awesome. A few tweaks and we've got this. Just remember how much I love you and that I've always got you, promise."

Gilbert

At this point, I don't give a fuck anymore. Coswell doesn't get to have a happily ever after with my woman and start a fucking podcast about it. I probably shouldn't have called in, but fuck it.

At least everyone will know what kind of woman she is. Let's see how everyone feels about their fiancé-stealing golden boy now. I hope he's canceled and gets benched before the big game.

"Hello," I answer my phone as it rings on my desk.

"We need to talk," my uncle growls on the other end.

"What about?"

"Have you lost your mind? What the fuck are you thinking? If your grandmother finds out what I just heard, you're finished. She isn't going to give you shit.

"She liked that girl and was devastated that you two didn't get married. She's been talking about putting a trust in the kid's name. Is he even yours, Gilbert?"

"I appreciate your concern, Uncle Theo. Grandmother isn't going to be a problem. She's not going to find out," I say dryly.

"I wouldn't be so sure about that. You're fucking up, Gil. There are some people who have been asking around about you.

They want to know what happened between you and Hamilton. Where's Hamilton, Gilbert?"

I work my jaw as I can't answer that question even if I wanted to. The news never reported the discovery of his body. I've been waiting, yet nothing has come to light. I refuse to return to the scene of the crime.

"I have no idea what you're talking about," I grumble.

"Yeah, sure. Listen, I don't care if you receive your inheritance or not. My brother would have wanted you to, so I'm trying to look out for you here.

"I'm warning you, you're about to fuck it all up. Fix your shit." He hangs up without another word.

I drop the phone on the desk and glare at it. Hamilton said he didn't mention me. Why the fuck are people looking for me and asking about him?

Better yet, where the fuck is Hamilton's body? Why didn't the housekeeper report finding him? I don't have time for this bullshit.

"Maybe it's time I get grandmother to take another trip," I muse.

I'm not against her leaving Aaron a trust. My boy will be my ticket one way or another. This might work out in my favor after all.

"Now this I can work with," I say and nod at my thoughts.

CHAPTER THIRTY-NINE

For the Win

Bentley

A month later ...

My hair is soaked under my helmet and sweat's dripping down the bridge of my nose. Adrenaline is pumping through me like crazy. My veins are buzzing with excitement and anticipation.

We're so close. The score is 24–28. We need to get this touchdown. They've been on our asses all game. My team is playing hard, and the defense has really shown up, but so has theirs.

However, I'm playing for something. I'm going to win this game for Zah and Aaron. I want us to grow our family.

I'm not losing that bet. When I walk off this field, I'm leaving with something. Zahirah might as well start picking out baby names.

"Come on, Coswell. We've got this. We're so close. There's enough time on the clock to take this home," Coach says.

It's the fourth quarter. There're still two minutes on the clock and we have both of our time-outs left. There're eighty yards to go, but my best receiver has gone down.

However, I still have my tight end and our running back, Jenkins, can catch it out the backfield. We have a real shot at this.

Everyone pats me on the helmet and back as I head back out onto the field into the huddle. I have tunnel vision. We've come too far to let this slip through our fingers.

"Blue, eighty-two, set, hut, hut."

I drop back as I see the blitz heading for me. The pocket is collapsing faster than I'd like. I roll out to the left and go with my legs. My guys block for me and I pick up the first down.

"Let's go, let's go," I call out as I rush to the line of scrimmage.

We need to keep this thing moving. I keep my eye on the play clock as I read the defense. I notice their safety coming in toward the line of scrimmage, which tells me I can throw a seam pass to my tight end.

I call an audible for a go route. The ball is snapped, and I drop back once again. The safety goes for the blitz just as I thought.

I look over the middle, and my tight end is wide open. I throw a bullet pass and hit Miller right in the hands. He takes off and makes it to the other team's thirty-yard line. We're ten yards out from the red zone.

"Fuck yeah," I fist pump the air.

Immediately, I call a time-out with fifty seconds left on the clock. I run to the sideline to get the next call. I can taste this win in the air.

"Okay, we have one time-out left. That means we can take another shot in the middle of the field to get deeper in the red zone," Coach barks out.

"All right, I noticed their linebackers are gassed. Let's try a swing pass toward the sideline to Jenkins. Dude, you catch it and get as many yards as you can then get out of bounds, bro."

"I got you," Jenkins says.

The time-out ends, and we head back onto the field. This is it. All I can think about is stopping the clock and getting this touchdown.

I drop back and look to my left. Quickly, I turn right and throw the ball to Jenkins. Jenkins catches the ball in space, planting his feet. Then he runs, avoiding one defender with a juke move. He runs and gets tackled by a linebacker in bounds after a twenty-yard gain.

We're now at the ten-yard line. I immediately call a time-out with ten seconds left. The stadium goes nuts. They're so loud I can feel it in my chest.

I don't have time to stop and take it all in. I get back to the sideline with my team. We have one more play. It's all or nothing.

"This is it. I don't have to tell y'all what this means. We have one play to get this done. Coswell, they're expecting you to throw to Miller and they're going to lock Jenkins down," Coach says.

"Let's use a pump fake to Stern. I'll take it in myself. Lattimore and Corby, you guys cover my ass. Darity, if I need it, you give a little push. We've got this."

"Nice, Coswell. A fake scene bootleg. I like it." Coach nods.

Me and the guys make our way out to the line of scrimmage. Getting into formation, I then get under center and give the signal call. I put Lattimore in motion toward Stern. Once Lattimore reaches Stern, he sets his feet and looks toward the end zone.

I look over the linebackers in the middle of the field then call a fake audible. This causes them and the safety to shift over to Stern and Lattimore.

I call a hike, drop back, then pump fake toward the scene. I roll out to the left side with no defenders in sight. I run as fast as I can. All I see is the end zone.

As I get closer, I notice a defensive back charging toward me from the middle of the field. Darity comes from my blind side and blocks him at the one-yard line as I hurdle into the end zone.

I lie on my back, staring up at the sky. This one feels different. It's like I can feel my father looking down on me. I'm finally the man I know he would want me to be.

Overwhelmed with emotions, I allow my teammates to pick me up and lift me into the air. We won. I've got a ring with my home team.

"Yeah, Coswell. That's what the fuck I'm talking about," Darity croons as I'm placed back on my feet.

None of this feels real. I know I promised Zah I would do it, but standing here with the mission accomplished is surreal. I always get a high from a touchdown, but this one will forever have a special place in my heart.

Zahirah

"How does it feel to be the MVP?" I ask with a smile on my face as we step off the hotel elevator and head to our room.

I'm so proud of Bentley; he earned that MVP trophy. He played his ass off all season, but tonight. Tonight was something special.

That game-winning touchdown was perfection. I held my breath the entire time. I couldn't breathe until I saw Bentley walking to shake hands with the other team.

"My heart was in my throat while you just lay there after that touchdown. I thought something was wrong," I say as we enter our suite.

We're finally here after all the press and celebrating with his team. Mom has Aaron back home in Arizona. I had a feeling my man was going to bring home the chip, and I would have to make good on our bet.

I have a little surprise for him tonight. We've come a long way in the last seven months. Our therapist has praised us on our progress repeatedly.

I'm proud of us too. We're able to communicate so much more effectively. If there's a challenge, we talk it out.

Bentley shows up for me day in and day out. I couldn't ask for a better partner. I know if we had to go through everything we went through in college now, we'd come out of it a lot different today.

"I had a moment. This one wasn't like all the others. I know Dad is always with me, but this time it felt like he was smiling down on me. I can't explain it, but I felt it," he says.

"I know he's proud of you. You played your heart out."

He tugs me into him and captures my lips in a searing kiss. I moan into his mouth as I wrap my arms around his neck. The amount of passion he kisses me with takes my breath away.

"I had something to play for. I love you so much," he breathes when he breaks the kiss.

"Is that right? What exactly did you have to play for?"

He growls into my neck and nips at my skin. Goose bumps rise and a chill runs through me. I can feel how hard he is as he pulls my body into his.

"You know what I was playing for. I'm not allowing you to back out of your promise, Zah. It's all I've been thinking about all day."

I laugh and shake my head. I'd be lying if I said I haven't been thinking about it too. I'm actually excited about trying for another baby.

Things will be so different this time. Bentley will be there with me, and our family will be a part of the entire process. I can never give them all back what they lost with Aaron, but this feels like something I need to do for our family and us.

"Is it okay if I take a shower?" I tease.

"Sure, take all the time you need. However, once I get my hands on you, you're mine for the rest of the night," he croons.

"Um, I'm not complaining at all. I love you. I'll be right back."

He dips his head and pecks my lips. Knowing if I stand here any longer, I'll never get to my surprise, I turn and head into the bedroom of the suite. Grabbing my bag, I then retrieve the little outfit I placed inside with tonight in mind.

I won't tell Bentley this, but I had decided I would let him get me pregnant again, whether he won or not. With a smile on my lips, I glide into the bathroom to freshen up. Game days can be superlong and exhausting.

This entire day was taxing, but I'm not going to allow that to ruin tonight. I make my way through a shower that does wonders to wake me up. Once out of the shower, I dress in the bra, panties, thigh highs, and garter set.

When I look in the mirror to take my scarf back off, I'm feeling myself. The knotless boho braids with the cornrows in the front look good on me. I figured they would be best for the busy weekend.

I flip them over to the left and smile at myself as I take one last once-over. I look sexy and happy. Swiping on some lip gloss to make my lips pop, I then head into the bedroom.

I turn on some music to play softly in the background. I made a little playlist before we flew out here. I've had this all planned out for weeks.

I climb onto the bed and settle into the middle of it. Leaning back on my palms, I push my breasts out and tilt my head to the side. I laugh to myself as anticipation buzzes through me.

"Hey, Bent, can you come here for a minute?" I call out.

It doesn't take long for him to appear in the doorway. His eyes fill with lust as he takes me in. He runs his hand through the front of his hair and licks his lips. My smile grows as he slowly saunters fully into the room.

"You look so fucking amazing, Zah. You drive me crazy. You know that, right?"

I bite my lip and nod as I look at him through my lashes. I was hoping this would be the response I would get. The look in his eyes says it all; he's going to fuck the shit out of me.

He unbuttons his shirt as he moves, tossing it to the floor as he gets to the foot of the bed. His jeans and socks are the next things to go. I sit watching this beautiful man bare himself to me.

His hard body is amazing. Airbrushing him couldn't make him more perfect. The definition and chisel of every muscle speak to his dedication.

He has a few bruises on his right side from the game. I pout a little, hating that he got hurt. Catching my gaze on the area, he looks down and shrugs.

"Hazards of the job. I'm all good, baby. Nothing is going to stop me from fucking you senseless tonight."

His words hit their mark. I begin to squirm on the bed as my juices start to flow. The hooded look on his face only turns me on more.

"Is that right?" I purr and spread my legs so he can see my panties are crotchless.

He groans and reaches for my ankles to drag me to him at the foot of the bed. I fall back with a little bounce. Once I'm where he wants me, he bends at the waist and leans in to devour me.

"Bentley," I cry out as he works that amazing mouth on me.

My panting, moaning, and keening almost drowns out the sound of Michelle Morrone crooning the lyrics to "Feel It". I bow off the bed, caving into myself as he consumes me.

"Oh God, yes," I moan.

He dives in deeper as he reaches up to palm one of my breasts. Adding two fingers to the mix, he pumps them in and out of me while he eats my pussy with determination. My body tightens as everything in me comes alive.

When he lifts his head to look down at my pussy, the look on his face is so sexy. It's as if he's in awe of the sight before him. He's looking down at me with so much lust and want.

I bite my lip, trying to wait him out. As if knowing I need him and can't wait much longer, he angles my body to the side then guides his length into me. I cry out in pleasure, matching the long, deep groan that falls from his lips.

Head thrown back, mouth open, hips thrusting, he makes a sight worth capturing. My pussy ripples around him as I take him in. I think I might come just from looking at him.

My toes curl and I fist the sheets. It's all I can do to keep from screaming out. He's so hard and deep.

He begins to rub my clit as he continues to thrust, swiveling his hips every few thrusts. I'm sobbing in pleasure at this point. The look of pleasure on his face is priceless.

He tugs the cup of my bra down and begins to play with my nipple. I'm so wet for him. The sound of my juices begins to compete with our loud moans.

"Fuck, baby. You feel so good. Your pussy is so wet."

"Only for you, babe. You make me feel so good. Please give me that hard dick."

His eyes light up and he pulls out. I keep my eyes on him as he climbs onto the bed while stroking himself, then lies on his back. He doesn't have to ask. I quickly move into position and take him into my mouth.

I hum as he slides against my tongue. Bent reaches for my braids to gather them in his hands and holds them up so he can watch me work. My mouth waters, helping to soak his shaft.

He begins to thrust his hips and fuck my mouth. I relax my throat and allow him to go deeper before I suction my cheeks and take back control.

"Fuck, baby. Yes," he grunts.

I wrap my hands around him and begin to stroke as I bob my head. He's getting harder by the second. The deeper I take him, the harder he gets.

"Come here, I want to feel that hot, tight pussy on me. Come fuck me, Zah."

I lift my head and smile at him. As I straddle him, he places his hands on my hips. I watch as he bites down on his lip while I seat myself. A look of love, hunger, and focus comes to his face.

Just when I think I'm going to ride him into next week, he plants his feet and takes over. I grab his hard biceps and let him fuck me as I hold on for all I'm worth. I'm breathless and coming all over him in no time.

"I love it when you come all over me like that," he growls and lifts me off his dick to place me beside him.

He shifts on the bed and turns me onto my stomach. Lifting my hips in the air, he enters me from behind. I bury my face in the sheets as he continues to fuck me.

Reaching beneath me, he bands his arm across my breasts and palms one in his hand. He uses that arm to tug me up against him, his hot breath fanning my shoulder as he pants and grunts. I'm so wet and he's so fucking hard.

"Bent, shit. I'm coming again, babe. You feel so good. Don't stop."

"You like that, baby? How do you want it?"

"I want it hard and nasty. Don't hold back. I can take it."

He groans. "I love it when you talk dirty to me. Knowing I'm the only one you've ever let inside you turns me on so much.

"That filthy mouth is all mine. The way you fuck, that's all for me. Zah, fuck, I'm going to come."

"Yes, that's how we're going to get our baby. Come for me, Bent. Let me give you another baby."

"Oh my God, oh my God. Baby, shit. Yes, milk my cock for that cum. Give me that shit. Give it to me now," he growls.

I begin to come so hard my sinuses start to burn. Bentley's hot seed spills into me, causing me to come again. He releases me and falls onto his side.

"You know that's not it," he says with a smile in his voice.

"Yeah, I know."

"Good girl," he croons and slaps my ass.

CHAPTER FORTY

Episode Two

Zahirah

"Hey everyone, we're back. This is Zahirah Nickels and I'm here with the MVP, QB Bentley Coswell, right off his champion win.

"Let's give it up for the man. Did you guys see that game-winning touchdown? You are totally amazing, babe, and I, for one, am totally proud of you," I gush into the microphone.

We're not in our home today. Bent said he wanted to try a new aesthetic for the podcast. He rented this place and had it set up for today's recording.

"It's good to be back. Even nicer to be back with another ring and the MVP trophy," Bentley says.

"Take us back to that moment. How did it feel to take the game-winning touchdown to the house?"

"I'll be honest with you guys. This one was different. If you have followed my career, you all know my father and Zahirah's dad were killed in a car accident a month before the draft. We're talking about two men I admired and respected deeply.

"They were at all my junior high and high school games and quite a lot of my college games. However, neither got the opportunity to see me play professionally.

"From the start of my career, the media didn't allow me to forget that they weren't there, which was harder than I let on to the world outside my close circle.

"I spent years trying to keep my head above it all. I've won championship games before, but this time … I don't know if it's because I play for Arizona or what, but that win was personal for me. I'm sorry," Bentley says as he begins to get choked up.

He clears his throat and continues. "I can best explain it as feeling whole this time around. The goal was before me and there wasn't any other option but to win."

"Well, you did that. At thirty-two, you now have three championship rings. What's next? How many more years do you think you have in you?"

"You know, when I'm in season and focused on the game, I don't feel any of the wear and tear the game puts on me. However, during the offseason, things that shouldn't begin to hurt," he chuckles. "It's only the beginning of the offseason and I think I'm starting to feel my age just a little."

I tilt my head at him and smile. He's been chasing me around every day trying to make a baby. I think that might have more to do with any aches and pains he might have, not the season.

"As for what's next, I want to enjoy my family. This place needs to be furnished and we're probably going to need to start looking at schools or decide if we want to homeschool.

"I'm leaning toward homeschooling. Our boy is so smart already. I don't want him to be bored in a classroom. Although there are some pretty elite options for us to choose from in the area.

"Sarah already has a list for us. I'm excited about spending time with you and the baby. I feel like I'm always on the run during the season," Bentley goes on.

I sit looking at him with my brows knit. He's just said several things that aren't adding up. He looks back at me with a huge smile on his face.

I open a chat box on my laptop and begin to type to ask him what's going on. He said he rented this place for the day. What does he mean we need to furnish it?

"Sounds like you're ready to get domestic," I say, so we don't have dead air.

"You have no idea. By the start of training camp, I'm hoping to have two under two. This new house I had built for you has more than enough room for the six kids you promised me."

"Bentley," I gasp. "Are you kidding me?"

"About what? Holding you to that promise of six kids or the fact that I had this place built for you."

I stare at him like he's crazy. From the time we pulled onto the property, I couldn't stop gushing about how gorgeous it is. Once inside, I was in awe.

Never once did I think this place was ours. I love my little two bedroom. I bought it with my own money for me and Aaron.

Since Bentley has been staying there with us, I haven't thought once about needing to move. We've become a family there. He had an entire house built just for me.

"First, babe. I'm not having five more babies. So I'm ignoring you and that comment. Second, you stinker. You said you rented this place to record today. This is our home?"

He winks at me. "It's about eleven years late but I finally did as I promised. Yeah, this is our home. I wanted to surprise you."

"Surprise," is cheered behind me.

I turn to find our family standing just off camera. My mother has a huge smile on her face. I sit frozen as I allow this information to sink in.

"Guys, I think I honestly surprised her. Let me know in the chat if you think she's surprised. Could I have done a better job?" Bentley croons.

"Oh my God. You're insane. I can't believe you did this, Bent.

"Thank you. I'm totally surprised. I'm blown away," I say as I tear up.

"Well, I have another surprise for our viewers. Garret dropped in with my new ring this morning. I realized I've never shown you the others. That got me thinking.

"Our viewers probably haven't seen a championship ring before. I figured, why not show you and them all three of mine," he says, pointing to the ring boxes he has set on the table.

"But you won three. There are four boxes there," I murmur.

"Open them up and show the camera," he says simply.

I open the first box and look at the ring. It's from the first year he won. I lift the box and allow the camera guy to zoom in on it. Then I close it and place it back down, opening the next one on the table.

This one is from the second championship he won. I show it to the camera too. Then I place it down and go for the third box on the table between us.

When I open it, I nearly melt right out of my seat. With shaky hands, I place it back down on the table and cover my mouth. It's not his newest ring. It's an engagement ring that's breathtaking.

Bentley has moved to kneel in front of me as I sit stunned. This has to be a dream I'm going to wake up from any minute now. Suddenly, it's like someone turned the heat on.

I'm sweating and the room feels so hot. The ring is absolutely stunning. The Asscher cut center diamond has to be over four carats. And it's surrounded by a halo of smaller diamonds.

"I promised we'd do the work together. If you don't think we're ready, don't hesitate to tell me no. I'll wait.

"But if you feel like you can trust me to always show up and be the man you need, I'd love for you to be my wife. It's always been you, Zah. Wanting to be a better man for you has made me the man I am today.

"I love you more than anything. Can you see yourself with me? Will you marry me, baby?" he says while holding my face between his palms as he's still on one knee.

"Yes, a million times yes. I love you too."

Our family cheers and claps behind us. I think I'm still in shock as he slides the ring on my finger. He tugs me up from my seat and pulls me to him for a searing kiss as he holds me tight.

"It's me and you, Zah. Nothing can take me away from you. I'm going to be here until the very end," he says into my ear.

"I'm holding you to that, Coswell."

"Please do, baby," he croons.

"Hey, guys. The chat is asking to see the ring," Erica says, reminding us we're still on air.

Oh my God, he just proposed to me live on the air. I shake my head. We're going to have to talk about what I meant about us not sharing too much of our personal relationship.

Right now, I'm too happy to care. I love this man and we're getting married. My little crush turned into the love of my life.

Who would have thought?

Gilbert

"That motherfucker." I seethe as I swipe my arm across the desk and knock everything to the floor.

My chest is heaving as I stand glaring at the laptop, now lying on its side across the room. I can't believe he proposed to her live on that piece-of-shit podcast. Even worse is how fast she said yes.

Was having a house built for her all I needed to do? I would have built her two. None of that matters now.

Everything is fucked. I had to drop my uncle and kill that old bag grandmother of mine, but not before I tortured her into signing everything over to me. The problem is, all the family assets were frozen the day after I buried the old bag.

I don't currently have the resources to find out why or how. I'm not supposed to have access to any of it yet, so I can't walk into the bank of the business and start asking questions until the documents I forced my grandmother to sign are filed.

"Everything is turning to shit," I roar.

I begin to pace as I try to figure my shit out. Not only do I need cash flow, but I also want to finish what I started. Coswell needs to pay.

I took Hamilton off the board too soon. He would have been helpful at the moment. Instead, I'm on this island hiding out with no answers.

I used the last of my money to bolt here. Other than the information I can get from the internet, I don't even know what's going on back home.

However, this—this bullshit Coswell has pulled, it's a sign I need to head back and handle some shit.

I get an idea and jump into action. Pulling my phone, I dial the one person who can help. I knew keeping her in my pocket would pay off someday.

"Hello, Gilbert. It's been a while. How are you?"

"Hey, Robin. I've been thinking about you a lot lately. I'm hoping you're not too busy."

"I'm on my way back to Arizona, but I need a favor. It's only a temporary ask. I have some big things in the works and can repay you after I arrive to see you."

"Oh, you're coming to see me? What do you need?"

I grin. That was too easy. I wonder what else I can get her to do.

CHAPTER FORTY-ONE

Looking Out

Bentley

A buzzing sound drags me from my sleep. Annoyed, I inhale a sharp breath and swipe at my face as if to knock the sleep away. As I begin to wake, I groan.

My phone is ringing, and I know it's not late enough for me to want to take a call. Aaron turns at my side and snuggles deeper into me. The last thing I remember is tucking him into me to get some more rest when Zah left this morning for a spa appointment.

It's my first day of truly not having anything to do with football, my team, or my career. No workouts, no meetings, no press, not a single endorsement or fundraiser. I'm officially in the offseason and I planned to sleep in until afternoon.

I'm not in the mood to talk to anyone. Realizing Zahirah isn't home and in bed with us, I pop up and answer the call. I would never forgive myself if she needed me and I didn't answer.

"Hello," I grumble.

"Coswell, it's Fred."

I knit my brows and fall back onto my pillow. Pushing a hand into my hair, I try to clear my head. I haven't spoken to Fred in nearly three years or longer.

"Fred, what's going on?" I say in confusion.

I haven't heard from him since I dismissed him and paid the final invoice. Once he told me Zah was engaged, I thought I could let her go. The best way to do that was to stop checking in on her life and having her tracked.

I've thought of how I regretted that decision after finding out about my son. If I hadn't called him off, he would have told me Zah was pregnant. All things of the past now. Nothing I can do about any of it.

We're moving into our new home, and we're engaged. I have everything I want. Life is going as it should.

"I know you terminated the job for Zahirah Nickels. I did stop monitoring her, but I had this gut feeling I couldn't shake. I stayed on that Manning motherfucker because he gave me bad vibes.

"I was right. I'm going to advise you to provide Miss Nickels with a security detail. Manning is extremely dangerous, and he's been targeting you folks with some type of vendetta.

"The bastard is sick. You should watch your back as well. I just thought you needed to know," he says.

I'm wide awake now. I sit up and swing my legs over the edge of the bed. I'll kill Manning if he tries some bullshit with Zah. A broken jaw will be the least of his worries.

Rage runs through me, causing my head to throb. I see red. Just when we're happy, and everything is going great, here this asshole comes. Not on my fucking watch.

I'll take Manning's head off. He hasn't even seen how bad my temper can get. I close my eyes and take a calming breath.

"Hold on, Fred. I need you to tell me exactly what's going on. Why do you think Zah isn't safe? What's Manning up to?"

I already know I'm not going to like whatever he has to say. I brace myself anyway. Gritting my teeth, I listen and allow him to explain.

He releases a heavy breath. "Like I said, I've been keeping an eye on him. He tried to murder his friend and left him for dead in his apartment. He would have died if I hadn't been on Manning's ass.

"I got into the apartment after Manning left and found the guy bleeding out. I got him to a buddy of mine in time to save his life.

"The guy asked me not to reveal he's still alive or his identity, so that's all I can tell you at the moment about that. However, he was very forthcoming with details of what Manning has been up to."

"Were you able to verify his story? Can you trust his word?" I quiz.

"I've verified every word. It all checks out. I wouldn't have called you if it didn't."

I nod my head as if he can see me. I had to ask and make sure. I know from experience people will bullshit you when they have a motive.

I try to figure out who this friend of Gilbert's could be. He didn't have a lot of close friends back in high school, maybe one or two who stuck around during college that I know of. Fred continues as my thoughts race to connect the dots.

"It seems he's wanted to get back at you for years. He's also wanted Miss Nickels for himself. He had been scheming to marry her for his inheritance, but he didn't plan on letting her out of the marriage once he got the money."

I scoff. "How the hell did he plan to pull that off?"

"The bastard is a lunatic. The feds are already on him, and some other nasty characters are hunting him down as we speak. I just don't want him to get to you guys before they get to him."

"Thanks for the heads-up, Fred. Are you available for the job?"

"I could be. I have a few guys I trust who I can bring in. From what I know, this guy has bodies on his hands. No one has heard from Christen Manning in weeks. His uncle, Theo Manning, is also missing. There's also information linking him to the murder and disappearance of his own father."

"What the fuck?"

"I'm telling you, this guy is unpredictable and highly dangerous."

"I'm going to text you Zah's current location. I want eyes on her as soon as you can," I bite out.

"I'm on it. Be safe, Coswell. Congrats on the chip."

With that, he hangs up, leaving me with my head spiraling. Snapping out of it, I quickly shoot off a text with Zah's location. I can't believe this shit.

Gilbert is fucking crazier than I thought. However, when it comes to my family, I can be crazy too. I'm not about to allow him to take everything from me.

I look at my sleeping son and my heart squeezes. Zah could be pregnant with our next child. My priority is to keep her safe.

I dial her number just to hear her voice and make sure she's okay. I don't want to alarm her, but I need to at least hear her. It only takes two rings before she picks up the line.

"Hey, babe. You guys finally up?" she sings.

"Hey, baby. I'm up. Aaron is still sleeping. I'm about to wake him and get us something to eat."

"Cool, I should be home soon. One of my services had to be canceled. You want me to pick anything up for you?"

"No, come straight home. Don't make any stops." I completely fail at keeping the panic out of my voice.

I glance at Aaron and think of getting dressed to go pick her up myself. However, as I think of the time it will take to get Aaron and me ready, I decide against it. Making her wait around for me could place her in danger.

"Is everything okay?"

"Yeah, everything is fine. I miss you and I want you home with me. You know what? I am concerned about you going out without security.

"With the podcast and all, I should be thinking about your safety more. I don't know why I didn't think of this sooner. Just come straight home, baby. We'll talk more then."

I'm becoming angry with myself. I really should have thought of giving Zah security sooner. She had been my own personal secret from the public until the podcast.

Now the world knows she's everything to me. I proposed before them all. I'm feeling like such an idiot.

"Okay, I'll call Erica and tell her not to meet me at the house. I had planned to go and pick a few things up."

"No, baby. Leave it for the movers. Anything you don't have, I'll replace it. Come home."

"I will … Bent, did something happen?"

"We'll talk when you get home. I promise. I love you."

"I love you too."

She hangs up and I sit staring at my phone. I text Fred to let him know she's on the move. I don't think I'm going to be able to relax until she gets home.

"Dada, water," Aaron says sleepily beside me.

I look at him and run a hand over his hair. He gives me a sleepy smile as he blinks up at me. I love his little face.

Being a father has become one of my greatest accomplishments. Seeing his smile and the trust in his eyes brings me so much happiness. God, I can't lose either of them.

Zahirah

My stomach has been in knots since I ended that call with Bentley. The spa I went to isn't that far from the new house, so I raced all the way home.

By the time I got home, Bentley had been coming out of the house still in his basketball shorts and tank top he slept in, looking as if he were about to jump in his car. He had Aaron in his arms, still in his pajamas.

A guy pulled up in a black sedan, not too long after me. He's a big guy with dark hair. Fred, that's who Bentley introduced him as.

"You have to be freaking kidding me," I breathe as I sit here listening to the story Fred just relayed to me.

"I wish I were. I got the call before I pulled up. If the authorities don't get to him first, he's going to meet up with some not-so-nice guys.

"However, he's in the wind. We know he's back in the country, but he gave everyone the slip moments after his arrival. As I told Coswell, it would be better to have you safe, so he doesn't get to you before someone gets to him," Fred says.

"Hold on, slow this crazy train down. Grandma Christen is dead? He killed his own grandmother?"

"And his uncle. He promised to pay a guy he got to help him with the bodies, but that backfired as the feds froze his family's assets after they dug into the information I tipped them off with.

"The guy didn't get the money, so he turned himself in and coughed up the details in exchange for a deal. He's escalating and leaving a trail in his wake," he says.

"It's Hamilton Deluca. That's who he tried to kill. That's who's feeding you information," Bentley says as realization lights his eyes.

"For the safety of everyone in this room, I won't confirm or deny that statement," Fred replies.

A knot forms in my throat. I try to swallow it down, but it doesn't work. I feel like I'm going to lose it any second now.

What does all of this mean? How could he have killed his grandmother? Why is he so hell-bent on destroying our lives?

A chill runs through me, causing me to feel ice cold. I allowed that man to manipulate me into being his fiancée. If Bentley didn't show up when he did, there's no telling what Gilbert would have done to me or my son.

I feel so stupid and violated. I thought he was my friend. I was trying to be a good friend to him.

I did care about his grandmother. She was always so nice to me. She loved Aaron.

I always felt so guilty for lying to her. I never did get to say sorry. Anger begins to boil up inside.

So many red flags are going off in my head now. Spain was never a coincidence. Gilbert knew I was there.

He had people watching me. Yes, Bentley had a PI looking for me too, but that was totally different. Gilbert had been doing some next-level stalker shit.

Erica and I were in danger from the time he conveniently ran into her in Spain. What kind of person comes up with an elaborate scheme like this? All because his jaw was broken in a high school fight.

"So I'm just supposed to live in fear while he's out there somewhere lurking like some psycho. All because Bent kicked his ass. Well, I have next.

"He was around my son with his crazy ass. I'm not about to allow him to hurt Aaron with his craziness," I growl.

"Baby, you don't have to live in fear. He's never going to get near you."

"After that call I received, I don't think either of you has anything to worry about. The feds are closing in, and his other problem knows that. They need to find him before he's in custody.

"I doubt they're going to fail. They happened to be highly motivated. Manning will be lucky to make it past the next forty-eight hours," Fred says.

"Then what do we do now?" I ask.

"We're staying in for the rest of the day. I want to give all the new security time to get in place and secure the property. Once they all coordinate, I'll feel better about you leaving the house, although I don't want you going anywhere without me," Bentley says.

"My head hurts. I'm going upstairs to lie down," I murmur.

Bentley pulls me into his arms and hugs me tightly. I try not to break down into tears. This is all so crazy and unsettling.

This morning, I was out getting a massage and relaxing, thinking about how great my life is and how happy I am. Now to come home to all of this.

I was being watched while in different countries. No telling if he was having me watched while I was in other states. I'm so creeped out right now.

Bentley gives me a squeeze and kisses the top of my head. I melt into him and take from the strength he's giving to me. I'm not going to allow Gilbert to take everything we've worked so hard for.

This isn't going to be the straw that breaks us. I get so mad as I think of someone trying to undo all the work we've done to get to this place of trust and love.

"It's going to be all right, Zah. I've got you and Aaron. Don't worry about that asshole."

"I'm here. I'm going to keep you safe. I love you," Bent says into my hair.

"I love you too."

"Go on upstairs. I'll be up in a minute. You want me to bring you something to eat?"

"No, I don't think I can stomach anything yet," I say as I shake my head.

CHAPTER FORTY-TWO

Best Revenge

Gilbert

I lie naked with only a sheet covering my waist as I stare up at the ceiling, plotting my next move. Robin might be useful for more than her money. Now that I'm thinking more clearly, I see all she has to offer in this situation.

As if reading my thoughts, she gets up from the bed, puts on a silk robe, and grabs her laptop. She comes to sit back on the bed with her back to the headboard. Reaching for one of her legs, I then run my fingertips up and down her soft skin.

"I'm so glad you're here," she says as she glances out the corner of her eye at me. "Who would have thought when I met you all those years ago, we'd keep in touch for so long."

I give her a smile. Little does she know, I planned that meeting after learning she was Zah's sophomore year roommate. I had tried to connect with the other roommate from her freshman year, but she brushed me off and didn't buy my charm like this one did.

I've had Robin in my pocket since that first run-in. That worked out in my favor as she's made quite the life for herself. Robin has gone into tech and built a multimillion-dollar company.

I've gotten her to fund a few things my family didn't need to know about. Getting her to help me sneak back into the country was like taking candy from a baby. Even now, she has stars in her eyes as she looks at me.

"It's good to see you too. Next time we shouldn't wait so long to get together."

"I've been so busy lately. This is the first time I'm getting to kick back. I barely have any time for a social life," she says as she clicks away on her keyboard.

I'm used to this. She's a workaholic computer geek. All the better for me as I'm able to get so much over her head. I don't have to put in much effort with her.

She talks a lot, but I ignore most of it as she has a habit of talking out loud to herself. I fuck her, give her a little attention and she's off like a little kitten. Whenever I need anything, I call, and she comes purring for a little more.

"Oh my God. This is so crazy," she gushes, suddenly pulsing with excitement.

"What's that?"

I look at her face to find it all lit up with joy. She's not a bad-looking woman. She had a glow-up after college. I'm actually curious as I wait for her to explain.

"It's my college roommate. I heard she started a podcast with her college boyfriend. They were such a cute couple. He just gave her a new house.

"Oh, he had it built for her. I knew he was always crazy about her. They were so in love back then.

"I felt like I was broken up with when they split. I was so heartbroken for both of them. Look, here's the last episode of their podcast. He proposed. I'm so happy for them," she rambles.

"Oh, congrats to them," I mutter.

"You have no idea how big a deal this is. He's actually Bentley Coswell. He just won the championship with the game-winning touchdown. That game was freaking amazing."

"I'm sure this is exciting for them. You want to get something to eat?"

"You still don't get it. Let me finish. Zah was a track star.

"I was there when she injured her knee and it ended her career. They went from the happiest couple in the world to ... they just fell apart."

"Robin."

She ignores me and continues. "First, her injury, then they both lost their dads in a car accident, then they broke up. Seeing them back together and engaged, that's so awesome."

"Robin, be quiet."

She sighs dreamily. "I spoke to Zah not too long ago. She sent me a pic of their son. He's so adorable. They should absolutely have more bab—"

"Shut up. Shut the fuck up," I snarl with my hands around her neck.

"Gil, stop, I can't breathe," she pushes out.

She's clawing at my hands, trying to pry me off her. I straddle her body and keep tightening my hold, refusing to release my grasp. Her face turns red, and her eyes widen.

"I told you to shut the fuck up. I don't want to hear about Zahirah and Bentley Coswell. I don't want to think about him with his hands on her, you stupid cunt," I snarl in her face.

I snap out of my rage as she stops struggling. Looking down at her lifeless body, I frown. She wouldn't shut the fuck up and I lost it. It wasn't just the talking.

It was the subject. She kept going on and on about Zah and Coswell. Gushing over him giving Zah that house and proposing.

The last straw was when she suggested the two would have more babies together. That's the last thing I want to hear.

"Shit, fuck, fuck, shit," I groan.

I wasn't done with her. I needed her help to find out why my assets are frozen. She wouldn't have questioned why I didn't just call the bank and find out for myself.

Suddenly, the sound of someone slow clapping pulls my focus. It's not Robin. Her eyes are vacant, and her chest isn't moving. Besides, the sound is coming from behind me.

"Would you look at this. Nothing has changed with you, old friend. Still leaving a trail of bodies. You might want to make sure this one is dead before you cut out this time."

I jump from the bed to my feet. My mouth falls open as I look at Hamilton glaring back at me. No wonder there was never any news of his body being found.

"Why, Gilbert, you look like you've seen a ghost. You're so pale. What's the matter? Aren't you happy to see me?"

"Ho ... how are you still alive? How are you here?"

"Patience, my friend. One question at a time. I'm alive because someone found me before I bled out, saving my life. Next time, I suggest you go for the head or heart or something with a better rate of success."

"Someone found you alive? Who?"

"You don't need to know that. You'll never have to worry about them. Now to answer your other question. How am I here?"

"You had a habit of telling me too much. All the details of your plans. The pawns you kept in your back pocket.

"It didn't take me long to figure out Robin would be your ace for getting back in the country and moving around to get back to Arizona.

"Once I found out she had a property here, I knew exactly where we would find you. So predictable." He clicks his tongue and sighs.

"What do you mean where *we* would find you?"

"Oh, you still think you're off the hook? News flash, Gilbert. I'm not dead. I also no longer have any reason to protect you or cover for you.

"You still owe, and my partners plan to collect. It was in my best interest to help them find you. You're about to learn what it looks like to do a job and make sure it's done."

I scoff. "Hamilton, this was all a misunderstanding. I wasn't thinking that night. I panicked and overreacted. Why do you think I didn't try to dispose of your body?" I say.

"Bullshit," he bellows. "You thought killing me would get you off the hook and you'd be able to walk away scot-free. You overplayed your hand, bro. Now you're going to pay."

"You don't want to do this. I got the money. I just need to figure out why the accounts are frozen.

"Then I can pay the money. We'll all walk away the way we planned," I say.

"Fuck you, asshole. Me, I'm the reason your shit is frozen, you dumb fuck. I made sure the feds had the right information to start digging into you and your family. You're fucked, Gil. No matter what, you're fucked."

"The feds? But—"

"Trust me, I won't be implicated in anything you've done. I've known for years you'd stab me in my back one of these days. I've been building my get-out-of-jail-free card all this time.

"Although they're not going to find you in time. You're not going to jail. You don't deserve that mercy," he seethes.

"How much do you want? Help me clean this mess up and we can undo whatever you've done and split the money," I say.

Hamilton throws his head back and laughs. "There's nothing you can pay me even if I wanted to help turn this around. You're done, Manning.

"You tried to fuck over the wrong people. Your money isn't going to save you from this. I wish you could see your face right now.

"How does it feel to know you're never going to get your revenge on Coswell? He has the money, the girl, and the dream. You have nothing," he chuckles and wipes the back of his hand across his mouth.

I glance out of the corner of my eye to where my bag is. My gun is inside. I think over my options.

"Do you mind if I put some pants on for this conversation?"

"Please do. I see the rumors were true. No wonder you've always led with your family's wealth.

"Damn, so much is starting to make sense. Shit, that's fucked up. That was her last dick before she died." He nods at Robin.

He snorts. "I wouldn't take Zah's rejection too hard if I were you. I was on the football team.

"Coswell makes your shit look like a Tic Tac. Sucks for you," he roars with laughter.

I frown and grind my teeth. However, I allow him his laugh as I move to grab my pants. I'll have the last laugh when I blow his fucking head off.

I fake like I'm going to grab my pants, but reach for the handle of my gun in my bag instead. However, before I can turn and fire, the sound of a gun goes off, and I know it's not mine. Suddenly, I feel a burning sensation tearing through my shoulder.

"You caught me by surprise the first time. It will never happen again. Thanks for confirming I'm doing the right thing. You can take him, the boss is waiting to see him," Hamilton says to the two guys who rush into the room.

I pull my hand from my shoulder, and it's covered in blood. My hand is shaking and I'm still standing here naked. The two guys come over, and one throws a bag over my head.

My hands are tied behind my back, and I'm shoved from the room. Hamilton's words ring in my ears.

How does it feel to know you're never going to get your revenge on Coswell? He has the money, the girl, and the dream. You have nothing.

This can't be how this ends. If I have nothing, Coswell should as well. I'm going to get out of this, and I'll get my revenge.

"As they torture you and kill you. I want you to think of one thing. Coswell was always the better man and Zah never wanted you. You're an entitled asshole and you're about to get everything you deserve," Hamilton hisses in my ear as he digs his finger into my bullet wound.

I try not to make a sound, but lose the battle as he applies more pressure. I scream and black out.

Zahirah

I tighten my hold on Aaron as Bentley spoons me from behind. I've been in bed since after dinner. I didn't eat much, and I didn't feel like doing anything else after.

Bentley and Aaron climbed into bed with me about an hour ago. I've been cuddling my son, needing to feel him safe in my arms. I get the feeling that's how Bent feels.

He's had us both in his embrace. I'll admit, I feel safer in his arms.

"What happened to him? He was such a nice guy in high school," I murmur.

"Baby, I'm sorry to burst your bubble, but I never liked that guy. There was always something off about him," Bentley replies.

"Really?"

"Yeah, he put on a face for everyone else. However, I've seen it slip before. That's why I was pissed off when he started showing interest in you.

"He has always given off this vibe … I don't know how to explain it, but he didn't belong around you, and I wasn't having it. He didn't back down like all the rest did when I told him there was no way.

"That's why I broke his jaw. It was the arrogant smugness, like he could buy you, that set me off. As if you didn't have a right to reject him.

"He swore he could have you if he wanted. That was the wrong thing to say to me. I blacked out and blinked. The next thing I knew, Hamilton was helping him to his feet," Bentley says.

"Wow, I never knew anything about that. Truth be told, I didn't know you were warning other guys off as well. I just thought guys weren't into me.

"I didn't mind because I was crushing on you so hard. Maybe if I wasn't, I would have noticed." I laugh a little, but it doesn't sound right to my own ears.

"You're out of your mind thinking guys weren't into you. I threatened more guys than I'd like to admit. With Gilbert, I don't think he wanted anyone to know. I remember him taking time off from school after.

"I only knew I broke his jaw because I saw it. I didn't announce it to everyone because I didn't want to get cut from the team or benched. All that mattered to me was that he knew."

I go to say something else, but Bentley's phone rings. He rolls to his side of the bed to grab the phone and answer. I kiss the top of Aaron's head and bury my face in his hair.

"I have you on speaker, Fred. Zah is right here with me," Bentley rumbles, causing me to sit up and look at him.

"Gilbert's body was found. Someone worked him over pretty bad. His eyes were missing, as well as a few fingers and teeth.

"There were several bullet wounds. I'd say they tortured him before putting him down. Sadly, it looks like he had one more victim before they got to him. Zahirah, do you remember your roommate sophomore year?"

"Oh my God, Robin?"

"Yes, Robin Gensis. He strangled her to death. It seems she's the one who helped him back into the country."

"I just spoke to her a few weeks ago. She was doing great. We made plans to meet up soon," I say sadly.

"I'm sorry for your loss. It looks like the threat is over. Manning won't be bothering anyone else in this lifetime," Fred says.

"I still want Zah to have security. Can you come in to have a chat with me tomorrow?"

"I'll be there. Glad things worked out for you guys," Fred says and ends the call.

I look at Bent with tears in my eyes. It's over. I can finally live my life without worrying about when Gilbert will show up. No more calls to our podcast, no more showing up at my door.

"It's over," I whisper.

Bent palms the back of my head and kisses my forehead. I wrap my arms around him and break down sobbing. He holds me tight and begins to rock me in his strong arms.

"We can move on with our lives. He can't ever threaten us again. It's over.

"Breathe, baby, breathe. I was never going to allow him to hurt you, no matter what. I love you so much," he says as he holds me.

"I love you too. God, I hope this is it. I don't think I can take anything else trying to tear us apart. I'm so tired," I say.

"This has only proved how strong we are. It didn't break us; it made us unbreakable. We're going to be fine. You want me to take Aaron to his room?"

"No, leave him here. I do want to take a bath with you. I just want to relax in your arms."

"I'll get the water going and go get us some wine. Sound good?"

"Yeah, I'll get him set and grab the monitor."

He pecks my lips and nods. I watch as he gets up and walks into the bathroom. Dropping my head in my hands, I take a deep breath. It seems like my entire life has settled on my shoulders.

However, as I sit here, I think about how it has all worked out. I have a baby I love, the man I love is back in my life, and we're building the life we want.

"I did it, Daddy. It wasn't easy, but we made it. It was all worth every obstacle," I breathe, hoping my father is looking down, proud of me.

Touchdown

Zahirah

I have a huge smile on my face as I watch Bentley and Aaron in the backyard playing football. Aaron pumps his little legs as he holds the ball tight against his chest.

"Oh my God, they're so adorable," my mother laughs as my daughter lunges for her brother and tackles him to the ground. Bailey jumps up and does a little dance.

Bentley is laughing so hard he's holding his belly. Aaron stands up with a frown on his face as he glares at his sister. The two remind me so much of their father and me at that age.

Aaron is starting peewee league this year. His sister loves to get out there and help him train. I cover my round belly with my hands and smile widely.

"They are, aren't they?" I reply.

"They are and so are these two," she coos at Peter and Autum in her arms.

Yup, we have four kids with one on the way. What can I say? The man does something to me. He looks at me and I'm pregnant.

The most important part is we're happy. This will be Bentley's last season. He's decided to retire at thirty-six.

He's had an awesome career. He wants to walk away on a high. They've come away just short of another chip this season. That would have been his fifth.

Could he try for one more? I believe he could, but what I'm looking at now as I stand on our deck is all that matters to him these days.

"Phew, I didn't think I was going to make it. That drive seems longer and longer each time," Fran says as she comes out of the house.

She immediately grabs Peter from my mom and smothers his face with kisses. These two love being grandmothers. Our house is always filled with family and love.

"The favorite uncle is here," Eddy croons as he comes out back.

At twenty-four he's as handsome as ever. The kids adore him. Garret appears and comes to rub my belly and kiss my cheek.

"Hey, sis. How are you guys today?"

I give him a hug. "We're doing great. Almost there."

"Favorite uncle," Erica snorts at Eddy, then croons. "But I'm the favorite auntie."

I shake my head at the two. Erica looks at me and smiles. I laugh as she comes to palm my belly.

"Hey, hot mama," she sings.

Aaron and Bailey prove her point as they come racing to hug her legs. She just might be the favorite auntie after all. She spoils them enough.

Bentley comes over and palms my stomach as he dips his head to peck my lips. I look up into his eyes and smile. I don't know how I got this lucky, but I love my life.

"I love you," we say in unison.

We laugh and smile at each other. He places his forehead to mine.

"I never thought I would find anything that brings me the joy I get when I score a touchdown."

"Are you saying that now you have?"

"You and the kids bring me twice that joy. Nothing could replace how you guys make me feel."

"I know exactly how you feel. I think I scored big time, but this is still our last baby," I snicker.

"We'll see about that," he says with a wink.

"Mommy, Aaron pushed me," Bailey whines.

Bentley groans. "So not helping."

I burst into laughter. I love him enough that he might get baby number six. Might.

ABOUT THE AUTHOR

Blue Saffire, award-winning, bestselling author of over eighty contemporary romance novels and novellas, writes with the intention to touch the heart and the mind. Blue hooks, weaves, and loops multiple series, keeping you engaged in her worlds. Blue writes for her own publishing company, Perceptive Illusions as Blue Saffire, as well as Royal Blue.

Blue and her husband live in a house filled with laughter and creativity in Long Island, NY. Both working hard to build the Blue brand and cultivate their love for the arts. Creative is their family affair.

Blue holds an MBA in Marketing and Project Management, as well as an MED in Instructional Technology and Curriculum Design. She is also an NLP Master Practitioner.

ACKNOWLEDGMENTS

I'm happy I got to complete this one. I didn't know what to do with it when the platform it started on closed down. I had a little window, so I went for it and finished it. I hope you loved Bentley and Zah as much as I do. This will be a standalone.

My dear reader friends, I can't go without saying thank you so much for your continued support and patience. So much more is to come.

As always, thank you for the encouraging reviews, emails, videos, posts, shares, comments, and DMs. Big thanks, friends. Remember, sharing is caring. If you have a friend who reads, let them know about me, please and thank you.

Big shout-out to my husband, who has me watching college football and has taught me so much about the game. I was so proud of myself for writing this one. I think he was proud of his student too.

Never to be forgotten. All thanks to my source. God knows the mission He set me on and I'm walking it out. Walking gratefully in my purpose. By faith and not by sight. To God be all the Glory.

I'll say it again. This is where passion meets fire. Thank you, Lord, thank you.

Next! Follow me. I'm on a mission.

Wait, there is more to come! You can stay updated with my latest releases, learn more about me, the author, and be a part of contests by subscribing to my newsletter at

www.BlueSaffire.com

If you enjoyed *Touchdown*, I'd love to hear

your thoughts and please feel free to leave a

review on my website. And when you do, please let me

know by emailing me TheBlueSaffire@gmail.com

or leave a comment on Facebook https://www.facebook.com/BlueSaffireDiaries or Twitter @TheBlueSaffire

Other books by Blue Saffire

Placed in Best Reading Order

Also available …

Legally Bound

Legally Bound 2: Against the Law

Legally Bound 3: His Law

Perfect for Me

Hush 1: Family Secrets

Ballers: His Game

Brothers Black 1: Wyatt the Heartbreaker

Legally Bound 4: Allegations of Love

Hush 2: Slow Burn

Coming Soon…
King of Gods Book 4: Immortal Iron Brothers Series
King of Past Book 5: Immortal Iron Brothers Series
Brooklyn Book 3: Kings of New York Series

Other Blue Saffire Series

Hold On To Me Series
My Funny Valentine
Be My Valentine

Hitter Squad Series
Remember Me

Work Husband Series
Unexpected Lovers
My Best Friend's Wish
The Ones Left Behind
The Last Ones Standing

The Lost Souls MC Series
Forever
Never
Always

The Moran Brothers Series
Love Notes
Stay With Me

The A**hole Club Series
Pit Book 1: The A**hole Club
Ox Book 5: The A**hole Club
Kelex Book 6: The A**hole Club

Immortal Iron Brothers Series
King of Knights Book 1
King of Inferno Book 2
King of Tides Book 3

Check out Blue Saffire exclusives on the
BlueSaffire.com website
The Fixer
His Miracle Baby

Dark Disciples Series
Razor
Dane
Trip

Discipline Disciples Series
Wounded
12 Rounds

Bay Breezes Series
Professor Jones
Room 112

Love's Brew Series
Heart to Heart
Beer With Me
Clouded Views coming soon …

Other books from Evei Lattimore Collection Books by Blue Saffire
Black Bella 1

Destiny 1: Life Decisions
Destiny 2: Decisions of the Next Generation
Destiny 3 coming soon…

Star

Other books from Royal Blue Gay Romance Collection written by Blue Saffire
Kyle's Reveal
Beau's Redemption